STRING ME A MURDER

String Me a Murder

A Murder

AN *All Aboard Bar* MYSTERY

COLTAN NICCI

INSTRINSIC LATCH BOOKS

INTRINSIC LATCH BOOKS

String Me a Murder
Copyright © 2026 by Coltan Nicci

Cover art and design: Julia Horobets

ISBN 9798994501603

FIRST EDITION
First Printing, 2026

Also available in ebook:
ISBN 9798994501610

For the young queer musicians
who practiced alone in their bedrooms
and dreamed of immortality.

San Francisco has always been a city of fog and facades.
I fit right in.

STRING ME A MURDER

CHAPTER ONE

F og already swallowed the train station across the street by
the time I clicked the switch for All Aboard Bar, its neon
sign dissolving into the mist. Most nights ended in perfect
harmony, the final chord of a string quartet fading to silence.
But tonight, a sour note hummed beneath the quiet, as
though the fog itself were alive with restless energy, stirring
the damp air in crowding whispers. From inside, a wall of gray
pressed thick against the window like a stranger hesitating at
the threshold, waiting.

Lucas leaned on the bar. "You're staring again."

"I can't help it. That fog… it feels off somehow."

"It does that." He shrugged. "Old-timers say it doesn't just
roll in. Sometimes it brings visitors who shouldn't be here."

Nervous laughter slipped out, though I told myself it was
just local lore.

Carefully, I balanced another pint glass atop my tower. The
stack wobbled before settling. Years of viola training had given
me a kind of grace, despite how often I bumped into door-
frames with these gangly limbs.

Behind the bar, Lucas's fingers flew across his laptop

keyboard, the rhythmic tapping oddly musical in the empty space. The screen's glow lit his face, highlighting cheekbones sharp enough to cut glass. His dark eyes focused intently, a slight furrow forming between his brows.

From his mother, Lucas Kemp had inherited distinctly Korean features—elegant bone structure, almond-shaped eyes, and straight black hair that fell across his forehead—which kept him looking younger than thirty-nine. But there was also a hint of his father's Scottish build in his tall, stocky frame and rugged nose. The sleeves of his Dark Knight tee had been strategically cut off, revealing biceps that looked more fitting for the Man of Steel than a brooding billionaire in a cape.

"That's quite the Jenga tower you've got going," he commented, still focused on his screen, yet somehow sensing my precarious balancing act.

"It's all about wrist control," I replied, sliding the stack on the bar. "Same principle as bowing technique. Just with more potential for shattering."

Lucas glanced up, and the way he looked at me nearly made me topple the whole thing. "Speaking of shattering, how about taking out the rest of tonight's trash before we add these glasses to the pile?"

"Aye aye, Cap'n." I gave him a mock salute.

He rolled his eyes. "At ease, soldier. And make sure you prop the door open this time. I don't want to have to rescue you again."

"That happened once!" I protested. "And in my defense, the lock is tricky."

"Whatever helps you sleep at night, Cass." He turned back to his spreadsheets, but not before I caught the hint of a smirk.

Yes, that's Cass with two s's. It was my mother's fondness for balance and symmetry that led her to choose Caspar with two a's. You learn to live with these family quirks, I guess.

I did a quick count of the three overstuffed trash bags lined up by the back door, courtesy of our busiest drag show yet. The queens had been particularly generous with their drink tickets tonight, which meant more empty bottles than usual.

"Think you can handle all three in one go?" he challenged.

I hoisted two bags over my shoulder. "Please. This is nothing compared to hauling a viola case stuffed with orchestra scores and a music stand across campus in the pouring rain. Though I still say these arms are better suited for viola than trash duty."

"Those long arms are the reason you got hired," Lucas said matter-of-factly. "Well, that and the way Jules lights up every time you walk by."

Jules Beaumont, our neighborhood retiree, had a fondness for ascots and cute twinks. He was all too eager to buy a drink for anyone he found adorable.

"Jules would flirt with a street sign if it wore skinny jeans," I retorted.

"True. But the street sign wouldn't blush nearly as prettily." Lucas's eyes met mine again.

I bent to grab the last trash bag, trying to hide my flustered reaction. "Says the guy who has half the neighborhood dropping by for a 'quick drink' whenever you wear those sleeveless shirts."

"Don't sell yourself short, kiddo." He stretched his arms with a tired yawn. "Now hurry up so we can finish closing."

"On it, Master Wayne," I called over my shoulder, pushing through the back door into the alley. The chilly night air hit me like a splash of cold water—a stark reminder of how far I'd come in just a few months.

♪ ♪ ♪

Five months ago, fresh out of college with a music degree and naive optimism, I'd decided to leave my parents' home in sunny, affluent Hillsborough, California, and make foggy San Francisco my permanent home. My brilliant plan included coming out to my parents before the big move. You know... a fresh start, live authentically. All that inspiring stuff they plaster on LGBTQ+ pride parade banners. Instead of the acceptance I'd hoped for, my father had cut me off faster than a wrong note in an audition.

On my own for the first time in my life, fate had led me to All Aboard. Or maybe it was just good geography. It's the closest gay bar to Bay Area Music Academy, where I'm still chasing the dream of making it into the SF Philharmonic. It was perfect. Students hung out there since it was only a short bus ride or walk away, and the train station across the street made it easy to get downtown for orchestra concerts, opera performances, or academy gigs.

Just around the bar, the West Portal neighborhood felt like a small slice of the past nestled inside the city. Candy-colored houses and storybook storefronts dotted the peaceful nook. A delightfully charming bookstore, with a cozy mix of local authors and new releases, sat a couple of doors down from a quirky vintage record store crammed with old CDs and DVDs. Farther along the avenue, a sweets shop offered handmade chocolate truffles and even a whimsical wooden swing hanging from the ceiling.

Family-run restaurants brought their own flavors to the street, from a bustling taqueria to a wine bar beloved by locals for its thoughtfully curated cheeses and a constantly rotating list of imported Italian wines. The dry cleaner's clerk knew you by name and knew your dog's name too, while the owner of the hardware store still wrote receipts out by hand. Together, they gave the neighborhood an old-school charm that didn't bother competing with the tech-fueled streets beyond the hill.

Above it all, Sutro Tower—the tall, three-pronged tower with alternating bands of red and white perched atop Sutro Hill—stood as a quiet reminder that even this friendly enclave belonged to a larger whole. It was the kind of place where everything felt familiar, even if you were seeing it for the first time. A threshold, a portal, it lived up to its name—always moving a beat outside the city's rhythm, much like the rest of us who'd found a home here.

The day after my parents' rejection, I drifted alone along West Portal Avenue in the slow early afternoon, unsure of my next steps. I could've taken the train over to the Castro, a neighborhood known for its flashy gay bars and rainbow-painted crosswalks, but I sought comfort in a place I already knew. When I wandered into All Aboard, the bar was empty, aside from Lucas—all biceps and quiet intensity as he prepped for opening.

As the general manager, he offered me a sympathetic ear and a job within the hour. He mentioned that a room in the apartment upstairs, normally reserved for bar employees, was available. After checking with the owner, he decided I'd be a good fit. That's how I met Micah Velasco, who became my best friend and roommate. And now, five months later, I was hauling trash bags to the dumpster in the alley—a small price to pay for the way Lucas had turned my life around.

♪ ♪ ♪

The fog had thickened in the narrow alley, and the outdoor string lights barely pierced the gloom, casting more shadows than illumination. The plastic lid thumped open, its hollow echo bouncing between the walls. I had just tossed the last bag in when a prickle of unease made me freeze. A whisper of movement? A shift in the air? My heart stuttered as instinct screamed danger. Years of watching conductors' cues and waiting for a beat to land had trained me to notice when something was off, when the world fell out of tempo.

"Hello?" My voice sounded thin in the fog. No answer came. Only the distant rumble of the last train.

Acutely aware of how alone I was, I hurried toward the door, but the handle refused to turn.

"Crap! No, no, no..." I jiggled it frantically. "Lucas! I'm locked out!"

An arm clamped around my torso and yanked me backward as a hand sealed over my mouth—fingers ice-cold against my skin, so cold they burned. I thrashed instinctively. My long limbs, usually precise from years of musical training, flailed uselessly. It was like fighting a statue, my struggles no more effective than a butterfly beating against marble.

My heels scraped the concrete as I was dragged deeper into the shadows, the rough surface shredding my canvas sneakers.

The dumpster's rusted edge slammed into my hip as we passed. The impact barely registered through waves of terror. My attacker's grip never loosened, never faltered, never hinted at weakness. The stench of rotting garbage filled my nose as I clawed for the bin, desperate to catch hold of something—anything—when a dark shadow enveloped me.

Then came the pain. A hard jab pierced my neck, and my world exploded into white-hot agony. The stab was immediate and brutal, but it was the wrongness—the unnatural cold of my attacker's touch and the inhuman strength pinning me in place—that made my mind recoil, sharper than the panic that gripped me on stage when a solo slipped from memory, every note unraveling under the audience's gaze.

This wasn't happening. Couldn't be happening. I tried to tell myself I was imagining things, tired after a long shift. But the steady pull of blood leaving my body felt like the slow, inevitable drag of a bow across strings—only in reverse, drawing life instead of giving music.

Darkness crept in at the edges of my vision. My struggles weakened as a heavy lethargy spread through my limbs. The last thing I registered was a sudden commotion and the sensation of falling.

♪ ♪ ♪

Consciousness returned in fragments.

A sense of floating.

The gentle sway of movement.

The feeling of being cradled against a broad, solid torso.

I forced my heavy eyelids open and lifted my head to find Lucas's jaw clenched tight, his nostrils flaring from effort. The hallway lights formed a halo around his dark hair as he carried me back into the bar, like an avenging angel who'd traded wings for superhero T-shirts. The thought drifted hazily through my mind, and despite the terror still coursing through my system, I felt oddly safe in his arms.

"Wha... what happened?" The words scraped past my raw throat.

"Shhh." His voice was soft but carried an undertone of steel. "You're safe now."

He set me gently on a barstool. I slumped forward, the cool wood soothing against my cheek. The burning in my neck ebbed, replaced by a strange tingling. My tongue felt thick, coated with a coppery taste I was too afraid to name.

"Rest," Lucas murmured, his hand firm on my shoulder. "We'll talk when you're stronger. I promise you'll be alright."

As consciousness slipped away again, I had the unsettling thought he was trying to convince himself as much as me.

CHAPTER TWO

The viola's strings vibrated under my fingertips as I drew the bow across them, but the sound came out more screech than song. I winced. My newly sharpened hearing made the mistake sting all the more. One week since the attack, and I still couldn't control my strength. My bow arm felt as if I were trying to paint watercolors with a sledgehammer. Meanwhile, every shift of position on the fingerboard risked crushing the viola's delicate neck—my fingertips threatening to punch straight through it—demanding fierce concentration to avoid snapping strings.

"Come on, Bach, work with me here," I muttered, invoking the composer as I adjusted my bow grip for what felt like the hundredth time. Outside, the rumble of the L-Taraval train rolling down the street kept its usual percussion to my practice session.

I closed my eyes, focusing only on the weight of the bow in my hand. Lucas had taught me a technique for managing my enhanced senses: *Isolate one sensation at a time until the rest fades into background noise.* But with music, it was harder. Every vibration rippled through my entire body. Each note amplified beyond what should be possible.

The memory of that first morning after the attack surfaced. Waking on the worn leather couch in Lucas's office, I was disoriented and thirsty in a way I'd never known. Lucas had been sitting beside me, his usual playfulness replaced by a grave tone as he explained what I'd become.

"The hunger will be intense at first," he'd said, pressing a medical blood bag into my trembling hands. "But it gets easier. You learn to control it, just like any other instinct."

My eyes had stayed fixed on the bag, disbelief holding me there. "How... how often?"

"Once a day is enough to maintain strength. Twice if you're healing or stressed." His hand had squeezed my shoulder. "We have an arrangement with the city's blood banks. Ethical sourcing only. No hunting required."

I'd expected a far more dramatic transformation. Sunlight might burn my skin, or I might have to start sleeping in a coffin. Maybe my fangs would pop out without warning. But none of that happened. Just a constant chill beneath my skin, and a faint hunger that refused to leave.

The high A string snapped with a sharp ping, yanking me back to the present. "Dammit!"

"Another casualty of the supernatural biceps?" Micah's voice came from the doorway, carried on the rich aroma of coffee. Her choppy dark brown hair, streaked with a few drug-store-blonde highlights, peeked out from under a bright orange-and-black knitted beanie, her bangs sweeping casually to the side.

She held out a steaming mug like a peace offering. "Made it extra strong, just how you like it." Crossing our small living room, she added, "Though I still think it's weird you can drink coffee but need blood to survive. Vampire biology makes zero sense."

I accepted the mug gratefully. "Lucas says it's evolution. Modern vampires adapted to blend in better." I could eat and drink like anyone else—and even enjoy it, every bite and sip amplified—but only blood truly fueled me. The coffee tasted different now that I could distinguish every flavor note, from the earthy undertones to the slight burnt edge left by our ancient coffee maker.

"Speaking of our favorite undead bar manager..." Micah perched on the arm of our secondhand couch. "He sure has been spending a lot of time teaching you... the ways of the night."

I busied myself with pulling a replacement string from my case. "He's my mentor. It's his job."

"Uh-huh. And those lingering looks between you two are purely professional?"

"Can we focus on the fact that I can barely play my instrument three weeks before my audition?" I held up the mangled string for emphasis. "I've gone through more strings this month than I usually do in a year."

"You'll get it back. Remember when you told me about switching from violin to viola? Back then, you thought you'd never adjust to the size difference, but look at you now."

"This is a little different than changing instruments." I gestured at myself. "Everything's different. I can hear our neighbors two buildings over arguing about whose turn it is to do laundry. I can smell what everyone had for breakfast. And don't even get me started on the heartbeats."

"The what now?"

"Heartbeats. They're like... background music I can't turn off. Yours is doing this even allegretto thing." I tapped my bow against my leg to demonstrate the rhythm.

"Okay, that's both cool and creepy." Micah stood, straightening her vintage Journey T-shirt. "But maybe you can use it? Like, work whatever's going on into your playing somehow?"

Before I could answer, a steady heartbeat approached our door, a few beats slower than a human's resting pulse. Lucas. My own heart skipped, a stutter I was sure he could hear.

Three sharp knocks followed by two slower ones. "Pre-shift meeting in ten," he called through the door. "Cass, bring your schedule for next week. We need to adjust your training times."

"Be right down!" I called, ignoring Micah's smirk.

"Oh, and Micah?" Lucas's voice came again. "Did Tita Isa drop off those ube ensaymada rolls I ordered for the meeting?"

"Yup! My mom delivered them fresh this morning," Micah called back. "She added extra ube since she knows it's your favorite. Said something about complex carbs supporting your workout regimen."

I smiled, thinking about how Micah's mother had practically adopted the entire bar staff into her extended family. Tita Isa's catering business in Daly City, just south of San Francisco, began as a small home-kitchen operation, baking traditional Filipino pastries for church events and family gatherings. Word spread quickly through the tight-knit Filipino community about her perfectly balanced ube halaya and cloud-soft ensaymada. Before long, she was catering birthday parties and baby showers across the Bay Area, her purple yam—

filled treats becoming her signature.

"Mom's actually looking into opening a proper storefront now," Micah said, gathering her things for the meeting. "She's got her eye on this cute space near the Daly City BART station. Says the morning commuter crowd would love her pandesal-and-coffee combo."

"The location makes sense," I said, packing away my viola. "Half of Daly City already stops by her house for breakfast anyway. Remember when your dad had to install that second doorbell just for food pickups?"

Micah laughed. "Yeah, and now she's got that whole system with the color-coded containers and pickup times written in Taglish on the whiteboard. Very organized for someone who still refuses to write down her recipes because 'measurement is by feeling, *anak*.'"

I watched her, charmed by the way she teased her mother's insistence on keeping her recipes secret. It seemed fitting that the only ones who knew about my transformation were Micah and her parents. Lucas had been reluctant to share our secret, but eventually agreed once it became clear that hiding it from my closest friend was doing more harm than good.

♪ ♪ ♪

Unlike Micah, whose family embraced their Filipino heritage with open arms and endless servings of pork adobo, my connection to the culture felt like sight-reading an unfamiliar score. I could follow the melody and recognize the notes, but never quite capture the soul of the composition.

My father, Agustin Reyes, had married into my mother's family from Hillsborough, a prominent suburb about a half-hour from the city when traffic cooperated. He worked for our family real-estate business, Hawthorn & Co., which rested on wealth my family had accumulated since the Gold Rush. Determined to shed his immigrant background like an ill-fitting suit, he polished away his accent and avoided Taga-log even when my *lola*—my grandmother—visited. While other Filipino fathers taught their children about their home-land, mine taught me which fork to use at the Crystal Springs Country Club.

The Hawthorn estate was a stage where I played the role of the perfect multicultural success story—ethnic enough to let my mother Angela's friends feel progressive when they in-vited us to charity galas, but never so ethnic that it made them uncomfortable. While Micah grew up learning to wrap lum-pia with her cousins, I was paraded through country clubs in pressed suits, performing Vivaldi and Kreisler for Silicon Val-ley executives and venture capitalists who praised my "exotic" features before asking if I'd considered applying to their alma maters. They'd smile indulgently at my "unique" name while mangling its pronunciation, then congratulate my parents for raising such a "well-assimilated" child. I learned early how to smile and nod, to serve as a bridge between two worlds while never fully belonging to either.

"At least your dad taught you something useful," Micah had once said, searching for a silver lining. "All those fancy business dinners made you comfortable performing."

♪ ♪ ♪

I snapped my viola case shut, its velvet interior now holding more broken strings than intact ones. The receipts from the music shop were piling up next to overdue bills. Between rent, utilities, and constant string replacements, my savings were bleeding out fast.

The reminder of my finances sent a fresh wave of anxiety through me. Five months into living on my own, I was still figuring out how to survive. The only thing I had was my viola—a gift from my grandmother on my mother's side, and my tether to the life I wanted, even when everything else felt uncertain.

"Earth to Cass?" Micah waved a hand in front of my face. "You're doing that vampire statue thing again," she said, describing my frozen state.

I blinked, disoriented. "Sorry. Just thinking about bills."

"Lucas would give you more shifts if you asked."

"I know. But I need practice time for the audition." If I picked up more hours, the little practice time I had left would evaporate. With my audition looming and Lucas diligently training me to control my new senses, I was already stretched thin.

I snagged my All Aboard work T-shirt from the back of a chair. "Besides, I don't want him thinking I can't handle things on my own."

Micah trailed me down the narrow stairs to the bar, balancing the carefully arranged box of ensaymada rolls. "Pretty sure he already knows exactly how well you handle things, considering he's probably listening to every word we're saying right now."

Supersonic hearing. Crap. Another vampire perk that made zero biological sense.

We stepped into the bar's main room, where Lucas was

setting up for the staff meeting. He didn't glance up from his clipboard, but the wry quirk of his lips was unmistakable, confirming Micah's theory about his eavesdropping.

The familiar scents of stale beer and cleaning supplies hung in the air, undercut by the distinct fragrances of each staff member drifting in for the meeting. Scent being another sense I was still learning to manage, I noticed that everyone carried a unique signature. Micah smelled of fresh coffee with a trace of vanilla, a comforting aroma that always felt like home, especially on days when I needed extra warmth. Lucas, though, hit me like a perfectly aged whiskey, rich and complex enough to be dangerously intoxicating. Yet beneath that allure lurked a darker note, one I couldn't place but ached to understand.

"Alright, everyone," Lucas began once we'd gathered. "New schedule goes up today. Drag night's turnout and bar sales were solid last week, so we're adding another show next month..."

I tried to focus, but my sharpened hearing betrayed me, picking up the ice maker's low hum, a mouse scuttling in the walls, and the symphony of heartbeats around the room. Through it all, Lucas's voice anchored me, as it had during those first disorienting days after my transformation.

The memory of our first feeding lesson surfaced. Lucas showed me how to pierce the medical bags, guided me to control the hunger, and taught me to recognize the warning signs before the thirst became dangerous—before I lost control and risked an involuntary attack on someone. His patience had made the terrifying transition almost bearable.

"Cass?" Lucas's voice cut through my thoughts. "Your training schedule?"

"Oh, right." I fumbled with my phone, pulling up my calendar. "I can do mornings before practice, or late nights after closing."

"Late nights," he decided, jotting a note. "Keep the mornings free. Between viola practice and your training sessions, you'll need the time to recover."

Our eyes met, tension flickering like static before he looked back at the schedule, all business again. "Alright, that's everything. Opening in thirty minutes. Let's get set up."

As the staff scattered to their tasks, I caught my reflection in the bar mirror. The changes were subtle but undeniable. Cheekbones sharper, skin clearer, eyes carrying a new kind of depth. I looked like myself, only... refined. Like an Instagram filter made flesh.

"You'll get used to it," Lucas said quietly at my side. "The senses, the strength, the changes. Just give it time."

I nodded, our reflections lined up in the mirror like two versions of the same story. "I know. It's just... a lot."

"It is." His hand brushed my arm. "Now go rescue Micah before she drops another rack of glasses trying to reach the top shelf."

CHAPTER THREE

The Bay Area Music Academy perched atop Golden Gate Heights like a fortress of sound overlooking the Pacific. As Northern California's premier music school, it drew the most gifted instructors and ambitious students, many of whom later claimed coveted orchestra seats or launched solo careers.

Inside Dolores Larsen's teaching studio, the air smelled of herbal tea and aged sheet music, a combination that wrapped around me like an old friend. Concert posters and framed programs lined the walls, alongside photos of past students cradling their instruments with proud grins. My own photo from four years ago hung among them, capturing a lankier, more uncertain version of myself holding my viola like a shield after placing second in a local music competition.

I claimed my usual spot by the bay window, where the ocean stretched endlessly before me. The view had always been captivating during lessons, but with my new vampire vision I caught details that once would've been impossible. Waves crashed against the distant rocks in a mesmerizing, hypnotic rhythm—nature's own metronome keeping time. I followed seabirds riding the air currents and read the clouds as they swirled in patterns that declared "rain coming" as clearly as sheet music. It was as if my eyes had been upgraded from standard definition to ultra-HD, and I couldn't decide if it was breathtaking or overwhelming.

I set up my music stand and lifted my viola with the delicacy of someone handling blown glass. These days, the slightest miscalculation of strength could snap my bow like a twig. The first few notes burst out too strong, my bow arm still learning to navigate its supernatural upgrade. I closed my eyes and tried Lucas's focusing technique. *Isolate the sensation*, his voice echoed in memory. I felt how the horsehair connected to the strings, vibrating through the bow into my fingers. *Nothing else exists.*

Gradually, the sound smoothed as I found the right balance of pressure. Perfect intonation came easier now that I could hear the slightest pitch deviation. Maybe being a vampire wouldn't completely wreck my musical career after all.

"Well, well." Dolores's voice carried its signature flourish as she swept into the studio. "Someone's been practicing."

I managed not to jump at her sudden entrance; my heightened hearing had caught her approach. She glided in wearing a flowing, colorful kaftan, silver hair arranged in her signature elegant twist. The scent of rosehip tea and honey followed her, warmed by a rich spice—probably the Indian takeout she favored for lunch.

"Good afternoon, Dolores." I adjusted my bow grip. "Just warming up with some scales."

"Mmmm." She studied me, squinting behind her cat-eye glasses. "Something's different about your playing today. The tone is… richer. More controlled."

"I've been working on even bow pressure."

"Indeed." She tapped her chin. "Your posture has changed too. More grounded, like you've finally grown into those long limbs of yours." Settling into her worn leather armchair, the throne of a thousand lessons, she added, "Let's start with the Bach. From the top."

If only she knew how much growing I'd done lately. I launched into the Prelude from Bach's Suite in D minor, hoping to steer her attention back to the music. The opening was meditative, almost hypnotic. A single melodic line descending into darkness, then reaching toward the light. The notes flowed more easily than they had in days, each vibration alive beneath my fingers. The piece felt like a reflection of everything I was going through, with its constant shifts between shadow and clarity, never quite finding a place to rest.

As I focused on keeping the bow pressure consistent, another kind of lesson crept into my thoughts. During last night's feeding session with Lucas, he guided my hands, showing me the proper angle for piercing medical bags. *Just like bow control, it's all about finding the right pressure.* The memory distracted me, and I botched a shift, the wrong note sticking out like a siren in a lullaby.

"Focus, Caspar." Dolores's voice snapped me back. "You're rushing. Remember what we discussed. Let the music breathe."

I nodded and adjusted my tempo. Her pulse maintained a perfect andante—moderately slow and steady—and before I realized it, I was using it as my metronome.

"The dynamics feel stifled, dear," she said when I finished.

"You're trying to control it too much. Let it unravel. The pain is in the unraveling."

She adjusted my elbow, and I had to concentrate not to flinch at her touch. Every heartbeat in the room pounded in my ears. Dolores's calm andante set the baseline, a piano student downstairs tapped out a quickstep rhythm, and outside a squirrel hammered a frantic prestissimo—the fastest of tempos—across the branches.

Lucas had tried to teach me how to tune out the heartbeats. *Think of them like background music,* he'd said. *Acknowledge them, then let them fade.* Easy for him to say. He'd had ten years of practice.

"Again," Dolores commanded. "This time, let yourself feel it."

I closed my eyes, remembering how the piece had felt before the attack—before everything got complicated. The muscle memory was still there, buried under all this new strength. I needed to learn to trust it.

This time the notes flowed more naturally, my supernatural edge actually helping once I stopped fighting it. I caught Dolores's approval in the subtle shift of her breathing, the slight uptick of her pulse.

"Much better," she said. "Though I still hear hesitation in the crescendos. You have the technique to let the volume rise. You just need to trust yourself enough to use it."

It took more trust than she could ever guess to hold the bow without snapping it in two.

"Speaking of trust. Or rather, trust funds," she added with a sip of tea. "I assume Brad still plans to audition?"

I shifted my stance, that familiar cocktail of resentment

and envy stirring at Brad's name. Brad Bennington and I had gone to Hillsborough High together, where his last name alone practically guaranteed him first chair in the orchestra. After graduation, we both got into the Bay Area Music Academy. My grandmother celebrated my acceptance with the gift of a brand-new viola, an instrument I cherished more than anything else I owned. Brad, meanwhile, played an authentic 18th-century Guarneri violin, crafted by one of the most revered luthiers in history. Its age and reputation made it worth more than all my years of private lessons and school tuition combined.

"Last I heard," I said, keeping my voice carefully neutral, "he's still planning to audition for the Philharmonic's one open string position."

"Ah yes, that coveted seat." Her lips pressed into a thin line. "Quite unprecedented. Violinists, violists, and cellists all competing for the same spot. The committee insists it's about finding the best musician overall, regardless of instrument."

I tried not to dwell on how Brad's Guarneri would sound to the judges compared to my viola, no matter how cleanly I played. The competition was brutal enough without factoring in instrument quality. Some of the best string players in Northern California would be clawing for a single chair. The San Francisco Philharmonic hadn't opened a string position in three years, and now, thanks to budget cuts, they were filling only one slot instead of the usual openings reserved for each instrument section.

"At least with different instruments, the judges can't do a direct technical comparison. They'll have to pay closer attention to musicality and interpretation..." My voice faltered as the truth settled. "Not that it matters, since Brad's father sits on the board of directors."

"Ah yes, Richard Bennington." Her voice held a curl of distaste. "I remember when he tried to convince me to take Brad on as a student. Even offered to double my usual rate."

Classic Mr. Bennington. Always ready to throw money at any obstacle in his son's path. Brad had cycled through the Bay Area's top violin teachers, each one carefully chosen to polish his pedigree. His father hadn't stopped there. Summer intensives at a renowned New York conservatory and master classes with every touring soloist money could buy rounded out his training. Meanwhile, I practiced in our garage, trying not to disturb my father's business calls.

"Why did you turn him down?" I asked. Few teachers managed to resist the Bennington influence.

"Money doesn't buy talent," she said simply, adjusting her glasses. "It buys opportunity, yes, and I've heard him in the practice rooms around campus—Brad is technically proficient, I'll grant him that. But there's no soul in his playing. No depth."

Dolores's comment brought back more than just memories of Brad's hollow playing. It dredged up years of rivalry that went far beyond orchestra auditions. The Bennington name had hovered around mine long before Brad and I ever ended up in the same orchestra. My father used to tense anytime the Benningtons came up in conversation—especially after their expanding real-estate arm outmaneuvered my grandfather's old-guard company for a lucrative commercial property in Burlingame, the small city bordering Hillsborough. I remember him pacing our kitchen afterward,

shouting to my mother about "corporate strong-arm strate-
gies," his voice sharp enough to carry down the hall. I'd
resumed practicing as loudly as I could, trying to drown him
out.

Even in high school, I understood that Brad and I weren't
just two musicians in the same ensembles. We were inheriting
a rivalry between families who'd been trying to outplay each
other for decades. The terrain had shifted, but the contest
hadn't—now narrowed to a single open chair.

"His father's connections won't matter if Brad can't deliver
in the audition," I said, though it felt more like I was rehearsing the argument in my own head than convincing her.

"Mmm." Dolores stirred her tea, the spoon clinking softly
against porcelain. "The politics of it all. Talent should speak
for itself, but..." She lifted one shoulder in a graceful shrug;
resignation wrapped in elegance.

My phone buzzed with a reminder about my upcoming
bar shift, the real world barging into this fragile sanctuary of
music.

"Still working late nights at the bar?" she asked, frowning
at me. "You look exhausted, Caspar. The audition is in three
weeks. You need to be at your best."

What she saw was the spillover, the part I couldn't keep
contained. The nightly training sessions with Lucas, the constant fight to control my strength, and the juggling act of
maintaining a human mask all left me teetering on the edge
of exhaustion. I took a steadying breath. "I'm managing."

I prepared to play the Allemande, a stately Baroque dance
movement Dolores had assigned at our last lesson. The piece
unfolded like a graceful walk through memory, gentle in

pacing, but layered with subtle complexity, each phrase a careful step forward.

To my surprise, it came out nearly perfect. My new reflexes translated musical intention into movement without the usual struggle.

Her eyebrows rose. "Well. That's... remarkable progress." She leaned forward, tapping a finger against the armrest. "You know, the Allemande has such beautiful structure. Think of it like walking through a house you used to live in. Each room is familiar, but filled with echoes."

The image touched a place I hadn't realized was still sore. My thoughts drifted back to my childhood home, to the grand piano in the living room where my mother used to play, the study where my father worked, and the bedroom that was once mine. All those spaces that used to feel like they belonged to me, now echoes of a life I'd left behind.

"Yeah," I said. "Familiar, but... not quite the same anymore."

Dolores studied me with that keen teacher's attention. "Perhaps that's why you played it so well today. Sometimes distance gives us clarity." She smiled, a rare full expression that softened her usual sternness. "I think it's time you attempted a more challenging piece."

She moved to her vast music library, pulling out a worn score. "Hindemith's Der Schwanendreher. The Swan Turner. Start with the third movement. It's ambitious, but... I think you're ready."

I accepted the score, my pulse quickening at the sight of the fiendishly difficult piece. Under ordinary circumstances, I would have argued it was too advanced. But ordinary had walked out a week ago, after the attack, taking my limitations with it. I'd dreamed of playing this work since I was fourteen, and now Dolores had placed the score in my hands.

"Thank you," I said, scanning the labyrinth of rhythms and double stops. But with these new vampire abilities, how could I know whether mastering this work would be the result of practice or from being handed some sort of supernatural cheat code? Was I becoming a better musician, or just something... other?

CHAPTER FOUR

The heavy door of Dolores's studio clicked shut behind me, and before I could even adjust the strap of my viola case, angry voices from a nearby practice room sliced through the hallway. Beethoven's Piano Trio in B-flat major drifted through the wall, its melody now fractured by tension and frustration.

"For effing sake, Wyatt! It's the same entrance we've been drilling for weeks. How hard is it to come in on time?"

I winced at Brad's sharp tone, recognizing his voice instantly.

"I'm sorry, I just—" Wyatt's softer voice was cut off by the violent scrape of chair legs against hardwood.

"Sorry doesn't win competitions," Brad snapped. "Do you think the judges at Fischer will accept 'sorry' when you ruin our chances?"

The Presidio Trio, as they were known in Bay Area classical circles, had been Brad's pet project since freshman year. They'd quickly gained recognition for their polished performances and were now preparing for the Fischer National Chamber Music Competition, the most prestigious chamber music event in the country. He'd handpicked Wyatt Cross for his rich cello tone and Jordyn Hurst for her technical precision at the piano, though everyone knew the real reason was their willingness to tolerate his leadership.

Brad's approach to leadership felt less like guidance and more like a constant stream of demands, delivered with a polished smile and perfectly styled hair. He'd criticize every minor mistake while glossing over his own, expecting his trio partners to bend their entire lives around his schedule. I'd known Brad long enough to recognize his favorite tactics. He compared Wyatt to more successful cellists, offered backhanded compliments about Jordyn's "adequate" technique, and never missed a chance to remind them they were lucky to have him. It was like watching a master class in musical manipulation, and part of me wondered if they stayed because they actually believed him when he insisted no other group would want them.

"We've got six days until Fischer," Brad pressed on, his Italian leather shoes tapping an agitated rhythm. "Six days to prove we deserve to be there. Do you know how many strings I had to pull just to get us considered for the preliminary round?"

What went unsaid was that Brad's father's generous donation to the Fischer National Chamber Music Association had probably done more for their acceptance than their audition tape. But even I had to admit. They were good. When Brad wasn't letting his ego get in the way, the trio achieved flashes of genuine brilliance.

"Maybe if you weren't splitting your focus with the Philharmonic audition—" Jordyn began, but Brad cut her off.

"Don't. Don't you dare suggest I'm not giving this my all."
His intake of breath carried through the wall. "I've got my
solo repertoire memorized. The trio pieces are solid. I can
handle both."

The strain in his voice and the uptick of his pulse gave
away how stressed he was. Between morning lessons with top
violin teachers for his Philharmonic prep, afternoon trio rehearsals for Fischer, and evening practice sessions that often
dragged past midnight, Brad was burning the candle at both
ends—yet his polished videos and photos made it all look effortless on his socials.

"From the development section," Brad commanded. "And
Wyatt, for God's sake, watch my bow this time. I'm leading,
remember?"

The music resumed, but the tension remained, vibrating
through the wall like an off-key note refusing to resolve. I
should've walked away, headed straight home, and left the
drama of chamber music politics behind. But every nuance of
their argument still reached me, in the tremor of Wyatt's
breathing, the agitated tap of Brad's Italian leather shoes, and
the even rhythm of Jordyn's heart as she tried to mediate.

"Maybe we should break for lunch," Jordyn suggested.
"We've been at this for hours. This used to be fun. Remember
fun?"

"We wouldn't need a break if some people could handle
basic counting." Brad's words dripped with disdain.

Footsteps approached fast, and the practice room door
burst open. Brad nearly collided with me as he stormed out,
his perfectly styled hair mussed from running his hands
through it in frustration.

♪ ♪ ♪

The last time I'd been this close to Brad was six months ago, after that disaster of a party at his parents' Hillsborough mansion. The memory still haunted me. Too much wine, a moment of weakness in his father's study, and the way Brad's fingers had traced my jaw before pulling me into that first heated kiss.

Afterward, we'd curled up together in his father's leather club chair. No snide comments, no playful arrogance—just the quiet intimacy of us together. His fingers absently traced patterns on my wrist.

"Sometimes I think I could be in a room full of people and still feel like no one sees me," he'd said, his voice barely above a whisper.

I didn't know how to respond to that kind of honesty from him, so I squeezed his hand, feeling the calluses on his fingertips.

The moment I touched him, his eyes widened, as if he'd only then realized how much he'd let show. His body had gone rigid, pulling away as the mask slipped back on, smooth as a practiced transition between movements.

The morning after, I'd dared to suggest it might have meant more than drunken fumbling. His laugh had cut deeper than any insult. "Don't flatter yourself," he'd said, adjusting his shirt collar in his father's antique mirror. "It was just a bit of fun. And let's keep it between us. Wouldn't want to ruin my reputation for having standards."

The casual cruelty in his tone had made it clear exactly where I stood in his world. Brad had never been shy about who he was or who he shared a bed with. "Standards" for him had nothing to do with gender or labels—only whether he thought someone was worth his time. And in his eyes, I wasn't.

♪ ♪ ♪

Out in the hallway, Brad fixed me with that same arrogant expression, his lips curling into a familiar smirk. "Eavesdropping, Reyes? Hoping to pick up some tips for your audition?"

I shifted my viola case, forcing myself to appear casual despite how my enhanced senses picked up the faint trace of cocaine beneath his cologne and the thin sheen of sweat at his temples.

"Just leaving my lesson," I said evenly. "Though I'm surprised you still need to practice, considering your father's influence on the board."

His eyes narrowed. "At least I can afford proper lessons. How many strings have you snapped this month trying to play on that standard-issue viola?"

Before I could answer, Wyatt emerged from the practice room, his tall frame managing to shrink as he clutched his cello case. The scuffed shell was covered in stickers from music festivals and coffee shops, etched with little doodles only they would understand. Tucked among them was a faded Polaroid of the Presidio Trio. It was from their senior recital earlier that year, a performance I'd attended. They were all smiling, back when making music together had still been fun and easy.

Jordyn followed, her usual composure intact on the surface. The crisp white button-down and perfectly pressed slacks projected confidence, but I caught the subtle tremor in her fingers as she smoothed her ash-blonde bob.

"The competition's less than a week away," she said, clearly trying to redirect the conversation. Jordyn reached into her tote bag and tossed a bottle of water to Brad, who caught it with a quick nod. "We should be focused on polishing the piece, not fighting about it."

"Assuming we even make it through the preliminary round," Brad said, shooting another glare at Wyatt. "Though I suppose Daddy's donation to the competition fund won't hurt our chances."

The scent of cocaine grew stronger as Brad wiped his nose with the back of his hand, a chemical undertone rising from his dewy skin.

Wyatt and Jordyn exchanged a look I couldn't quite decipher. There was history there. Layers of unspoken communication built through countless hours of rehearsal and performance.

My phone buzzed in my pocket: Remember to feed before your shift. Bags in usual spot. -L

"I might stop by All Aboard later," Brad announced. "I deserve a little playtime after all this hard work."

"Finally, a good idea. Caspar, is there a show tonight?" Jordyn asked, her eyes flicking to me with barely concealed interest. "I heard Lilith's playing piano again."

Of course Jordyn would bring up Lilith Fox, our resident piano genius at All Aboard who played for all the live drag shows. They'd been practically inseparable at the academy until Lilith made the bold choice to leave school and forge her own path.

"You mean that basic lounge act?" Brad scoffed. "Though I suppose bar piano is all she can manage now, since transitioning ruined her performance career. As if changing her name to Lilith makes her any less—"

"Stop." I cut him off, a growl barely held in check. "Just stop." His arrogance was endless. I knew his words were meant to sting, not reflect reality. Transition or not, Lilith's talent hadn't disappeared.

He raised his hands in mock surrender, though the smirk never left his face. "Touchy subject? Or are you just worried about your own little secret?"

My heart would've skipped a beat if it still followed normal rhythms. There was no way he could know, but the sly edge in his tone set off warning bells.

"See you at the bar, Reyes," he said, shouldering past me. "Try not to break any strings before then."

He strode down the hallway, every step calculated to project confidence and control. But I caught the slight hitch in his breathing and the too-fast rhythm of his heart.

Wyatt mumbled an apology of sorts as he hurried after Brad. Jordyn lingered, her hazel eyes fixed on me with an intensity that made me wonder how much she noticed.

"Be careful around him," she said. "He's been more unstable than usual lately."

I nodded, not trusting myself to speak. Brad's presence in my world, both musical and supernatural, felt like an invasion. The predator inside me, the one Lucas was teaching me to control, bristled with intensity, hunger prickling beneath my skin.

My phone buzzed again, snapping me back to the

moment: Seriously, Cass. Don't skip meals. —L

I thumbed back a quick *I know* before turning to Jordyn. "You should be careful too."

She gave me a small, sad smile. "We all should."

CHAPTER FIVE

A sudden pang of distress tightened in the pit of my stomach as I stopped short. Micah turned to face me, her expression equal parts patience and determination.

"Do I have to?" I asked, deploying my best puppy-dog face, the same one that worked on Dolores when I needed an extension on new repertoire. We'd walked the last three blocks along West Portal Avenue in a rare patch of gusty sunshine. As luck would have it, a woman passed us, one hand clamped on her sunhat to keep it from flying off while her golden retriever puppy bounded at her side. I couldn't help giving the little fluff-ball a small wave as it trotted by.

"F'real? Cass, we're literally five steps from the door." Micah wasn't falling for it—her fondness for cats and disdain for canine theatrics made her immune to my pleading expressions.

Through the front window of The Lotus Yoga Studio, a handful of mid-afternoon clients in skin-tight Lululemon watched our sidewalk standoff, drawing more attention than I was comfortable with. Micah wore one of her vintage rock T-shirts—blue tie-dye with the iconic Pink Floyd prism—

loosely tucked into charcoal-gray tights. I glanced down at my plain white undershirt and baggy black joggers, realizing how out of place we looked.

"You're totally stressing over the audition. You're all wound up," Micah pressed. "This will help calm whatever the heck's going on in that big head of yours. Plus," her eyes narrowed like a cat in the sun, "you already promised."

I had never exercised a day in my life. Unless you counted rushing between practice rooms or hauling overstuffed trash bags at All Aboard. Still, after that night in the alley, I'd developed a new appreciation for lifting those bags without breaking a sweat. The academy teachers strictly forbade students from weight training to avoid injuring our precious fingers. Dolores, a lifelong yogi, kept pressuring me to give it a try, insisting it could help with breathing and performance anxiety.

"But we're gonna get all sweaty," I said, catching myself before the whine fully escaped. "We have shifts at the bar after class, remember?"

"Bruh, I signed us up for Intro... to... Yoga," Micah said, drawing out each syllable as though she were talking to a particularly stubborn child. "Not Hot Bikram."

"Fine," I conceded—I couldn't argue; she was the one paying for the session.

The moment I stepped through the studio's glass door, the scent of sandalwood essential oil hit me like a wall. Apparently, another vampire enhancement was a heightened sensitivity to aromatherapy. Great.

The studio itself was peaceful enough. Natural light streamed through large windows, and the pale bamboo flooring was smooth beneath my bare feet. About a dozen other students were already unrolling their mats, their heartbeats forming a symphony of rhythms that threatened to overwhelm my senses.

That's when I heard it. One heartbeat that stood out from the rest. Strong, with an unusual, syncopated pattern that caught my attention like a perfectly executed rubato. I followed the sound to its source and found myself staring at a guy about my age adjusting his mat in the back corner.

"Oh em gee! Jackson Nolan?!" Micah's exuberance snapped me out of my trance. She waved enthusiastically at the guy, who looked up with a warm smile that crinkled his eyes behind stylish glasses. "I didn't know you came to afternoon classes."

"Hey, Micah," he replied, his voice carrying a pleasant resonance that matched his unique pulse. "Yeah, just switched my work schedule around. Tech companies are finally admitting not everyone does their best work before sunset."

As they chatted, I tried not to stare while setting up my borrowed mat. Jackson was attractive in an understated way. Tall and fit with a sturdy frame, though softened around the middle, which only added to his appeal. His chestnut hair had a subtle wave, and across his T-shirt, *goto sleep(); Counting Sheep in Binary* was emblazoned. I had to bite back a smile. Anyone who'd ever spent hours debugging MIDI interfaces would appreciate the programmer humor.

"This is my roomie, Cass," Micah said, pulling me into their conversation. "He's a musician too. Classical. Viola."

"Nice to meet you," Jackson said, extending his hand. I hesitated for a split second, remembering Lucas's warnings about controlling my strength during casual contact. But Jackson's handshake was firm and warm, and I managed not to crush his fingers. Progress.

The instructor called the class to order before I could say anything embarrassing. As we moved through the poses, I was surprised to find my new vampire grace helped more than it hindered. My balance and flexibility made even the trickier positions feel natural. I lifted into Half Moon, torso rotated to the side, one hand brushing the floor while my back leg extended behind me and the other arm pointed skyward—like I was auditioning for Cirque du Soleil. Then I sank into Chair Pose, squatting low with my hands pressed together and elbows grazing my knees until my thighs screamed. Of course, I wobbled a bit to avoid looking suspiciously adept for a first-timer.

"Beautiful form on that Warrior Three," the instructor called out, and I immediately slouched, remembering Lucas's advice about blending in. Jackson, two mats over, caught my eye and smiled. I pretended to struggle with the next pose, though I overheard his whispered "show-off," more admiring than accusatory.

The rest of class passed in a blur of controlled breathing and careful calibration of my strength. Each pose brought new challenges to appear humanly imperfect without completely failing the movements. By the final Savasana, I had to admit Micah and Dolores were right. The practice had eased my racing thoughts, even if I spent more energy faking normal than actually relaxing.

"So," Jackson said as we rolled up our mats after class, "viola, huh? Don't meet many violists outside the classical world."

"Yeah, we're a rare breed," I replied, trying not to notice how his post-workout scent blended with his natural chemistry. "Most people assume we're just confused violinists."

He laughed, the sound blending with the lingering quickness in his pulse. "I actually know the difference. I've been working on a music education app that includes string instruments. The viola's role in quartets is fascinating, the way it bridges violin and cello."

"You know about string quartets?" I couldn't hide my surprise. Most tech people I'd met thought classical music began and ended with *Für Elise*, the universal beginner-piano anthem.

"Bruh, Jackson's like a secret music nerd," Micah chimed in, giving me a look that clearly said *you're welcome* for dragging me to class. "He's been coding this game that teaches people instruments through, like, actual fun methods instead of boring scales."

"It's still in development," Jackson said, pushing his glasses up in a gesture that was both self-deprecating and adorable. "But hey, if you're interested, I could show you some prototypes. Maybe get your professional opinion?"

"That actually sounds really interesting," I said, surprising myself with how much I meant it. "I've done some basic music programming—just small MIDI and sequencing scripts for an electronic music class—but nothing that advanced."

I caught Micah's slight intake of breath, her tell when she was about to play matchmaker. Sure enough, she jumped in. "You should totally come to our drag show tonight. Cass helps with the music arrangements and sound tech, and the queens are always looking for new tech solutions for their performances. Plus, you've got to see my costume work. I help create most of their gowns and accessories."

I shot Micah a look—her matchmaking instincts were in overdrive—but Jackson was already nodding enthusiastically. "I've heard about your shows from her. I'd love to see how you incorporate live music, check out the technical setup. And of course, finally see these amazing costumes she keeps bragging about."

His eyes met mine, holding contact a moment longer than necessary. The quickened pulse in his chest matched the flutter I tried to suppress in my own.

"Speaking of music," Jackson continued, "I've been experimenting with a feature in the app that uses gaming mechanics to teach guitar. The algorithm adapts to each player's learning style."

"Like Guitar Hero, but actually educational?" I asked, grateful for the shift toward a more technical topic. Easier to think about code than the way his scent kept tugging at my attention.

"Exactly!" His face lit up. "But with real music theory built in. I'd love to expand it to other instruments. Maybe..." he hesitated, "you could help me figure out how to adapt it for viola?"

Before I could respond, Micah's phone chimed. "Shoot, we better jet if we're gonna make our shift," she said, though her expression suggested the interruption wasn't entirely unwelcome. "Jackson, I'll text you the show details?"

"Looking forward to it," he replied, then turned to me. "And maybe we can talk more about the app then?"

I nodded, not trusting myself to speak without giving away how his proximity threw me off. As we left the studio, Micah waited until we were halfway down the block before unleashing her grin.

"Don't even start," I warned.

"I didn't say anything!" She raised her hands in mock surrender. "But, like, his heartbeat totally picked up when he was talking to you."

"You can't hear heartbeats," I pointed out, then immediately regretted it when her expression turned triumphant.

"No, but you can. And you were definitely listening to his."

I groaned. "I hate you."

"You love me," she corrected. "And you're gonna love me even more when Jackson shows up tonight in his tech-nerd-tries-nightlife outfit."

I almost hated how much I was already looking forward to it.

CHAPTER SIX

Micah and I had barely made it through the bar entrance before she started in on me. "So, about Jackson..." she sing-songed, dropping her bag behind the bar.

"Nope." I busied myself with the day's pre-opening checklist, pretending to study Lucas's neat handwriting instead of thinking about the way Jackson's eyes crinkled when he smiled after class.

"I'm just saying, the way he kept watching you in Downward Dog—"

A piercing shriek of feedback cut through her words as the microphone onstage wailed in protest, the sound bouncing off the walls like an angry banshee. I flinched; the aural assault felt like ice picks driving directly into my eardrums.

"Jesus, Mary, and Joseph!" Micah yelped, clapping her hands over her ears. "Can somebody turn that down? That's loud enough to scare the sequins off a showgirl!"

She shook her head, amusement softening her wince before she pulled out the register drawer to start her count. The ritual of organizing bills and checking the till calmed her.

"Sorry about that!" Adda's voice carried from the small

stage area as she adjusted the mic stand. When she spotted me, genuine warmth lit up her face. "Cass! Just in time for my soundcheck. I need an honest opinion on this new number."

Even from across the room, Adda Miration commanded attention like a force of nature. She wore an elaborate sequined gown that caught the dim stage lights and scattered starbursts across the walls. The dress hugged her tall frame perfectly, gold thread running through the emerald velvet like veins of precious metal. Even without her full makeup, she carried herself with the confident presence of someone who knew exactly how much space she deserved in the world.

Adda was a legend in the city, renowned for her commanding aura and razor-sharp wit. Her performances weren't merely shows, they were master classes in artistry and humor, inspiring both laughter and admiration. Over the years, she had built a fiercely loyal following that flocked to bask in her charisma. Watching her move through the space, I understood why. There was a magnetic quality to the way she inhabited her body.

The air around the stage buzzed with pre-show energy. Dim lights flickered to life above the small performance space. There was no real backstage at All Aboard, just a loosely agreed-upon strip of floor beside the stage where mirrors leaned against the wall and everyone politely ignored the extension cords underfoot. The chemical bite of wig glue mingled with clouds of setting powder, while floral notes of perfume created an olfactory symphony, the scent of ritual and anticipation. Beneath it all, the metallic spice of adrenaline clung to the back of my throat.

The   queens   whirled   through   their   elaborate transformation rituals. Brushes swept across faces with artistic intent, and practiced hands adjusted and readjusted wigs to perfect angles. I watched, fascinated and overwhelmed, as they shed their day selves and emerged more vibrant, more fearless.

The details threatened to drown me. Powder brushes rasped over skin. Rhinestones clicked into place with the snap of tweezers. Fabric rustled as costumes shifted and settled. Every heartbeat in the room added its own rhythm, layering into a dense, dizzying percussion.

Adda crossed over to me, her heels clicking an even rhythm against the hardwood floor. Up close, the sequins on her gown formed an almost hypnotic pattern, each tiny disc catching and reflecting light like a constellation map.

"Sweetheart," she said, her voice warm with concern that made me straighten involuntarily, "you look like someone trying to hold it together with a glue stick and a prayer."

She leaned against the bar beside me, close enough that I caught the subtle scent of her perfume—sophisticated with notes of rosewood and bergamot that cut through the competing fragrances in the air. "I've helped enough baby queens to know when someone's wearing something that doesn't quite fit yet, inside or out."

"I'm fine," I said, the words automatic and hollow even to my own ears.

Adda's laugh was gentle. "Cass, you're looking at everything like it doesn't quite fit anymore. Like the world's the same, but it feels different on your skin. You alright?"

Her observation wasn't wrong. Everything had felt different lately. Not only the vampire transformation, but the way

I moved through spaces, related to people, even held my viola. It was like someone had changed the prescription on glasses I hadn't realized I was wearing, leaving me constantly adjusting to a world that looked familiar but felt foreign.

I gave her what I hoped was a reassuring smile. "Just processing everything that's been happening, I guess. Big crowd tonight?"

She studied me a moment longer, her expression telling me she wasn't buying my deflection but was willing to let it slide for now. There was a maternal warmth in her gaze, protective and understanding without being pushy.

"Adda, mother darling!" Hella's voice rang out from the stage as she struck a dramatic pose, one hand on her hip, the other reaching toward an imaginary spotlight overhead. Her makeup was a stunning transformation, electric blue and silver geometric lines bold against her deep-toned complexion, glowing with a satin finish.

Hella Centrique was a whirlwind of creativity, her outfits a kaleidoscope of textures and colors, each one a testament to her bold vision and avant-garde spirit. Tonight she wore a bodysuit adorned with mirrors and crystals, catching every available photon and throwing it back tenfold.

"Tell me I look absolutely devastating," she demanded, spinning in a circle that sent light refracting across the walls like a disco ball explosion. For all the glitter and confidence, she still checked Adda's face before committing to the moment.

Adda grinned. "Honey, you look like you could blind a pilot from three miles away."

"Good. Then it's giving what it's supposed to give." Hella

threw a hand up toward the ceiling. "Micah!" she called, her voice slicing through the chatter. "I need your expert eye! These costumes won't accessorize themselves, and if I have to sew one more rhinestone on this bodysuit, I'll lose my mind!" She gestured at a pile of sequined fabrics and glittering embellishments scattered across a nearby table.

"On it!" Micah replied, giddy as she crossed the room. "Just try not to blind me with all that sparkle, okay? You know I can't resist a rhinestone emergency." Her fingers were already diving into the colorful chaos, quick and sure, sorting through the glittering accessories with the keen eye of someone who understood exactly how each piece would catch the stage lights.

Watching Micah work was like watching a master craftsperson in her element. She'd always been a natural with needle and thread; her skills forged in her *lola's* sewing room amid bolts of fabric and the whir of the sewing machine. There, she learned how to transform scraps into garments, how a few careful stitches could turn plain cloth into creations that were functional and beautiful.

Fashion design wasn't Micah's primary focus, but she thrived on the challenge of bringing the queens' extravagant visions to life. Her approach was methodical yet intuitive, understanding not only how fabric moved but how it would look under stage lights, how it would feel during a high-energy performance. In return, the queens admired her craftsmanship, marveling at how she could whip up a gown with the precision of a seasoned tailor and the flair of someone who knew exactly where the spotlight would hit.

"This needs to catch the light right here," Micah offered,

holding up a strip of rhinestones against Hella's shoulder, "but it can't compete with the mirror work on the bodice."

Hella nodded seriously, as if they were hashing out military strategy rather than accessory placement. "Exactly! You get it. Beauty's in the details, sis."

Adda regarded them with the cool, confident eye of a queen who'd spent years helping others find their footing.

"Mind your turns, Hella. Micah constructed that to show a shape, not a blur—let the crowd see it."

Hella nodded. "Got it. Clear shape, keep the pace."

As Micah and Hella dove deeper into their rhinestone consultation, soft piano music drifted from the stage. Lilith sat at the electronic keyboard, her long fingers tracing each note with calm intent. The melody was haunting and melancholy, *Falling* by Harry Styles. We'd worked on the arrangement weeks ago, but she continued refining it, layering in subtle variations that made it uniquely hers.

The music slowed time around me, each note hanging in the air like drops of honey. The delicate shifts in her touch and the way she used the sustain pedal to let certain chords bleed into the next phrase created a sound that was beautiful, sad, and somehow familiar, like a half-remembered dream.

I found myself drawn to the piano, the melody wrapping around me, pulling me into its gravitational field. The way Lilith played felt like a conversation, each phrase a carefully chosen word that spoke directly to the heart.

She looked up as I approached, her fingers never pausing in their dance across the keys. Her makeup was more understated than the others', elegant rather than theatrical, enhancing her natural features instead of transforming them completely.

"Hey, Cass," she said softly, her voice barely audible above the music.

"You always play like you're trying to tell a secret," I said, settling onto the bench beside her, careful to leave enough space that I wouldn't interfere with her playing.

Her lips curved into a small, mysterious smile. "Maybe I am."

There was a depth in Lilith's expression I recognized, a complexity beneath the surface. I'd seen it before—in quiet moments at the academy when she thought no one was looking, and in how distant she'd grown before leaving school. It spoke of heavy truths carried in silence, the weight of choices made and paths taken, forging a kind of kinship between us— two people who understood what it meant to reinvent ourselves, even if our circumstances were worlds apart.

The music flowed steadily from her fingers, every note exactly where it needed to be. I thought about her story—how she had bravely chosen to live as her authentic self, despite the challenges she knew transitioning would bring. There was a courage in that choice I deeply admired.

"Did it get easier?" I asked tentatively, unsure if I was overstepping but needing to know. "Becoming yourself?"

Her hands paused for a moment, cutting the phrase short. When she resumed playing, the melody shifted to a softer, more introspective mood.

"Not easier," she said after a long pause. "Just... more mine."

There was a truth in her words that resonated in places I wasn't ready to examine too closely. A beat of shared understanding passed between us, unspoken but real. She didn't press for details about why I was asking, and I was grateful for that restraint.

I stood from the piano bench, offering Lilith a small smile. "Break a leg tonight," I said. She nodded in understanding, her fingers finding a new melody.

I made my way back to my usual spot behind the bar, grateful for the familiar rhythm of checking inventory and arranging glasses. A few minutes later, Micah appeared beside me, her rhinestone emergency with Hella evidently resolved. She gave my side a playful nudge.

"You're doing good, you know," she said, pulling a cloth from under the bar and joining me in polishing glasses. "Keeping it all together."

I let out a short laugh, though it didn't quite hide the exhaustion in my voice. "Harder than it looks."

Her expression softened. "Yeah, I bet it is." She was quiet for a moment, then added, "I get that you're not ready to tell everyone yet, and that's okay. But you're not alone, you know? We've got your back."

I wanted to believe her, though part of me still struggled. The isolation of the past week since the transformation had left me feeling disconnected even in this warm, supportive community.

She sensed my lingering unease, and she studied my face with an intensity that left me feeling both seen and exposed.

"You sure you don't want to be up there in sequins?" she asked, nodding toward the stage, where Hella was now rehearsing a dance routine. "You've got that dramatic, brooding thing down pat."

Despite everything, I found myself smiling. "I think I've hit my rhinestone limit for the day."

"Fair enough," she said, smiling back. "But the offer stands if you ever want to try it. I could whip up something that'd make Jackson's eyes pop right out of his head."

I hesitated, already talking myself out of overthinking Micah's grin, when Hella's voice rang out again. "Micah! Crisis number two! This strap is being absolutely impossible!"

Onstage, Hella yanked at a slipping strap, letting out an exaggerated sigh and giving the ceiling a long-suffering look.

Micah glanced between me and the stage, clearly torn between helping her friend and staying to offer support.

"Go," I said, nodding toward Hella. "I'm okay."

She gave me a long look, then squeezed my arm gently. "If you need anything..."

"I know where to find you."

With Micah back to handling costume emergencies, the bar settled into its familiar rhythm. The queens continued their preparations, their chatter and laughter forming a warm backdrop of sound. I busied myself with practical tasks, arranging bar trays, checking the ice supply, and making sure the sound system was properly connected.

For a few minutes, it felt almost normal. The overwhelming feelings that had weighed on me all day began to ease, becoming more manageable. I still caught snippets of conversation and the layered scents of perfume and makeup, but it no longer felt like a sensory assault.

The calm shattered with a loud crash outside, the unmistakable sound of a heavy object toppling, followed by the clatter of trash cans or recycling bins hitting the pavement.

Everyone in the bar froze. Conversations halted mid-sentence, and makeup brushes paused mid-stroke as commotion spilled in from the street.

Micah was the first to react, looking up from the strap disaster she was helping Hella untangle. "What the hell was that?"

I tilted my head and closed my eyes, focusing on the sounds filtering through the walls. Footsteps echoed on the sidewalk, unsteady and aggressive, followed by a voice shouting in anger. Recognition prickled across my skin. I knew that voice; I'd heard it raised in fury countless times during orchestra rehearsals.

"Brad," I said, the name coming out low and clipped, carrying more weight than a single syllable should.

CHAPTER SEVEN

"Holy crap, Wyatt, get it together!" Brad's voice sliced through the wall like a hot knife.

Micah paused mid-fix on the stubborn strap. "Heads up, folks," she called. "Brace yourselves—incoming attitude and designer cologne."

The front door swung open and Brad stalked in, his tailored clothes doing little to hide his rigid posture.

"Well, well," Adda drawled, "aren't we a little high-strung?"

She shot me a knowing look that made me want to crawl under the bar.

Adda stage-whispered loud enough for Brad to hear, "Honey, you're not the only one who's sampled *that* particular vintage." She threw me a playful wink. "Some of us just have better taste than to go back for seconds."

I focused on wiping down the bar, willing myself not to react. That night at Brad's parents' mansion was ancient history. Still, the memory made my skin crawl. And I definitely didn't need the mental image of Adda and Brad... together.

"Ladies," Brad acknowledged, forcing politeness. "Reyes, I

need a drink before heading to the academy. Lucas around?"

"Office," I replied, noting Lucas's absence behind the bar. "I can make you something."

"The Presidio Trio's star violinist drinking before rehearsal?" Adda clicked her tongue. "My, how the mighty have fallen."

Brad's jaw flexed. "It's a meeting, not rehearsal. Some of us have actual careers to manage."

The door chimed as Enzo Dodson—built like a wine barrel—rolled in a delivery cart loaded with liquor bottles, his daughter Irene trailing quietly behind.

"Hey, Enzo. Hey, Irene," I called out, grateful for the interruption. "The usual Friday delivery?"

From her spot at the keyboard, I caught Lilith watching the delivery with unusual interest.

"How've you been, Irene?" I asked, remembering our AP music theory classes at Hillsborough High—part of the school's competitive orchestra track—where we'd both stumbled through harmonic analysis. "Still playing violin at all?"

She tucked a strand of dark hair behind her ear, smiling shyly. "Oh, um, just for fun sometimes," she murmured, her voice barely carrying across the bar. "Nothing serious anymore."

I remembered how she used to command attention in orchestra, her violin playing so beautiful it silenced even the chattiest freshmen. Back then, everyone expected her and Brad to battle it out for the concerto competition's solo prize. Her technique had been flawless, the result of raw talent and dedication, not wealthy parents funding extra coaching. But everything changed senior year, after Mr. Dodson's business partner passed away unexpectedly. Irene began missing rehearsals to help at Spirit Haven, their family-run liquor distribution business with a small retail storefront. By graduation, she'd abandoned her dreams of music school entirely.

"Remember when you played the Tchaikovsky concerto at that pre-competition recital?" I couldn't help asking. "I swear the entire audience was in tears."

A flicker of emotion—pain, regret—crossed her face before she looked down at her clipboard. "That was a lifetime ago," she said softly. "The business needs me now. Dad can't manage deliveries and inventory alone."

I caught Brad watching her. He'd ended up playing the same concerto after Irene dropped out. Not quite as masterfully, though his expensive Italian violin did most of the work for him. Notes that should've scraped or wobbled came out warm instead. Sometimes I wondered if he remembered he'd only gotten the solo by default.

The awkward silence broke with the clink of glass bottles. Enzo wheeled his delivery cart closer to the bar, his cheerful energy taking over the room.

"Wait until you see what I've got!" Enzo announced. "This Brazilian banana liqueur is trending all over social media for its real banana flavor. None of that artificial stuff. It's taking over craft cocktail bars everywhere!" He pulled out a sleek bottle with a geometric label.

"Oh my goddess, yes!" Hella exclaimed, practically bouncing over to the bar. "That's the stuff everyone's been obsessing over for those Banshee cocktails." She ticked off the ingredients on her fingers. "Crème de cacao, banana liqueur, and milk. Basically an adult banana milkshake that's breaking

TikTok right now."

She leaned over the bar, examining the bottle with genuine excitement. "How did you even get this? I heard it's virtually impossible to find."

Enzo beamed with pride. "Let's just say I have my connections. Twenty years in the business, you learn a few tricks." He winked, setting the bottle on the bar with a flourish.

"I'll try it," Brad said, cutting off Enzo's enthusiastic presentation. "Make me a Banshee."

I hesitated, mentally running through Brad's allergies—nuts and dairy. Back at high school orchestra camp, he'd made everyone miserable by loudly complaining about having to sit at a separate table when the cafeteria couldn't accommodate his needs. Food allergies are no joke, but his over-the-top dramatics had always made the rest of us roll our eyes.

"With oat milk," I specified.

Brad waved dismissively. "Whatever. Just make it strong."

The cocktail came together smoothly. I'd seen the trending videos and knew the steps. By scent alone, I detected the perfect balance of ingredients, and my newfound grace made the pour into the delicate coupe glass look effortless, elegant even. The pale cream-colored liquid settled into a perfect crescent against the rim, not a drop spilled despite my still-adjusting strength.

Brad took a long sip, nodding appreciatively. "Not bad, Reyes. Maybe you've got a future in bartending, since that Philharmonic spot is basically mine."

"Careful, honey," Adda called from across the room. "Pride comes before a fall, and those Italian leather shoes aren't made for stumbling."

Brad's retort was cut short by a sudden grimace. "Bathroom," he muttered, heading toward the back hallway.

When he slid his empty glass back across the bar, the lingering scent drew my attention. The banana liqueur was supposed to be trending for its natural flavor, but beneath it I detected faint chemical notes and a bitter scent that didn't sit right. My vampire senses were still new, so I couldn't be sure if it was a real flaw, or if I was picking up details no one else could.

"Alright, darlings!" Adda's commanding voice cut through the low murmur of conversation. "As riveting as this little drama is, we've got a show to put on." She swept her emerald-clad form toward the keyboard, where Lilith's bench sat conspicuously empty. "Has anyone seen our resident piano princess?" she called. "Lilith, honey? These arrangements don't play themselves."

The question lingered in the air unanswered as footsteps echoed from the back hallway.

Lucas emerged from the office. The moment he walked in, his eyes locked on me and he tipped his head, subtle but enough for me to know something wasn't right. I gave him a quick nod, understanding we'd have to wait to discuss it away from the others. Bitter chemical traces in the air still had my senses buzzing.

"Enzo," he greeted warmly. Lowering his voice, he asked, "Hey, that Brazilian liqueur... who's your supplier?" He must've heard our entire conversation from his office.

"Ah," Enzo's face lit up, and he checked the room before answering. "Between you and me? Got it through that new distributor in Hayward. Very exclusive. They're only selling to a handful of venues."

Their words barely carried as they discussed pricing and availability. Lucas's hand tightened imperceptibly on the edge of the bar when Enzo mentioned the shipment had come through an unusual route.

"Just came in yesterday," Enzo added. "Had to clear customs separately from our regular imports, but the paperwork checked out."

Lucas nodded, pulling out his phone. "Send me the details?" he asked.

The front door chimed again. Wyatt and Jordyn walked in, their anxious energy palpable even across the room.

"Brad here?" Jordyn asked, her impeccable posture held a little too carefully. "We've got that meeting with Professor Yates."

"Bathroom," I said, noticing how Wyatt's fingers tapped out a nervous rhythm against his thigh until a pointed look from Jordyn cut it short.

"Still?" Micah looked up from helping Hella with rhinestones. "It's been like ten minutes."

That wasn't like Brad. He wasn't the type to vanish this long for a bathroom break. His vanity wouldn't allow him to risk raising questions.

"I'll check," I said, already heading for the hallway. With each step, the scents intensified, the pungent bite of cocaine giving way to the cloying sweetness of the banana liqueur, and beneath it all, that unsettling chemical edge...

I pushed open the bathroom door to see Brad's legs sprawled beyond the stall door. What hit me was the terrifying absence of his heartbeat.

"Oh god," I whispered.

CHAPTER EIGHT

The bathroom stall door swung open, revealing Brad's crumpled form in his designer clothes, stark against the white tile. His limbs sprawled at unnatural angles, a bluish tinge creeping into his perfectly manicured nails. Light traces of white powder ringed his nostrils. Calluses from years of violin practice marked his pale hands, now unnervingly still.

The chemical trace of cocaine surfaced, followed by the sour reek of vomit. Beneath it all, a bitter note lingered, persistent and unnamed. The combination stopped me where I stood.

"Cass." Lucas's voice cut through the overload. He appeared in the doorway, reading my sensory shock in an instant. Without hesitation, he pulled me back, one steadying hand on my shoulder.

"I need you to breathe," he urged, positioning himself between me and the bathroom. "Focus on my voice."

Behind us, Micah was already on her phone. "Yes, we need an ambulance at All Aboard Bar," she said, her voice level despite the tremor in her hands. "It's one of our regulars. He's not responding—in the bathroom."

Lucas caught Micah's eye and signaled her to close the bar as he surveyed everyone present. His protective instincts were subtle but unmistakable in the way he kept himself between me and the bathroom door.

From the main room, Adda's commanding voice rose above the growing chaos. "Alright, ladies, show's canceled. Pack it up. And no social media posts, understood? This isn't the kind of publicity we need." The drag queens responded instantly to her authority. "Well, darlings, this is one show I never wanted to headline," Adda muttered.

Hella appeared at her side, rhinestones forgotten. "Should we call the other venues? Warn them about..." She trailed off, turning towards Adda as if waiting for guidance.

Lilith slipped back in, face pale beneath her makeup. "I can't believe this is happening," she whispered. "One minute he's ordering a drink, and now he isn't moving."

"Darling, in this business we learn fast to handle the unexpected," Adda said, her tone gentle despite her flair for drama. She touched Hella's shoulder before turning to Lilith. "Now come help me make sure everyone's accounted for. Heaven knows we've had enough surprises tonight."

The queens exchanged glances as their quick wit gave way to crisis management. Chairs scraped and heels clicked as someone reached instinctively for the house lights. They fanned out through the bar, checking booths and dressing corners, voices overlapping in clipped exchanges.

The next few minutes blurred into sirens and uniforms. The paramedics worked quickly, but I already knew what they'd say.

"Time of death, 6:17 p.m.," one paramedic murmured.

A detective who looked to be in her early thirties arrived as Brad's body was being covered. She moved methodically, cataloging the scene as though piecing together a puzzle only she could solve.

I couldn't shake the feeling that her careful observation carried more than routine procedure, hinting at a deeper understanding of the situation than she revealed. Her eyes paused on Lucas, and unease pricked at me. Was it recognition? Curiosity?

The way she studied him with a blend of scrutiny and respect made me wonder if she sensed the layers of our world beneath the bar's ordinary facade. I'd watched Lucas navigate the fragile balance of human and vampire interactions with ease, but she seemed intent on peeling those layers back, searching for truths beyond reach.

She approached with measured steps, her badge catching the bar lights as she extended a hand to Lucas.

"Detective Kerri Martinez, SFPD Homicide. You're the general manager here?" Her voice carried authority without aggression.

Lucas nodded, the picture of composure, perfectly balancing helpful civilian and polished professional. "Lucas Kemp. Yes, I manage All Aboard." He gestured toward me. "This is Caspar Reyes, one of our bartenders."

They exchanged a brief handshake before Martinez looked up, taking in the security cameras mounted strategically around the bar. "Those cameras active?"

"All of them," Lucas confirmed. "Including the one covering the bar area where the drinks are made."

"I'll need that footage."

"Of course. Give me a few minutes to pull it from the system." Lucas headed toward his office, leaving me alone with the detective.

When Martinez turned her full attention on me, the weight of her scrutiny pressed down. A subtle edge in her bearing suggested she might understand more about our world than she let on.

"Mr. Reyes," she said, her gaze holding mine, unnervingly intense. "Walk me through what happened."

"Brad came in for a drink before his trio's meeting at the academy," I explained, focusing on the facts to steady my voice. "Lucas wasn't around, so I offered to make it."

"Tell me about the drink preparation." She pulled out a small notebook, her pen gliding in neat, methodical strokes.

I described making Brad's drink, emphasizing the substitutions.

"He's allergic to nuts and dairy, so I used oat milk instead of regular milk or cream. The recipe also called for crème de cacao and that new Brazilian banana liqueur."

"The Banshee cocktail," Martinez noted, her pen pausing. "I've seen it all over social media."

"Yeah. Enzo, our distributor, just brought the banana liqueur today. First time we've used it."

"And you're certain about using oat milk?" Martinez pressed, her dark eyes locking onto mine.

"Absolutely. I double-checked because of his allergies. We keep the alternative milks in separate containers to prevent mix-ups."

Her expression remained unchanged. "We recovered cocaine in his pocket," she said, watching for my reaction. "Did you know about his drug use?"

The discovery wasn't surprising. I'd already noticed his erratic behavior at rehearsal and caught the chemical traces under his cologne. But before I could answer, a commotion erupted from the main room.

Wyatt blurted, "This is my fault," to an officer. "The competition pressure, the way we fought—" His words tumbled out between sobs.

Jordyn stood apart from the others, posture rigid and hands clasped neatly in front of her, as she answered questions.

"Brad had been... difficult lately. More aggressive than usual. Paranoid about the competition. But he was brilliant. We had disagreements about interpretation, about rehearsal schedules, but nothing that would..." She trailed off, swallowing hard.

Lucas returned from the office with his laptop. "Detective, I have the security footage ready."

The grainy video captured Brad's heated argument with Wyatt and Jordyn outside, his solitary entrance into the bar, and every subsequent movement until he entered the bathroom. I watched myself make the Banshee cocktail, meticulously measuring each ingredient. Nothing appeared amiss, yet off-screen, that faint, bitter scent lingered in the room.

Between interviews, I found myself drawn back to the bar, following that elusive aroma. Lucas caught my eye from across the room, a subtle shake of his head warning me not to hover where there was nothing to see.

Micah had somehow corralled the drag queens into giving

coherent statements, though their flair for drama still peeked through.

"There I was, adjusting my contour," Hella declared, "when I heard the most theatrical argument outside. And let me tell you, when a drag queen calls something theatrical—"

"Focus, dear," Adda interrupted gently. "Just the relevant details."

Detective Martinez approached the bar and examined the bottle of banana liqueur. She bagged it as evidence, along with Brad's glass.

"Detective," Micah called, waving a notebook. "I've got everyone's preliminary statements organized by time and location. The queens can be... elaborate storytellers, so I highlighted the actually relevant parts."

Martinez raised an eyebrow, accepting the notebook. "Efficient."

"Girl, you try keeping track of drag queen drama without a system," Micah replied, earning a small smile from the detective.

Wyatt's voice cut in, as if cued by an orchestra conductor. "He'd been using more," Wyatt revealed through fresh tears. "The cocaine. Said it helped him focus, but he was getting paranoid. Kept saying people were trying to sabotage him before the competition."

"Mr. Cross," Martinez interrupted gently. "When exactly did you notice the changes in Mr. Bennington's behavior?"

Jordyn answered instead, her academy-trained voice carrying clearly. "About a month ago. After we got accepted to the Fischer Competition finals." She paused, as if choosing her phrasing with care, then continued, "He became obsessed with winning. Said his father's connections had guaranteed us the prize, but we had to be 'worthy' of it."

"And how did that make you feel?" Martinez asked.

"Angry." Jordyn's admission was clipped, like a perfectly articulated staccato note. "He threatened to have me black-listed. Said one word from his family would end any chance I had at a professional career. As if I need to be reminded of how this industry works."

Lucas and Martinez exchanged a look, and I had the sense they'd done this before. When Martinez had me review the drink preparation a second time, Lucas kept his distance but remained close enough to support me while still appearing professional.

"The security footage shows Mr. Bennington entering the bathroom at 5:41 p.m.," Martinez noted, consulting her note-pad. "Mr. Reyes discovered him at approximately 5:50 p.m. In that time, did anyone else enter or exit?"

"No," Lucas replied firmly. "The cameras cover both en-trances. Brad was alone."

If no one else had entered the bathroom, and Brad's aller-gies were well-known...

"The liqueur," I said. "There's something about it."

Martinez's expression sharpened. "Mr. Reyes, are you sug-gesting..."

"The bottle," Lucas finished, his voice carrying an author-ity that silenced the room. "It needs to be tested."

The detective was already pulling out her phone. "I'll ex-pedite the lab work. We'll test everything involved." She paused, making sure Lucas was following. "Both standard and... specialized analysis."

As she stepped away to make the call, I couldn't shake her composure. She hadn't questioned Lucas's authority, accepting it without hesitation, and it left me wondering how much of the supernatural world she could already see.

The scene cleared, leaving our core group in the empty bar. Micah began stress-cleaning glasses, while Adda supervised the other queens as they packed up their costumes. The normal post-show bustle felt hollow, like musicians trying to play a piece with vital notes missing.

"I should have noticed something was wrong," I said quietly, more to myself than anyone else. "The scent was there—in the drink. I just couldn't place it."

Lucas's hand landed on my shoulder. "You couldn't have known," he said, but there was a careful neutrality in his tone that made me wonder what he wasn't telling me.

CHAPTER NINE

The early morning stillness shattered as I drew my bow across the viola's strings, the day outside still colorless through our living room's small window. My hand trembled as I tackled a particularly difficult passage. The bow still felt as if it might snap beneath my fingers, dread coiling tighter with each measure. The Philharmonic auditions were approaching fast, and there wasn't nearly enough time for me to adjust to my newfound strength and sensitivity.

"Focus, Reyes," I muttered, trying to center myself as Lucas had taught me.

It didn't work. My thoughts kept circling back to Detective Martinez. Not the questions she'd asked, but the way she'd watched me. The pauses she allowed. The moments she didn't rush to fill. Even then, it had felt like she was paying attention in a different way.

A familiar knock pattern interrupted my thoughts. Three quick taps followed by two slower ones. Lucas.

"Come in," I called, lowering my bow. The door opened, revealing Lucas balancing two coffee cups in one hand.

"Thought you might need this," he said, handing me one.

His fingers brushed mine longer than necessary, sending a jolt through my sensitized skin. "Early morning practice?"

I caught myself studying how the morning light played across his features, highlighting the strength in his stance, protective even in casual moments.

"Couldn't sleep. Too much processing."

"About Martinez's questioning?" He leaned against the doorframe, a posture that managed to both block the exit and appear completely relaxed.

"Among other things." I took a sip of coffee, the flavors exploding across my taste buds. "She seemed... different from the other officers asking the usual questions."

"You noticed that, did you?" His knuckles rapped softly on the wall. "Some law enforcement officials work closely with our community. They help maintain balance, keeping certain incidents from drawing unwanted attention."

"Wait, Martinez knows about vampires?"

"I can't confirm anything specific," he said carefully. "But there are signs if you know what to look for. The way she maintains eye contact without discomfort, the focus on scent-related questions."

I thought back to her methodical examination of the banana liqueur bottle. "That reminds me, there was something off about that bottle. An indistinct, bitter scent. Slightly chemical."

Lucas snapped to attention. "Time for some training," he announced, heading downstairs to the bar. I followed, trying not to focus on how gracefully he moved despite his size.

We slipped behind the bar together, and he guided me into place with a light touch at my waist.

"Stay there," he said. Before I could ask what he had in mind, he added, "Close your eyes."

I hesitated, then did as he asked.

Behind me, I heard him move along the back bar. Glassware clinked and liquid poured, one measured splash, then another. Bottles were set aside with a faint scrape.

"Here," he said, returning to my side. "Let me show you how to isolate specific scents. It's a crucial skill for our kind."

He positioned himself behind me, close enough that I could feel the solid presence of his chest against my back as he guided my hands to the first glass.

"Focus on separating each individual aroma," he instructed.

The proximity was... distracting.

I tried to concentrate on the glasses rather than Lucas's hands guiding mine between them, but my senses seemed determined to catalog everything about him instead. The subtle spice of his cologne mingled with the rhythm of his breathing, along with the controlled strength in his cool touch.

"Focus, Cass," he breathed, stirring the hair at the back of my neck.

The shiver that followed had nothing to do with vampire sensitivity.

Without meaning to, I found myself leaning back into his solid frame, breathing in the intoxicating mix of coffee, cologne, and something indefinable that was uniquely Lucas. My head spun.

Footsteps from the back hallway broke the moment. I opened my eyes as Micah burst in, carrying a familiar pink box from Tita Isa's kitchen.

"Good morning, my fav-... oh," she paused, taking in our position. "Am I interrupting something?"

"Training," Lucas said smoothly, stepping back. "Scent identification."

"Uh-huh." Micah's knowing grin suggested she wasn't buying it. "Well, my mom sent breakfast. Coconut pandan ensaymada and ube pandesal. She says you're too skinny, Cass. Vampire or not."

She arranged the pastries on the bar, the familiar scents of coconut and ube mingling with the lingering aromas from Lucas's training exercise. "Also, everyone in West Portal has a theory about Brad. Want to hear the top three?"

"Do we have a choice?" I asked, reaching for an ensaymada.

"Nope!" Micah hopped onto a barstool. "Theory one: Brad was secretly dating a married symphony patron who poisoned him when he threatened to go public."

Lucas raised an eyebrow. "And where did that come from?"

"Mrs. Nguyen at the dry cleaners. She swears she saw Brad getting into an expensive car with an older woman." Micah grabbed her phone. "Oh wait. Speaking of Brad—"

A news anchor's voice burst from the phone's speaker: "...CEO of the Bennington Development Group, Richard Bennington, is demanding a full investigation into his son's death at a local San Francisco bar. Bradley Bennington, age twenty-two, was an accomplished violinist expected to join the San Francisco Philharmonic..."

B-roll footage showed Brad performing, his Italian violin gleaming under stage lights. The camera panned to showcase his father's stern face at a press conference.

"The circumstances of my son's death are suspicious," Bennington declared. "I expect every aspect to be thoroughly investigated."

"Great," I muttered. "Because this wasn't enough of a circus already."

My phone buzzed with a text: Hi Cass. It's Jackson. Got your number from Micah. Saw the news. You okay? Yoga buddy if you need one.

Despite myself, a reluctant warmth rose at the message. When I looked up, Micah's smile was already in place.

"What?" I asked.

"Oh, nothing," she said brightly. "Just clocking the timing." She glanced pointedly at my phone, then over at Lucas. "Speaking of which—Lucas, don't you have some very important... manager things to do in the back office?"

Lucas's expression remained neutral. "Actually, yes. Cass, we'll continue training later."

"And no eavesdropping!" After he left, Micah turned to me. "Okay, spill. What's going on with you three?"

"Nothing's going on," I protested. "Lucas is my mentor, and Jackson is... Jackson."

"Sure. And I'm the Queen of England." She popped a piece of pandesal in her mouth. "Want to hear theories two and three about Brad?"

Before I could respond, movement outside drew my attention. Even through the window's UV filtering, I could make out Wyatt's uneven steps and the anxious energy in the way he moved.

"Speaking of complications," I murmured.

Wyatt pushed through the door, making a beeline for the

bar. "Macallan. Neat."

"Geez, hitting the hard stuff already? It's not even noon," Micah pointed out.

"Please," Wyatt's voice cracked. "I just... I need something."

I poured the whiskey, noting how his fingers shook as he lifted the glass. "Want to talk about it?"

"The trio..." he started, then took a long swallow. "We had rehearsal yesterday morning. Before we ran into you in the hall. Brad was... he said..." Wyatt's breath hitched. "He threatened to replace us after the competition. Said we were holding him back."

Lucas emerged from his office, positioning himself casually but strategically between me and Wyatt. I wondered if he'd been listening the whole time.

"He called my technique sloppy," Wyatt continued, voice rising. "Said my scholarship was wasted on second-rate talent. That his father's connections could blacklist us if we didn't shape up."

A presence in the doorway drew my attention. Detective Martinez stood watching, her notebook already in hand. She didn't approach immediately, instead observing the scene with that same unnaturally measured composure Lucas had mentioned.

Wyatt didn't notice her. "He was sabotaging our rehearsals. Missing cues, playing out of tune, then blaming us when things fell apart. Said we were lucky he even bothered with us, that any decent musician would have replaced us months ago."

Martinez's heart rate remained perfectly controlled despite

the emotional scene unfolding. She was likely *in the know,* as Lucas had suggested.

"The worst part?" Wyatt said. "He wasn't wrong. My technique's slipping. I'm late on entrances, the trio feels it." He scrubbed a hand over his face. "I'm tired, Cass. I keep staying up late trying to fix it. And I don't have money for extra coaches. My scholarship barely covers tuition."

His voice dropped. "And when I couldn't make rent last spring... he covered it. No questions, no lecture. Just sent a Venmo with a single violin emoji."

That didn't fit the Brad I knew. Had there been a rare moment of actual decency buried beneath all that narcissism?

"If he was awful to you the rest of the time... why help with rent?" I asked.

Wyatt shook his head quickly, as if brushing off his own words. "I don't know. He still made me feel like I didn't belong in every other way. Like I was just some charity case he kept around to make himself look good."

Martinez chose that moment to step forward, her voice cutting through the tension. "That's interesting, Wyatt. Did Brad help you financially on other occasions?"

Wyatt's grip tightened on his glass. "A few times. But it always came with strings attached. He'd bring it up whenever I questioned his decisions."

I found myself staring into my coffee. The Brad I'd known growing up had been cruel, entitled, manipulative. But this painted a picture of someone messier, more complicated. Someone who could write a check to save a friend from eviction, then use that same generosity as a weapon.

Martinez stepped closer, her questioning style gentle but

focused. "Wyatt, could you tell me more about these rehearsal tensions?"

I noticed how she watched his physical responses more than listened to his actual answers. Her pen moved across the notebook, but her eyes never left his fidgeting hands.

"It wasn't just me," Wyatt continued. "He'd been horrible to Jordyn too. Said her interpretation was rudimentary, that she played like someone who learned piano at the mall."

Martinez set her pen down deliberately, her attention fixed on Wyatt's face. "Help me understand something, Wyatt. If Brad's behavior was this problematic, why didn't you address it sooner? Why wait until now to speak up?"

His thumb traced a restless line along the glass. "It's... it's complicated." He took another sip. "In classical music, you don't just... complain. There's a hierarchy. Brad had connections, reputation. If you speak out against someone like that..."

"But this affected your performance," Martinez pressed. "Your career prospects."

"Yes, but—" Wyatt's voice caught. He set the glass down. "Look, I tried to handle it professionally. We all did. You adapt, you work around it, you hope things improve."

"Even when it was damaging your own opportunities?"

Wyatt scoffed. "You don't get it. My parents think classical music is this... respectable, civilized thing. They'd never believe someone could actually..." He trailed off, staring into his whiskey. "They sacrificed so much for my education. My dad's a middle school math teacher, and my mom works in school food service. To them, it's this polished, elegant world where everyone just gets along and makes beautiful music together."

He looked up, blinking hard. "What am I supposed to say? That the whole music scene they've poured everything into is just politics and power games? That talent and hard work alone aren't enough?"

Martinez's expression softened. "So you protected their illusions."

"I protected their hope," Wyatt replied. "And mine, I guess. I kept thinking if I just worked harder, practiced more, maybe Brad would respect the music enough to stop sabotaging us." He shook his head. "Turns out I was protecting a lie."

I watched Wyatt's shoulders shake as he finished speaking, his voice striking a chord deep enough to capture the desperate need to protect the people who believed in you. Listening to him describe Brad's systematic cruelty, watching him crumble under the weight of safeguarding his family's naive hope, I realized how complicit we'd all been in the lie. We'd let people like Brad get away with their behavior because calling it out meant admitting the entire system was flawed.

Detective Martinez took detailed notes on Wyatt's statement before escorting him out. The morning stretched over the now-silent bar. I wiped down the already spotless counter, but my mind kept replaying the events, piecing together patterns in everyone's behavior, trying to make sense of it all.

"Break time," Lucas called out. "Micah, Cass, you both look like you need a breather."

I set down the cloth, realizing I'd been polishing the same spot for several minutes. "Thanks," I said, hearing the slight strain in my voice. The morning's revelations and tangled emotions had left me mentally exhausted. Even my vampire senses felt overworked, stretched like muscles pushed past their limit.

"Come on," Micah said, tugging my arm. "I need your freakishly long arms to help me with Hella's new costume. And you could use a distraction from all this music and vampire mess."

I followed her up the narrow stairs to our apartment, the familiar creaks of each step a welcome relief from the tension downstairs. "What about theories two and three? Or are you holding those under lock and key until I help with sequins?"

"You know me too well." Micah flung open her bedroom door, revealing what looked like a fabric store had exploded. Swaths of iridescent material draped every surface, and a half-finished gown dominated her dress form. "Theory two: Brad was actually running some kind of secret side operation, and his past finally caught up with him."

"What?" I carefully moved a pile of rhinestones to her bed. "Where did that come from?"

"Mr. Petrenko at the hardware store. He swears Brad bought duct tape and rope often enough to raise an eyebrow." Micah thrust a handful of gold trim at me. "Hold this while I pin."

"Buying duct tape and rope that frequently raises a question," I pointed out, stretching the trim along the gown's hemline. "But honestly? With Brad, that could be something dark... or just something embarrassingly personal."

"Exactly. His life always had undertones that weren't exactly... vanilla." Micah worked skillfully, pins appearing almost magically between her lips as she spoke. "But theory three is my favorite: apparently Brad was secretly learning drag makeup from Adda."

I nearly dropped the trim. "No way."

"Way! Jules saw him watching YouTube tutorials on contouring at the bar last month." Micah's grin was wicked. "Can you imagine? All that drama about his father's expectations, and he was planning a grand debut as..." she paused dramatically, "Bradney Spears."

The laugh burst out before I could stop it. "That's terrible."

"I know!" Micah cackled. "But admit it, you needed that mental image."

She wasn't wrong.

"There," she declared, stepping back to admire our work. "Now we just have to survive tonight's shift without any more drama."

"Don't jinx it," I warned, though I was smiling.

CHAPTER TEN

My phone buzzed, snapping me awake at precisely 8:00 a.m., an unfamiliar number with SFPD listed beneath it glowing on the screen.

"Mr. Reyes," Martinez said. "Could you come to the SFPD Headquarters downtown this morning? We have follow-up questions about Bradley Bennington's death."

"What time do you need me there?" I asked, striving to clear the sleep from my voice despite the early call.

"By nine would be ideal," Martinez replied, her tone still guarded.

"I'll be there in thirty minutes," I said, already grabbing the cleanest shirt from my laundry pile.

The precinct loomed ahead, its gray, institutional facade stark against the fog-diffused morning light. Inside, the stinging scent of industrial cleaner cut through the air, barely masking the bitter trace of stale coffee. Dozens of heartbeats thrummed nearby, their rhythms intertwining with the frantic clatter of computer keys in a restless duet.

I was escorted to a hallway and instructed to wait on a bench. The officer gestured vaguely toward a closed door at the end of the corridor before disappearing back toward the reception area.

The fluorescent lights above buzzed with an electrical hum that set my teeth on edge, and somewhere down the hall, a phone rang incessantly without answer.

Then I caught Lucas's voice, muffled but unmistakable, coming from behind the closed door.

Lucas was already here? Being questioned?

I shouldn't have listened. I knew that. But before I could stop myself, I focused on the conversation filtering through the door.

It wasn't easy. The buzzing lights created a constant interference, like static overlaying a radio station. I closed my eyes, trying to isolate Lucas's voice from the clamor.

"...good worker. Reliable..." his words came in fragments, broken by the ambient noise. "...keeps to himself."

I strained harder, blocking out a passing conversation between two officers discussing lunch plans.

"But he's... sensitive," Lucas continued, his voice clearer now. "You know how some people are. Things get under their skin."

Was that how Lucas saw me? Sensitive? Fragile?

Martinez replied, but the words blurred into the static.

"No." Lucas's voice sharpened. "Cass wouldn't hurt anyone."

The conviction in his tone set a small warmth blooming in my chest, even as my anxiety ratcheted higher. This wasn't the casual follow-up questioning I'd anticipated. This was an interrogation.

I leaned forward, the background noise fading as I locked

onto their conversation.

"Tell me about your liquor suppliers," Martinez said.

"We work with several local distributors," Lucas replied. "All properly licensed and vetted."

"Including Spirit Haven? I understand they delivered that Brazilian banana liqueur the day Brad died."

My pulse quickened. *The banana liqueur. The drink I'd made for Brad.*

"The timing of the delivery has been noted," Lucas said, his diplomatic tone firmly in place. "We've provided all supplier documentation, including our long-standing contract with Spirit Haven for liquor and wine."

A chair scraped against the floor inside the room, the sudden sound making me flinch.

"Thank you for your cooperation, Mr. Kemp."

The door swung open, and Lucas stepped out. His eyes found mine immediately, and as he passed, his fingers tapped once against his thigh. I took it for what it was: caution.

Whatever happened in that room, it wasn't good.

Martinez appeared in the doorway, pinning me with the same unnerving scrutiny I recalled from the night Brad died. "This way, Mr. Reyes."

I stood, my legs feeling less sure than I would've liked, and followed her into the interrogation room.

The space matched every crime show cliché, with bare walls, a metal table, and uncomfortable chairs, yet my senses caught what cameras would miss. Faint rings and dried droplets of coffee clung to the table's surface. The trace of fear-sweat, lingering from past occupants, soaked into the chair cushions and the porous ceiling tiles. The residue of cleaning products that couldn't quite erase the room's history.

Martinez gestured to a chair across from her. "I hope you don't mind," she said as I sat. "I asked Mr. Kemp to come in as your employer and character witness."

I nodded, not trusting my voice yet. My mind was still processing what I'd overheard.

She slid a folder across the table, the sound harsh in the small room. "The preliminary autopsy results are in," she began. "Brad died from anaphylactic shock. We're still determining whether it was caused by an allergic reaction, a contaminant in the cocaine, or a combination of factors."

She paused, pen hovering over her notebook.

"You mentioned knowing about Mr. Bennington's allergies?"

"Everyone at the academy knew," I answered. "Brad had a dramatic episode after eating a cookie with ground almonds at a donor reception. No one could forget it."

"And your relationship with the deceased?" Her pen moved in sharp, precise strokes, each scratch a percussive beat.

"We went to the same high school and college," I said, keeping my tone even. "Played in orchestras together. Him in first violins, me in violas." I traced a pattern on the table, focusing on its cool surface to anchor myself against the flood of memories.

"Did your relationship ever extend beyond professional?" She stilled, her unwavering stare locked on my face.

I swallowed, memories surging unbidden. "We hooked up once, six months ago, at a party at his parents' house. It didn't mean anything. At least not to him."

"Tell me about that night."

Martinez continued watching me with unrelenting intensity as I recounted the basics, her pulse holding that eerily even rhythm Lucas had noted. When I mentioned Brad's cocaine use, her pen froze mid-stroke.

"You're very observant, Mr. Reyes," she said, her tone sharp with scrutiny. "Especially about... details others might overlook."

"I'm a musician," I replied cautiously, heeding Lucas's warnings about revealing too much. "I guess I'm used to paying attention. Miss one cue in an orchestra and everyone notices."

Martinez gave a thin smile, then flipped a page before shifting gears. "About Brad's allergies," she pressed, "the bar must have strict protocols for handling orders from customers with severe reactions?"

"Absolutely," I replied. "We're trained in allergen awareness. We keep detailed logs of ingredients and use separate equipment for alternative milk preparations."

"Yet preliminary results indicate anaphylaxis," she added firmly. "Specifically, signs pointing to a severe allergic reaction."

"That's impossible. I used oat milk. I checked the container. Nothing with nuts went into that drink."

Martinez's foot tapped lightly under the table. "Witnesses reported Brad acting erratically in the weeks before his death. Arguments with his trio members, missed rehearsals, cocaine use..."

"That wasn't new," I countered. "Brad was always..."

"High-strung?" Martinez offered. "Demanding? His father thinks otherwise. Richard Bennington insists his son was under unusual pressure recently."

The mention of Brad's father sent a chill through me, despite my vampire-cold skin. Brad had never seemed fazed by his father's controlling nature. I recalled watching them at benefit concerts, Richard scrutinizing Brad's appearance before performances, while Brad beamed, proud to be the perfect prodigy son.

"If Richard thought Brad was under pressure, he wasn't wrong," I said. "He'd been stressed about his trio's competition. And the Philharmonic audition on top of it... it's a big deal."

"Yes, I understand you're both competing for the same position, Mr. Reyes?" A restrained edge crept into her voice. "Viola versus violin. Unusual for them to compete directly."

"Only one string opening," I explained. "They're considering all string players, regardless of instrument."

"High stakes," she noted. "Especially given your... recent financial situation."

I stiffened. Martinez's choice of words made it clear she knew more about me than I realized. Somehow Richard Bennington must've learned that my father had cut me off, and that information had made its way to her. The thought that Richard might even suspect me, that my circumstances could somehow be tied to his son, clarified the situation. I wasn't just a witness anymore.

"My personal circumstances have nothing to do with Brad's death," I said firmly.

"Of course not," she replied, her voice neutral, but I caught a faint uptick in her pulse. "Just trying to understand the dynamics at play."

Martinez nodded, a brief spike of adrenaline in her scent quickly fading. "About that bottle of banana liqueur," she said, folding her hands on the table. "You said something felt off about it. Can you elaborate?"

The question felt like a trap. She was fishing, probing how much I'd reveal about my abilities.

"Just… something didn't seem right," I said cautiously. "But I'm still learning the bar's inventory, so I could be wrong."

"Indeed." She folded her notebook closed. "We're done for now, Mr. Reyes." She paused, her attention fixed on me with an unsettling stillness. "But be careful after dark. The city can be… dangerous for those who notice too much."

Martinez's warning hung in the back of my mind as she escorted me out of the room. A few steps down the hallway, I caught her low voice behind me, exchanging words with another officer that seemed to include "Todd's territory," though I couldn't be sure.

In the precinct lobby, Micah paced in tight circles, her boundless energy coiled like a spring. Seeing her there, waiting faithfully despite the early hour, tightened my throat with emotion. She spotted me and launched forward with the unstoppable force I'd come to expect from my best friend, enveloping me in a fierce hug that made me stagger. Even with my vampire strength, Micah's enthusiasm almost overcame me like a force of nature.

"Got Lucas's text and came straight over," she whispered against my shoulder, then pulled back to study my face. Her eyes searched mine, her tense posture betraying the worry she tried to mask. "You okay?"

"I'm fine," I assured her, though fine felt like a stretch. Martinez's knowing looks still pressed at the back of my mind.

Lucas's hand rested lightly on my shoulder. "Her questions weren't all about the murder," he said gently.

We stepped into the fog-diffused sunlight, the air heavy with traces of coffee and exhaust from morning traffic. The realization that Martinez knew, or at least suspected, what I was left me off balance. If she was aware of vampires, she'd be scrutinizing every detail I'd noticed with my senses. Finding Brad's killer wasn't only about clearing my name. It was about protecting the secrets I'd stumbled into since my transformation, secrets Lucas guarded with an intensity that both reassured and unsettled me.

"We'll help," Micah declared, her fierce loyalty unwavering as she linked her arm through mine. "West Portal's small. People talk. And the queens hear everything." Her voice brimmed with the unshakable certainty that had carried us through crises since we met at All Aboard Bar months ago.

Lucas's expression was thoughtful yet resolute. "I'll make inquiries of my own. Discreetly." His measured authority hinted at resources and connections I could only guess at. Standing between Micah's steadfast friendship and Lucas's protective presence, I felt a knot inside me loosen.

But in that moment of letting my guard down, of finally exhaling after Martinez's interrogation, my control slipped. A passing car's exhaust stung my senses, the coffee from a nearby café seared my nose, and conversations half a block away crashed into my consciousness.

Lucas noticed instantly. "Time to get you home," he said,

leaving no room for debate. "Sensory overload won't help anyone."

"But—" I began to protest.

"He's right," Micah interrupted, her voice firm. "You look like you're about to vibrate out of your skin. Go rest. I'll cover your shift."

As Lucas guided me toward his car, I caught Martinez watching from the precinct steps. She didn't look away, her heartbeat holding that same steady rhythm, like a metronome set to a flawless tempo.

CHAPTER ELEVEN

Sleep eluded me that night. I still needed to rest, but the knowledge that Detective Martinez's attention had turned toward me kept it out of reach. Every time I closed my eyes, Brad's face appeared. Not his usual arrogant smirk, but the fearful expression from our final moment. Every creak of the old building, every passing car on West Portal Avenue, and Micah's rhythmic breathing in the next room wove into a restless symphony, mirroring my racing thoughts.

Martinez's interrogation replayed in my mind. The assessing look she'd given me, as though she saw more than she let on. And her warning about being careful after dark. Was it caution or a veiled threat?

I sat up, shoving aside tangled sheets, and crossed to the window. My instincts stirred, like my body was urging me to catch a detail I'd missed.

"This is stupid," I muttered, even as I pulled on an old black sweatshirt, edges frayed with wear. I should've waited for Lucas or texted Micah. But an urgent need to act drove me toward the door.

The stairs to the bar threatened to creak under my steps, but

I'd learned which spots to avoid. Sneaking down for late-night blood bags kept discreetly in a small fridge beneath Lucas's desk had honed my silent navigation. The main room stood eerily quiet without its usual crowd, the space feeling hollow, like a stage after the audience had gone and the house lights dimmed.

I took a deep breath, drawing the bar's familiar scents into focus. The stale beer soaked into the floorboards lay alongside the lingering sweetness of simple syrup from tonight's cocktails and the metallic tang of the refrigerator's motor. Beneath it all ran a chemical note that didn't belong, cutting across the others instead of blending in.

My feet drew me toward the restroom before I fully registered the decision. Pausing in the doorway, I let my senses adjust. The industrial cleaner used after... everything... stung my nose, but beneath it, that same bitter scent remained, frustratingly indiscernible.

At first glance, the bathroom appeared ordinary, but as I stepped into the stall where they'd found Brad, I spotted a subtle discoloration in the grout near the toilet's base, a barely perceptible gap where the tile met the floor. I ran my fingers along the edge, feeling a slight give. The tile pried loose, revealing a small cavity.

A plastic bag glinted in the dim light, white powder inside. Cocaine.

"Well, I'll be damned," I muttered. Who was Brad's dealer? Was it laced with anything?

Hurrying back to the bar, I grabbed a clean sandwich bag from behind the counter and carefully sealed the cocaine inside. I was likely contaminating evidence, but leaving drugs in the bathroom of a bar already under scrutiny felt like a worse mistake. The cavity under the tile was easy to miss during an initial sweep.

Footsteps approached from outside. My heart lurched as I ducked behind the bar, angling to watch the entrance while staying concealed. The front door opened with a soft click, the bell conspicuously silent.

Lucas stepped inside, and for a moment, I forgot to breathe. In the darkness, his presence shifted the room's energy, stripped of the clinking glasses and chatter that usually softened it. Without his polished professional mask, he was more predator than proprietor. His eyes locked onto mine instantly, their subtle glow catching the chrome bar fixtures like twin moons.

I'd seen him daily for five months, but that late-night encounter made me aware of him in a way I couldn't ignore. The fluid grace of his stride as he crossed the room. The slight tilt of his head, conveying both amusement and disapproval. His scent of cedar, with a note uniquely his, turned the space intimate and charged.

Lucas crossed his arms, still in his work clothes. Dark jeans and a charcoal button-down, sleeves cut off as usual. Had he even gone home tonight? Or had he been out in the darkness, patrolling his territory?

"Next time, call me first," he said, his voice low but clear in the silent bar. It wasn't quite anger. More a blend of concern and frustration, perhaps with a flicker of pride at my initiative he'd never admit.

I straightened slowly, masking the sheepishness creeping in. "Technically, I didn't break in," I said. "I came down, and the back door was unlocked."

"Because I unlocked it when I sensed you on the stairs,"

Lucas replied, stepping closer. "I hadn't gone home yet."

His eyes dropped to the bag of cocaine on the counter. "And what were you planning to do with that?"

"I found it in the bathroom," I said quickly, watching his expression. "Hidden near where Brad... where we found him. The grout was loose, and I smelled something chemical underneath."

Lucas picked up the bag and examined it. "Your senses are sharpening," he noted. "But your judgment needs work."

"I couldn't sleep. Certain details keep nagging at me. Brad's behavior that morning, his arguments with everyone, how the drink hit him so fast..."

"So naturally, sneaking into the bar was the logical next step?" Lucas raised an eyebrow.

"I didn't break in," I insisted. "And I found something, didn't I? This could explain Brad's erratic behavior. Maybe he was using more than usual, or something was laced in it."

Lucas set the bag down and stepped closer, his hand brushing dust from my sleeve. The touch sent an unexpected shiver through me. "You don't have to do this alone," he said, his voice softer now. "That's what I'm here for."

I wanted to step back, to keep some professional distance, but his eyes held me in place. The protective concern there made me hesitate, though I'd never admit it.

"I'm not some fragile newborn needing constant supervision," I muttered, even as part of me leaned into his touch.

"No," Lucas agreed, "but you're not indestructible yet, kid. And I'd rather not find out how breakable you still are."

The "kid" jab stung and I pulled away. "I just... I need to do something, Lucas. If I don't, I'll—" The words caught in my throat, choked by the helpless weight of suspicion and uncertainty crushing me.

"Then let's do something. Together." He motioned toward the cocaine bag. "First, we need to figure out who supplied it. Discreetly."

"You have contacts?" I asked, already knowing the answer. Lucas seemed to know everyone in West Portal, human and otherwise.

"A few," he said, a sly smile tugging at his lips. "Get some rest, Cass. I'll start inquiries in the morning."

I stalled, reluctant to leave now that we had solid evidence. Lucas must have sensed it, his expression hardening. "I mean it, Cass. No more rogue moves. We do this together or not at all."

As we moved toward the rear exit, Lucas's hand rested briefly on my lower back, guiding me out. The touch felt protective, not controlling, and despite my earlier defensiveness, I leaned into it.

The night air cooled my skin as we stepped into the alley. Lucas paused long enough to check the lock behind us. I expected him to slip into the shadows, as he sometimes did, but he turned to face me instead, the overhead string lights carving sharp angles across his profile.

"Cass," he said, his voice close and grave. "Whatever we find, wherever this leads... I've got your back. Remember that."

Before I could respond, he vanished, leaving me with the weight of his words and the lingering glow of his touch. Tomorrow, we'd start unraveling this puzzle. For now, I headed upstairs, alone.

CHAPTER TWELVE

While I restocked glasses, the gentle clink of crystal served as a soothing counterpoint to my racing thoughts. Behind the bar, Lucas methodically counted bottles for inventory. Familiar footsteps sounded outside—Dolores's measured pace blending with Jules's lighter, quicker steps. The door chimed as they entered, dressed for the opera downtown, at the Civic Center, where the city's grand performance halls lined the same street. Jules sported one of his signature ascots, this one a vibrant peacock blue that complimented his ash-gray hair. Dolores floated in behind him, resplendent in a flowing kaftan of deep amethyst.

"Darlings!" Jules exclaimed, settling onto his usual barstool. "You won't believe what Mango has been up to now."

"Mrs. Nguyen's new cat?" I asked, already smiling. Jules's neighborhood updates had become my favorite part of the afternoon shift.

"The very same! That feline felon has graduated from stealing gloves to pilfering entire chess sets from Mr. Petrenko's sidewalk display. Piece by piece, mind you. Mrs. Nguyen found a neat little army of pawns arranged in formation on her doorstep this morning."

Dolores laughed, warm and musical. "At least the cat has good taste. Those chess sets are carved from Grecian marble."

"An entire marble battalion waiting at her door..." I said, picturing the neat row of pawns. "Mango might be planning a coup."

Lucas didn't bother looking up from his clipboard. "Honestly? A Mango-led coup would be the most organized development this week."

"Mrs. Nguyen swears she's going to start locking him inside at night," Jules added, "but we all know that's an empty threat. She's already knitting him a little collar with a bell."

"As if that would stop him," I said, setting down the last of the champagne flutes. "Mango strikes me as the type who'd learn to move silently despite the bells."

Jules glanced toward the door as if checking for eavesdroppers, his eyes glinting with mischief. "Between you and me, I think Mr. Petrenko is secretly charmed. Yesterday I caught him leaving a pawn out on the edge of his display. *Un petit cadeau*—a little gift—for Mango."

Dolores's expression softened with affection, her fingers absently smoothing the fabric of her kaftan. "That cat has the entire neighborhood wrapped around his paw."

Jules settled back on his barstool, one knee crossing over the other. Dolores's attention shifted my way.

"And how are you holding up, dear?" she asked. "Have you been able to keep up your practice schedule with everything going on?"

Her genuine concern touched me; even with everything

swirling around Brad's death, she focused on my musical growth.

"I've been trying," I admitted. "The Bach suite is coming along, though the fourth movement still trips me up."

"Ah, that's where everyone struggles at first," she said with a nod. "Remember what we discussed about letting the bow do the work? The notes will flow naturally if you don't force them."

Her words carried a double meaning, and I felt myself relax. From behind the bar, Lucas caught my eye, a smug smile curving his lips.

"Let me make you a drink," I offered. "A French 75, right? My treat. For everything you've done."

"Oh, you don't have to—" Dolores began, but I was already reaching for the gin.

"*S'il vous plaît*, let the boy show his appreciation," Jules interjected. "Besides, your guidance deserves celebration. Did you know," he turned to me, "that our dear Dolores once made a grown man cry during a master class simply by raising one eyebrow?"

"That's an exaggeration," Dolores protested, though her eyes sparkled. "He was already emotional about the Brahms."

I was measuring gin when the door slammed open, hard enough to rattle the glasses behind the bar. Wyatt stumbled in, the sour-sweet reek of expensive whiskey rolling off him in waves. His tie was askew, his tan wool coat rumpled and smudged at the cuffs, and his face flushed an alarming shade of red.

Lucas and I exchanged a look as he collapsed onto a barstool, his hands clamped around the edge like it was the only thing keeping him upright. Without thinking, I poured a glass of water and set it in front of him.

"Wyatt?" Dolores's voice carried the same gentle concern she'd used with countless struggling students. "What's happened?"

He ignored the water, his breathing ragged. Each exhale carried traces of aged single malt. Definitely not his usual drink of choice. "Brad," he mumbled, the word barely audible. "We were... we were gonna..." His voice cracked.

"Take your time," I said softly, watching Wyatt's pulse jump erratically.

"We were gonna replace him," Wyatt managed, his speech slurred. "He was... God, he was so out of control." His grip on the bar tightened. "Drugs, sabotaging rehearsals, the constant yelling. He wasn't... wasn't the same Brad anymore."

Jules and Dolores exchanged glances while I tried to process the weight of his words. Brad's own trio had been planning to cut him loose, a move that would've destroyed not only his career but his very identity. Had he known? Was that why he'd been spiraling so erratically?

"Last month," Wyatt went on, "he showed up high to a donor reception. Started arguing with Jordyn about tempo in front of everyone. Called her a 'talentless hack riding his coattails.' Mr. Bennington practically had to drag him out."

I frowned as he spoke. I hadn't been there, hadn't even known about it, but it lined up with the aggression and turbulence I'd seen in Brad that morning.

"The worst part?" Wyatt stared at his reflection in the bar's polished surface, his eyes unfocused. "He kept saying we were jealous. That we couldn't handle his 'artistic vision.' But he was falling apart, and we just... we just watched it happen."

Behind me, Lucas shifted, close enough that I felt his steadying presence at my back. Not a warning. Just reassurance.

"There was this rehearsal," Wyatt continued. "Two weeks before... before everything. Brad showed up an hour late, completely strung out. We had donors arriving in thirty minutes, and he couldn't even hold his bow straight." His heart rate spiked at the memory, the rhythm jagged enough to make me worry. "Jordyn lost it. Said if he didn't get help, she'd tell his father everything."

"And what did Brad say?" I asked, though I'd seen enough of his reactions to threats.

Wyatt's laugh was hollow. "He said we were jealous. That his father would never believe us over him. Then he played the entire donor showcase flawlessly. I mean, absolutely flawlessly. Like he wasn't even human." The ice in his glass rattled, punctuating the silence between his words. "That's when we knew we had to do something. He was going to destroy himself and take us down with him."

The late afternoon sunlight caught the wetness in Wyatt's deep brown eyes, turning them amber. For a moment, he looked younger than twenty-two, lost in a way that made my chest ache.

"The thing is," Wyatt's voice cracked, "he wasn't always like that. First year at the academy, he was... he was brilliant. Not just dedicated but relentless. He'd spend hours in the practice rooms, shaping every phrase until it was competition-ready. Even when exhaustion hit, he kept pushing." His pulse jumped again. "I keep thinking about that Brad. The one who treated music like a battlefield he had to conquer. When did winning become more important than the music itself? How did we not see him unraveling?"

No one spoke. I noticed Dolores's hands tighten around her glass, saw the shadow of old pain flicker across her face. She'd been teaching long enough to have seen this story before. Probably more than once.

I nudged the water closer, and this time Wyatt took a small sip.

"My dear boy," Dolores said softly, "we can't save people who aren't ready to be saved. Sometimes the kindest thing we can do is step back and let them face the consequences of their choices."

"But if we'd told him sooner," Wyatt insisted, "if we'd tried harder to help instead of just planning to replace him…" His voice cracked. "Maybe he'd still be here."

"Ah, *non*," Jules cut in. "As my grandmother used to say, *'On ne peut pas sauver quelqu'un de lui-même.'* One cannot save someone from themselves. We can only extend our hand and hope they take it."

The inflection in Jules's tone, or maybe the plain truth of his words, drew a weak laugh from Wyatt. Even Dolores smiled, though her eyes stayed troubled.

"*Mon dieu*," Jules murmured, his accent more pronounced than usual. "Surely your family understands the pressures you've been under?"

Wyatt stared into his water glass as if it held answers he desperately needed. "They try, but it's not that simple. My sister…" His voice caught, and he had to clear his throat before continuing. "My sister took a gap year to help pay for my final semester. She's starting college next fall, and of course she's excited."

There was a ragged edge to his voice. "How do I tell my family I wasted it on... *this*?" He gestured vaguely around the room. "Dana's been working double shifts at that coffee shop, saving every penny, talking about her freshman year like it's going to be the best thing that ever happened to her. And here I am, part of a trio that's falling apart because we couldn't handle one spoiled rich kid."

Dolores looked at him. "Oh, sweetheart, you haven't wasted anything. Music isn't just about the trio. Your talent, your education. None of that disappears because of Brad's problems."

"Doesn't it?" Wyatt's eyes shone, glassy with either tears or alcohol. I couldn't tell. "My parents think I'm going to be the next Yo-Yo Ma. They have no idea how brutal this world is. They think because I got into the academy, because I can play Dvořák without breaking a sweat, that success is just... automatic." He shook his head. "They don't know about the politics, the connections, the way people like Brad can just take up all the oxygen in the room."

Jules reached across the bar and gently patted Wyatt's hand. "Perhaps," he said carefully, "your family's faith in you isn't misplaced. Perhaps they see something you cannot right now, through all that's happened."

"Or perhaps," Dolores suggested softly, "what you need most is rest. Time to catch your breath and simply *be* for a while."

Jules nodded, already pulling out his phone. "I'll call an Uber. I absolutely refuse to let you attempt navigating a Muni bus in your state."

"Come on," Dolores said, rising as she gathered her elegant shawl. "We'll wait with you outside. The fresh air will do you good."

Through the front windows, I watched them guide Wyatt into the waiting Uber. In the fading light, Dolores steadied his elbow as Jules kept his tone light, staying close in case Wyatt stumbled. I hadn't realized how much this place had come to matter, this makeshift family we'd found at All Aboard. Dolores offered instructions about hydration and sleep that managed to sound both motherly and professionally authoritative. Jules chimed in with a remark in French that drew a weak smile from Wyatt.

The bar felt different after they left, like a theater after the house lights rise, all the magic of the moment giving way to reality. As I wiped down the bar, my mind circled back to what he'd revealed. The weight of family sacrifice pressed down on everything Wyatt did. No wonder he'd been so desperate to hold the trio together, even with Brad's increasingly erratic behavior. But Brad's spiral hadn't only been about drugs or missed rehearsals. It was about control. He was losing his grip on everything—his talent, his relationships, his future—and instead of accepting help, he lashed out at the very people trying to save him. If Brad had known about the trio's plans to replace him, that gave both Wyatt and Jordyn potential motives.

"You're thinking too hard," Lucas observed, his voice cutting through my brooding. He leaned against the bar in that effortlessly graceful way of his, watching me with those eyes that always seemed to see more than I wanted.

"I'm processing," I corrected, scrubbing at a particularly stubborn water ring beneath my hand. "There's a difference."

"Is there?" The amusement in his tone made me glance up. "You're good at this," he said after a beat.

"At what?"

He gestured toward the space Wyatt had left behind. "Getting people to talk. Listening. You make people feel... safe."

I scoffed, uncomfortable with the praise. "That's just working in a neighborhood bar. Everyone talks to their bartender."

"No." His certainty caught me off guard. "It's more than that. You notice things, and not just because of your senses. You pay attention to people and to what they need. That's rare."

He turned away, leaving me to wonder what he wasn't saying. But that was typical Lucas. Always seeing more than he revealed, always holding parts of himself back. Sometimes I wondered if that was a vampire thing or simply a Lucas thing.

CHAPTER THIRTEEN

The familiar scent of sandalwood and sweat drifted over me as I approached Lotus Yoga, where Jackson stood waiting. My schedule had been a mess lately, pulled apart by audition practice, bar shifts, training with Lucas, and the fallout of the past few days, but I'd finally carved out time to take him up on his offer. Micah hadn't let me hear the end of it all morning, teasing me about "playing hard to get."

Jackson wore fitted black workout clothes that clung in all the right places, his skin dewy from the walk over. He was effortlessly put together, appealing in all the ways I didn't need right now.

I shoved the feelings down. Way down. This wasn't about attraction; this was about getting his help to find Brad's killer. Even if he did look distractingly good in those pants.

"Hey," Jackson said, waving me over. "Ready to pretend we're Zen for an hour?"

"Honestly? After everything lately, I could use some actual Zen." I followed him inside, doing my best not to obviously check him out while he signed us in.

"About that..." Jackson's voice dropped as we unrolled our

mats. "I wanted to apologize for not being there that night. By the time I heard about Brad, the bar was already blocked off." He lined his up mat, nudging the edge with the side of his foot until it was perfectly straight.

"Nothing you could've done," I said, lowering onto my mat. "Unless you wanted to enjoy the thrill of being questioned by Detective Martinez."

At the detective's name, Jackson's pulse kicked up. "They're still treating you as a suspect?"

"Main suspect, actually." I tried for lightness but probably missed by a mile. "Apparently serving someone their last drink earns you extra suspicion."

"We'll figure it out," Jackson said firmly, then let a grin soften the words. "But maybe, for the next hour, we focus on not toppling over in tree pose?"

The instructor entered before I could answer, her voice calm and commanding. "Find your center. Focus on your breath."

I tried to focus on my breathing, but the soft whoosh of twenty bodies inhaling around me overlapped the rhythm of their heartbeats. Beside me, Jackson's breathing sank into a calmer cadence as he eased into the flow. His scent, clean sweat laced with a trace of citrus, kept tugging me back to him.

Even after that first session, it still caught me off guard how naturally it all came with my new abilities. Everything felt effortless, even the poses that should have left me wobbling. Bodies shifted around me, mats dragged softly across the floor, fabric whispered as it stretched, all of it tugging at my focus and pulling me out of the flow.

And then there was Jackson. Right beside me, moving with unexpected grace for someone who usually lived hunched over a keyboard.

He muttered under his breath about his hamstrings staging a rebellion, and a low chuckle slipped out before I could stop it.

"Less talking, more breathing," the instructor scolded, her tone that uncanny blend of gentle and deeply judgmental.

Jackson and I exchanged guilty glances before forcing our focus back to the poses. I closed my eyes, trying to center myself. The temperature shifted as bodies moved in unison, and I caught the tiny hitch in Jackson's breath when he stretched too far.

After class, the cool San Francisco air wrapped around us. Jackson stretched his arms overhead, his shirt riding up enough to reveal a sliver of skin. I caught myself staring and looked away too late, his mouth quirking as he noticed.

"So," he said as he lowered his arms. "Want to do something more productive than ogling my mediocre yoga form?"

I sputtered. "I wasn't—"

"Cass." His tone was warm, teasing. "It's fine. I was watching you too."

The words threw me, but he shifted gears without waiting. "I was thinking about Brad's social media. People leave digital footprints everywhere. Could be worth checking the trio's online presence. See if any conflicts spilled out in public."

"I wouldn't even know where to start," I admitted.

"Good thing you know someone who would." He grinned. "Want to head back to my place? I can show you a few tricks of the digital-investigation trade."

My brain immediately jumped to places it shouldn't. I blamed the yoga endorphins. "Yeah, that would be... helpful."

♪ ♪ ♪

Two train stops away, we arrived at Jackson's apartment in the Castro, San Francisco's premier gayborhood. His place was exactly what I'd expected. Minimalist, but warm. Shelves lined with programming manuals and gaming consoles framed a sleek desk with dual monitors, a custom-built rig glowing beneath. Nearby, a mahogany acoustic guitar rested on its stand, its understated elegance suggesting it had been chosen with care. The whole space felt curated, nothing out of place, as though order itself kept him anchored.

"Beer?" Jackson asked, already heading for the kitchen.

"Sure," I said, even though I knew the bitter hops and malty undertones would overwhelm me. Another reminder of how abnormal my new normal had become.

He came back with two bottles and powered on his laptop. I settled beside him on the couch, keeping what I hoped was a friendly, professional distance. Harder than it should've been.

"Okay," Jackson said, fingers flying over the keyboard. "Let's start with the obvious. Public posts, performance reviews, that kind of thing."

I watched, impressed by how easily he moved between platforms. His focus tightened until the room around him seemed to recede, leaving only the puzzle before him.

At first, everything looked routine. There were concert announcements, glowing reviews about the trio's technical precision, and the usual PR polish. The comments told a different story.

What began as standard musician gripes—scheduling complaints, passive-aggressive digs about preparation—quickly turned darker. Entire threads surfaced where Jordyn and Brad went back and forth, their exchanges intensifying with every reply.

"Look at the timestamps," Jackson murmured, scrolling. "Three a.m., four a.m.... these weren't heat-of-the-moment rants. She was stewing."

I leaned in, scanning the text. Brad's responses were flippant, almost deliberately provocative. He brushed off missed rehearsals with jokes or vague promises. Jordyn's replies, by contrast, grew angrier and more personal as the thread wore on.

"'Your selfishness is destroying everything we've worked for,'" I read from one particularly venomous post. "'Four years of building this trio, and you're throwing it away for what? Your ego? Your addictions?'"

Brad's response was a single shrugging emoji, infuriating in its simplicity, a slap in the face to someone as driven as Jordyn.

"Wait." Jackson's fingers flew faster across the keyboard. "There's more." He pulled up a string of deleted posts from a private group for professional musicians. "Look at how she talks about him when she thinks he's not watching."

The picture that emerged was ugly. Jordyn cataloged every slight—every late arrival, every missed cue—her words steeped in resentment. But it went deeper. She wrote about the trio as if it were her child, a precious creation Brad was slowly strangling.

"'If you can't get your act together, we'll have to take matters into our own hands,'" I read aloud. "Wow. Subtle."

"Gets better." Jackson dug deeper, pulling up fragments from Jordyn's private account. I leaned in, fascinated by how quickly he tore through what looked like layers of security.

"You're good at this," I murmured.

He grinned without looking up. "Let's just say it's a handy skill in game development. Testing for vulnerabilities, you know?"

"Is this... legal?"

"Mostly." His grin widened. "Besides, solving a murder feels a little more important than terms-of-service violations."

Then he froze, eyes narrowing at a post dated only days before Brad's death: "You can't sabotage us if you're gone."

"Do you think she meant it literally?" I asked, though my stomach was already twisting with the possibility.

Jackson took a long pull from his beer before answering. "She was angry," he said. "But angry enough to act on it? That's a bigger leap."

I ran through what we knew, my mind arranging it like a piece of music, motifs and variations threading together into patterns pulled from chaos. "Brad was spiraling in the days before he died. Wyatt said they were planning to replace him, and Jordyn seemed the most vocal about it."

"Motive's one thing," Jackson said, tapping the side of his laptop. "Evidence? That's a different story."

He shifted closer, and my whole body went hyper-aware. His shoulder brushed mine, sending sparks of warmth through my skin. The clean citrus of his deodorant mingled with his natural scent, amplified by the heat lingering from yoga.

I hesitated, holding myself from making a reckless move. Like finding out if his lips tasted as good as they looked—and whether, despite having already fed earlier, I trusted myself to stop at that. This was about the case, not whatever was sparking between us.

"You okay?" Jackson's voice was softer now, threaded with concern. It took me a beat to realize he meant more than this moment.

I glanced down at my hands, flexing my fingers. Even that small motion felt different now, more controlled, more powerful. Everything was different. "I swear, I'm playing detective in a case where I'm also the prime suspect."

Jackson studied me, then reached out and brushed his fingers against my wrist. I tensed at the contact but didn't pull away. His skin was so warm against mine.

"Then we'll just have to prove you're not," he said simply, as if it could be that easy.

Silence stretched between us, broken only by the low hum of his laptop. His fingers hovered a breath from mine, and part of me ached to close that small gap. But the rational part of my mind reminded me what a spectacularly bad idea that would be. I could barely manage being a vampire under suspicion of murder. I didn't need to throw dating complications on top of it.

We both straightened, clearing our throats as if on cue, our attention snapping back to the screen. Jackson saved everything we'd uncovered, promising to back it up securely.

"Next step: real evidence," he said.

I agreed.

CHAPTER FOURTEEN

The final notes of Bach's Courante hung in the air of Dolores's studio, the fast-paced dance leaving my fingers buzzing with residual energy. I lowered my bow, aware of every micro-adjustment in my arm muscles. Dolores tapped her pen against the music stand.

"You're chasing the beat again," she said, the slight crease in her brow deepening. "That's not what this is. The courante pulls at you. It's like trying to run through a dream. You're fast, but never quite in sync."

I resisted the urge to sigh. Even with supernatural reflexes, I couldn't seem to master the rhythm she wanted. The courante's tricky pulse kept slipping through my fingers like sand, no matter how precisely I counted.

"Your fingers need to dance, not sprint," she said, rising from her chair. "Control with flair, not panic." Her hands moved through the air, tracing the rhythm's elusive flow. "You're treating it like an obstacle course, when it should feel like… like being swept along by a current that carries you if you let it."

Her words lingered, uncomfortably familiar. Lately,

everything felt off balance, like I was always half a step behind, moving too fast to stay grounded.

"Let's try the transition again," she said, settling back into
her chair. "And this time, stop fighting the rhythm. Even
when it feels unstable. That's the point of the courante. It's
meant to feel like you're about to lose your footing. Trust
yourself to—"

"I haven't had time to focus on the Hindemith," I con-
fessed, the guilt I'd been dragging around breaking loose. The
piece she'd assigned last week had loomed on my stand, untouched.

To my surprise, Dolores waved the concern away. "The
Hindemith is a long-term challenge, Caspar, not the priority
right now." She adjusted her cat-eye glasses. "Perhaps I was
too ambitious. We'll stick with your original audition pieces.
The ones that draw out your musicality, not just your technical ability."

"But—"

"One battle at a time," she said lightly, though the words
carried unexpected weight. "You're already trying to prove
yourself in so many ways."

I fumbled with my bow, nearly dropping it as her point
sank in. Was I that easy to read? Or was Dolores simply that
perceptive?

"You know," she continued, leaning back in her chair, "I
spent two years of my life trying to live up to someone else's
idea of the perfect musician." She gestured toward a faded
photo on her piano. A younger Dolores stared back at me with
poker-straight hair and a stiff, rehearsed smile; more corporate
headshot than musician's portrait. "I was convinced I was

falling behind because I didn't look the part. So I ironed these curls flat, bought concert gowns that felt like someone else's skin, and filled programs with flashy pieces I thought people expected."

I stilled my nervous fiddling with the bow, struck by the rare vulnerability in her usually confident voice.

"The harder I tried to prove I belonged," she said, "the hollower my playing became. Audition after audition, failure after failure." She shook her head, her wild curls bouncing freely with the motion. "Then one morning, I overslept for the biggest audition of my career. I showed up looking like I'd been dragged through a hedge backward, wearing the most comfortable dress I owned, and carrying only the piece I'd been playing for joy that week."

"Let me guess," I said. "You got the job?"

"I got the job." Her eyes crinkled. "It wasn't until I stopped pretending to be someone else that the music came alive again." She leaned forward, her focus settling on me. "Sometimes the only proof we need to offer is our authentic voice."

As I packed up my viola, her words echoed in my head. Trying to prove myself. To her. To the Philharmonic. To Lucas. To me. Would it ever be enough? Would I ever stop feeling like I was falling behind, even with literal superhuman abilities?

The familiar weight of my viola case settled across my shoulders as I stepped into the crisp San Francisco afternoon. The academy's hallways were unusually quiet, save for the cascade of piano notes spilling from a practice room where someone wrestled with a Chopin nocturne, full of enthusiasm and short on finesse.

From the city below, traffic sounds rose in layers, every engine note distinct, weaving into a chaotic urban symphony. Overhead, a seagull's cry cut through it all, and I found myself tracking its path against the cloud-scattered sky, its wings sharp against the shifting light.

I exhaled, adjusted the strap of my case, and headed toward the bus stop. My thoughts were still tangled in techniques and timing when movement caught my eye. Jordyn sat at the academy's front entrance, her fingers tapping out a restless rhythm against the stone bench—eighth notes beating in a nervous 6/8 time.

She looked up sharply as I approached, lips pressed into a thin line before forcing a smile. "Caspar. Hey."

I slowed, taking in the tension coiled in her posture. Her shoulders hunched forward like she was bracing for impact, and her pulse ticked a little faster than normal.

Before I could speak, she pushed off the bench and fell into step beside me. "Reyes, hold on. I wanted to ask you something." Her voice aimed for casual but cracked a note too high.

I tilted my head, waiting while she wrestled with the thoughts crowding her. Her fingers kept tapping that nervous rhythm against her thigh.

Finally, she blurted, "I'm thinking of leaving Presidio Trio."

I stopped dead. "You're what?"

Jordyn folded her arms, glancing back at the academy as if the building itself might argue. "Wyatt and I have discussed keeping it going, but I need a fresh start. I need to get out from under... everything."

"That's a big move," I said, though I understood the impulse. Sometimes breaking free completely was the only way to find your own path.

She exhaled slowly, her fingers resting lightly at her throat. "Even when he was alive, it was always Brad and His Trio. Not Jordyn, Wyatt, and Brad. Just Brad." Her composure clouded before she went on. "And even now, with him gone, I still feel like I'm playing in his shadow."

I studied her, noting the uneven rhythm of her breath and the tension thrumming beneath her skin like an out-of-tune string. I knew that feeling too well. The desperate urge to prove your talent wasn't only a reflection of someone else's light. Between his role as concertmaster and the single Philharmonic spot we were both chasing, I'd spent enough time in Brad's shadow myself.

"It's hard to be seen for who you are when you're always standing next to someone else," I said quietly.

Jordyn's fingers stilled against her thigh. She glanced at me, a shift in her expression. A wall coming down, maybe.

She hesitated, then her voice dropped, quieter and more reflective. "You know what's weird? For all the ego and the drama... Brad never lied to me. Not once."

I raised an eyebrow, expecting sarcasm, but the earnestness in her tone caught me off guard.

"Not about music, not about who he was, not even the messy stuff," she continued, her attention locked on the pavement ahead. "He'd say awful things, sure. But if something really mattered, I could count on him to be honest. Even when it hurt."

She paused, a small smile tugging at the corner of her

mouth. "Last year, this ensemble director offered me what seemed like an amazing summer gig. Great pay, prestigious venue. I was ready to sign on the spot, but Brad pulled me aside afterward. Told me the guy had a reputation for taking advantage of young female musicians, that the 'prestigious venue' was basically a vanity project where nobody important would hear me play." Her voice softened, carrying a trace of guilt. "He was right. I found out later the director had been blacklisted from half the conservatories in the state."

This didn't match the Brad I knew, the one who'd mocked the quality of my instrument and treated our rivalry like a personal vendetta.

"I hated him sometimes," she said. "But I also trusted him. That's a strange thing to say about someone who never let you forget they were better than you."

"It's funny how grief makes space for things resentment never could," I offered.

She nodded, then brushed off her sleeves and straightened her posture. When she spoke again, her voice carried a different energy. Forward-focused, determined.

"Anyway, I've been thinking about what's next." Jordyn watched me for a beat, gauging my reaction. "I'm considering Irene Dodson for the new trio."

"Irene?"

"Yeah." Her voice grew more animated. "I heard she used to be a prodigy. Serious about music before her family's business pulled her in." She turned to me, eyes searching. "Do you think she'd be interested?"

The question gave me pause. Irene had the skills once. But whether she still had the interest or the time was another story. Running Spirit Haven with her father seemed to take everything out of her.

"She's busy with the family business," I said carefully. "But maybe this could be what pulls her back."

Jordyn didn't wait. "Then I'll ask."

I hesitated only a moment before pulling up Irene's contact. "Just... don't push if she's not ready," I warned, handing over the number.

Jordyn hummed noncommittally, though the fire in her eyes said she'd already made up her mind. She walked a few steps ahead, pulling out her phone, and I slowed my pace on purpose.

I told myself I wasn't eavesdropping. Besides, this involved a friend and a potential murder suspect. That had to justify a little supernatural surveillance, right?

The call connected after a few rings. Irene's voice came through, soft and guarded. "Hello?"

Jordyn's tone shifted instantly, smoothing into a polished and persuasive cadence. "I have an exciting proposition for you. A chance to return to music. To pick up your violin again." Her words carried both genuine enthusiasm and the edge of calculation, like she'd already mapped out every move.

Silence stretched, Irene's hesitation almost tangible.

"Can we meet up to talk?" Jordyn pressed.

"Um... sure," Irene said at last, her voice quiet, reluctant. "When?"

"Tonight," Jordyn answered quickly. "I'll meet you after you finish up at All Aboard."

Another pause, longer this time. "I have deliveries scheduled after All Aboard. Could we meet tomorrow instead? After

I'm done with work?"

"Perfect." Satisfaction warmed Jordyn's tone. "Thank you, Irene. This means a lot."

The call ended, and a lingering feeling clung to me as I resumed my walk toward the bus stop. Irene hadn't sounded particularly excited. More like she'd been nudged into agreement. Maybe it was merely nerves. Returning to music after so long would rattle anyone.

Still, I couldn't' shake the question. Was this truly Irene's choice or a past she'd deliberately left behind?

I boarded the bus, my thoughts snagging between my own troubles and Jordyn's plan. I told myself it wasn't my concern, that this could be a good chance for Irene to reconnect with her music. So why did the whole situation feel off?

CHAPTER FIFTEEN

As I sliced citrus and refilled the garnish trays behind the bar, the clean scent of the peel pulled Jackson into my thoughts. Us alone together in his apartment.

I pictured the way his eyes softened behind his glasses when he laughed, the warmth of his smile—then my mind lingered on the pouty curve of his lower lip, how soft it would feel to kiss, to bite into.

I caught myself rubbing an orange slice on my lips and paused. *Right,* I thought. *Public place. Very public place.*

Apparently, along with heightened senses and sharper instincts, new hormones had decided to join the party.

Maybe I needed an extra feeding tonight. *Preventative,* I told myself.

I lowered my hand slowly, heat creeping up my neck.

When I glanced up, Adda was already turning away. She had absolutely noticed and wasn't saying anything. Yet.

Across the room, Micah knelt beside Hella, her nimble fingers fussing with the thigh-high slit of sparkling pink tulle gathered beneath a sculptural gold bodice, an ethereal creation unmistakably Hella's.

Their voices carried the passionate intensity only artists achieve when locked in debate over craft.

"This is everything!" Hella exclaimed, giving a twirl. "The way you constructed this bodice? Girl, you ate."

"Just wait till you see how it moves under stage lights," Micah replied, pins pressed between her lips.

Adda lounged nearby in one of the bar's plush chairs, still keeping her attention away from me, while Lilith sat beside her, absorbed in sheet music.

"A little higher on the left, darling," Adda said. "We want to show just enough leg to keep them guessing, but not enough to answer all their questions."

The playful energy was a welcome change from last week's heavy atmosphere. Amazing how quickly things could shift, from finding Brad's body in the bathroom to now watching Hella practice her runway walk in Micah's latest creation. The contrast wasn't lost on me.

The back door creaked open, and Irene emerged from the storage area, clipboard in hand.

"Hey," I greeted, keeping my tone casual. "How's the inventory looking?"

"You're running low on the craft vodka." She glanced down at her tidy columns of numbers.

"Listen," I began. "About Jordyn's proposition..."

Irene's pen tapped against the clipboard. Tap, tap, tap in perfect eighth notes. "Oh, um, yes. That." She shifted her weight, uncertainty etched into her posture. "I'm... considering it. It's just complicated with everything else..."

Before she could elaborate, Lilith materialized beside her, practically vibrating with uncharacteristic enthusiasm. "Irene!

Just the person I wanted to see!"

I watched as Irene's shoulders loosened, and a small but genuine smile broke through.

Interesting. I hadn't realized they were that close.

"I need to order more of your amazing hand cream," Lilith said, leaning casually against the bar. "My hands have never felt better, and it doesn't leave any residue on the piano keys. Do you know how hard it is to find a product that actually works without making everything greasy?"

Wait, what? I kept my face carefully neutral, arranging glasses even as my mind spun. Irene made beauty products? How had I never known this?

"Yes, of course," Irene said, her face brightening at the praise. "I just made a fresh batch, actually..."

"Cass!" Micah's voice sliced through their conversation. "I need your freakishly long arms over here! This bodice is being stubborn."

I wavered, torn between helping Micah and hanging back to catch more of Irene's unexpected reveal. I could follow the conversation from across the room, no problem, but...

"Go," Irene said, mildly. "We can talk more about the trio thing later."

I crossed to where Micah wrestled with an intricate row of hooks and eyes along the gown's back. Every stitch, every layer, every shimmer in the fabric caught the bar's lights, the patterns shifting like constellations under her hands.

"Hold this exactly here," Micah instructed, positioning my hands as if guided by a scalpel. "Don't move a millimeter or the whole thing will pucker."

While I stood frozen in place, more mannequin than man,

I tuned my hearing toward the bar. Lilith's voice carried easily, even though she kept it low.

"I've been thinking," she said to Irene, "about everything that's happened with Jordyn. Maybe it's time to extend an olive branch."

My eyebrows rose. That was new. Lilith had been ice-cold toward Jordyn since their falling out years ago. A mix of artistic differences and betrayal, apparently. At least, that's how the rumors went. Neither of them had ever given me the full story.

"Oh?" Irene's reply was cautious, careful.

"I was thinking of putting together a little gift basket," Lilith continued, tone casual in the way people use when they've already made up their minds. "Since everything's been so awful lately."

From across the room, I caught the subtle shift in Lilith's posture as she leaned in, studying Irene's reaction. The movement felt calculated, though I couldn't quite pin down why.

"That's such a lovely idea!" Irene said, her enthusiasm sounding genuine enough. "I've been working on a new salve. It's perfect for spots that need extra love, and it's oil-free like the hand cream."

"Perfect." Lilith's smile spread wider. "And maybe something special from Spirit Haven. A peace offering should include a good bottle, don't you think? Jordyn favors scotch, neat."

The weight she put on Spirit Haven made my skin prickle. I adjusted my grip on the bodice and earned a sharp, "Don't move!" from Micah.

"I could put it all together," Irene offered quickly. "I'm

meeting with Jordyn anyway to discuss... you know." She gestured vaguely, probably referring to the trio proposition.

"Speaking of which," Lilith segued smoothly, "that's quite an opportunity she's offering you."

I recognized the technique. Brad used the same gentle pressure, making suggestions feel like natural conclusions rather than manipulation.

"Yes, well..." Irene's pen resumed its nervous tapping. "We'll see."

"Is Enzo still around?" Lilith steered the conversation. "I could use his advice on the best bottle for Jordyn."

"Out back with the delivery van," Irene said, nodding toward the rear exit.

Lilith thanked her and moved to the back door, her steps purposeful beneath the veneer of casualness. The whole exchange felt off, like watching a perfectly choreographed dance without knowing the rhythm it followed.

"Earth to Cass!" Micah's voice snapped me back to the fitting session. "You can let go now. Crisis averted."

I released the bodice, flexing my fingers as my eyes drifted back to Irene. Her expression had gone distant, her fingers tracing slow, abstract shapes on the bar top, movements more listless than the nervous tapping from earlier.

"You good?" Micah asked quietly, noticing where my attention had settled.

I nodded slowly. "Just thinking about Irene. She's juggling a lot. The family business, this beauty product thing I didn't even know about, and now Jordyn's offer..."

"Girl's got range," Micah agreed, sorting through her pins. "Remember when you said Irene used to play violin? You told me she could've gone pro without breaking a sweat if she'd stuck with it."

"Yeah," I murmured, recalling those high school performances where Irene's talent had burned so brightly. "It was heartbreaking when she walked away for the family business."

As I helped Micah pack up her sewing supplies, my thoughts kept circling back to the strange choreography I'd witnessed. Lilith's careful nudging, Irene's mixed signals about the trio, the way they moved around each other like players in a game whose rules I didn't yet know.

My focus shifted toward the rear exit where Lilith had disappeared. Whatever she was discussing with Enzo, I doubted it was only about picking the right bottle for a gift basket.

CHAPTER SIXTEEN

"Thanks again for all your help!" Hella called out, tugging on her black denim jacket scattered with rhinestones and crystals. "This is going to be iconic."

"*Iconic* indeed," Adda said with a knowing smile, turning to Micah. "You really outdid yourself."

"See?" Hella said, already angling for the door. "Trusted the vision."

"You trusted impulse," Adda replied, following her. "There's a difference."

Hella glanced back, unfazed. "Impulse is why anyone's looking in the first place."

Adda adjusted her coat as they stepped outside. "Just don't let the look wear you."

"I never do," Hella said, the crystals on her jacket flashing once before the door closed behind them.

Micah turned to me, already reading my expression. "I can cover if you need a break," she offered. "You've got that 'I need to investigate something' face."

I tried to look innocent. "What? No, I just..." I patted my pockets theatrically. "Think I left something in the office.

Important... thing."

Micah rolled her eyes. "Sure, Cass. Just try not to get murdered while you're being nosy."

"That's literally impossible now," I whispered, already backing toward the hallway.

"Don't get too cocky," she called after me.

♪ ♪ ♪

The back office was dimly lit, the old fluorescent tubes casting everything in a muted greenish glow. Lucas sat behind the desk, organizing inventory sheets, his usual neat stacks fanned out beside his desktop keyboard. The bookshelves were overstuffed with binders and half-open cardboard boxes of merch, but even the clutter had a kind of intentional order. A small potted echeveria succulent sat by the monitor, the only splash of color in the room.

On the wall hung a framed photo from a decade-old staff party, everyone caught in silly poses. A younger Lucas was bent over while another guy clung to him piggyback-style, both of them laughing so hard their eyes were squeezed shut. The rest of the group looked like ghosts from an era long before my time.

I tried to move casually toward the adjacent storage room, aiming for "just looking for something" vibes rather than "definitely eavesdropping." The bar's backup stock of liquor bottles was ordered by type and height on the open shelving, and the mixers were stacked in labeled crates, aligned like they'd been squared with a ruler.

Through the frosted window past the shelves, muffled voices drifted from the alley. Lilith and Enzo. I angled myself closer, pretending to rummage through a box while actually positioning for optimal listening.

Lucas's eyes narrowed, catching my less-than-subtle behavior. I pressed a finger to my lips, nodding toward the window where the voices rose. Understanding flickered across his face as he moved beside me, his presence both reassuring and distracting. The familiar scent of his cologne made it harder to focus than I wanted to admit.

"You promised me more time." Lilith's voice carried clearly through the glass, tense and frustrated.

"I can't keep fronting you product if you don't pay on time." Enzo's reply was calm but firm, the voice of a businessman managing risks. "People are asking questions."

Lucas and I exchanged looks. The silent communication was immediate. I made a subtle gesture: *Did you know about this?* He shook his head: *No.* This wasn't about Jordyn's gift basket at all.

A clipped sigh from Lilith cut through the tension. "I just need things to calm down. Brad's death... everything's a mess right now."

My muscles tensed at Brad's name. This was connected. Of course it was connected. Everything seemed to lead back to Brad these days.

Enzo stepped closer to Lilith, the gritty cement crunching under his shoes. "I always hated that smug kid," he muttered under his breath, "and his father too. Back when my business partner Bill was alive, those Benningtons... they outbid us for that warehouse. Cost us the whole expansion. Bill carried that stress with him every day after. He had a heart attack at the store not long after. I blame Richard for it."

Lilith's shook her head. "I—I didn't know... I mean, I didn't realize it was personal."

"It's personal," Enzo replied. "Every move they make reminds me of that day. Watch your step and keep your distance. Especially now that I've heard Martinez is on the case."

I froze. *Enzo knows Martinez?*

He leaned closer. "We met the day Bill died. She was a rookie cop in Burlingame. Showed up early at the scene—saw the grief, my anger—and she didn't flinch. Handled it like she belonged there. I remembered her. Knew she could become a problem... or an advantage... down the line. Smart kid."

Martinez worked in Burlingame? She was that close to us and we never knew?

He paused. "Bennington noticed her too, through his connections. Started nudging her career along—promotions, opportunities—got her where she is now. Whatever you do... don't let her notice you."

Lilith's pulse quickened. "I'll be careful. You can trust me."

I glanced at Lucas, trying to read his expression in the dim light. Was Lilith being genuine, or was this another performance? After years of watching her on stage, I knew how convincing she could be when she wanted to be.

Enzo exhaled sharply, a sound of skepticism if I'd ever heard one. "Fix it fast. And remember what I said about Martinez." Then he turned and headed back toward the bar, where Irene was taking inventory.

Beyond the window, Lilith stood alone in the alley, her figure blurred but unmistakably tense. The late afternoon light caught the edges of her silhouette, making her look almost otherworldly. Or maybe that was my vision playing tricks on me.

Lucas's fingers brushed my wrist lightly, a silent signal: *Hold still. Don't react yet.* The touch sent an unexpected shiver through me, but I forced myself to focus on Lilith. After several deep breaths, she turned and headed back inside through the rear entrance.

Once her footsteps faded, Lucas and I stepped fully back into the office. I blinked hard, the tension ebbing. "Well, that was... something."

Lucas crossed his arms, his expression grim. "She's in deep," he murmured. "And Enzo's history with the Benningtons? I didn't see that coming."

"Yeah," I breathed. "Or that he knew Martinez. How does that even happen?"

Lucas stared toward the doorway, making sure no one could hear. "Bennington's influence runs deeper than he lets on. And Martinez... if she was at the scene when Bill died, she knows more than we thought."

"And Richard Bennington boosting her career? That feels... dangerous." I began pacing, my mind racing. "Lilith was Brad's supplier. If he was using too much, causing problems..."

"She had a reason to cut him off," Lucas finished, his voice tight.

"Or get rid of him?" I pushed, watching Lucas's reaction carefully.

He shook his head. "Supplying someone with drugs is one thing. Killing them is another."

"What if she thought he'd expose her?" I challenged.

Lucas didn't respond immediately, which told me he wasn't dismissing it outright.

I kept moving, unable to stay still as I processed everything. "Think about it. She's been acting weird lately. Distracted. Disappearing at odd times. The peace offering to Jordyn... and now Enzo warning her about Martinez like she's a liability. That can't be nothing."

"Drug dealers rarely want their clients to die," Lucas pointed out reasonably. "They need consistent buyers."

"Unless," I countered, "the buyer turned into a walking disaster."

Lucas leaned against the desk, his posture deceptively casual. "There's still no proof she actually did anything beyond dealing."

"But—"

"Murder isn't only about motive," he interrupted, voice firm. "It's also about opportunity."

I sighed, running a hand through my hair. I hated when Lucas was right, which happened frustratingly often.

"Okay." I began ticking points off on my fingers. "Lilith was Brad's supplier. She's having money problems. Wyatt and Jordyn wanted Brad out of the trio. And now Enzo's apparently got this whole... mob-adjacent personal vendetta with Richard Bennington and a career-favoring cop who might be watching all of us."

Lucas watched me carefully, his dark eyes tracking my movements. "This is getting dangerous," he said quietly. "If we keep poking around, someone might push back."

I shrugged, trying to appear more casual than I felt. "It's

not like I can die twice."

Instead of laughing, Lucas's expression tightened. "I wouldn't be so sure of that."

I blinked. *What was that supposed to mean?*

I didn't press. Not now. There were more urgent problems than unraveling cryptic vampire warnings.

"Should we confront Lilith directly?" I suggested, more thinking aloud than actually suggesting it. "If she had any involvement in Brad's death, she could be covering her tracks."

Lucas shook his head. "Let's wait. Watch her behavior. If we tip our hand too soon..."

"Right." I frowned, recalling another detail. "That conversation earlier with Irene about the peace offering for Jordyn. If Lilith really wants to make amends, why does it feel like she's manipulating something?"

Lucas tilted his head, considering. "Or maybe she knows someone's onto her. Maybe Enzo isn't the only one watching her closely."

We exchanged another look laden with shared understanding. This was bigger than Brad. Bigger than Lilith. And far messier than we were prepared for.

"We should head back," Lucas said, straightening up. "Try to act normal."

I snorted. "Right. Normal. Like that's even possible these days."

CHAPTER SEVENTEEN

By late afternoon, All Aboard Bar filled in after the trains rolled through West Portal Station. Regulars drifted in with jackets still on, loosening ties and shrugging off the day as they claimed stools and booths. Some ordered quickly, one drink before heading home to partners and kids, while others settled in, laughter coming easier now that the workday was done.

A group of thirty-somethings spilled out of an old school bus, painted vivid blue and parked crookedly at the curb. They wore matching T-shirts celebrating a joint bachelor party, printed with a collage of snapshots spanning the two grooms' relationship across chests flushed with excitement, their heartbeats threading through it all.

After closing, the noise and movement fell away. Each drip from the beer taps cut through the silence like a solitary note, the sound echoing off the bare stools with startling clarity.

Jackson, Micah, and I had claimed a corner booth, empty glasses scattered across the table like remnants of an unfinished ritual.

"Okay," Jackson said, snapping open his laptop. "Let's go

through what we know about our suspects." The screen's cold blue light washed over his features as he scrolled. "Starting with Jordyn."

His eyes narrowed, and his jaw flexed as he read through the harsher comments.

"Look at this pattern," Jackson said, scrolling through post after post. "The fights with Brad kept escalating. Public arguments about missed rehearsals turned into private threats. See here?" He pointed at the screen. "She went from complaining about his lateness to literally writing, 'I won't let you destroy everything we've worked for.'"

Micah leaned forward, the soft jingle of her bracelets punctuating the silence as she studied the screen. "Damn, girl had receipts for days. Look at this one: 'You can't sabotage us if you're gone.' That's intense."

"But was she actually capable of murder?" I crossed my arms, thinking back to my encounters with Jordyn. "She was dramatic, sure, but killing someone takes a different kind of..." I paused, remembering how she'd sit in rigid silence during critiques in our academy classes, her fingers tapping out aggressive rhythms on the piano lid, or leave rehearsals with perfectly composed tears streaming down her face. Dramatic, yes. Murderous? "I mean, this is the same person who wrote a three-page Yelp review because Starbucks used 2% milk instead of whole."

"Sometimes the loudest threats are just that—noise," Micah pointed out, settling back in her seat. "Like how Adda threatens to end careers over missed cues but really just wants everyone to shine, you know?" She paused, tapping her fingers thoughtfully on the table. "What about Wyatt's drunken confession the other night? That whole 'we were going to replace Brad' bombshell?"

"Could be guilt talking," Jackson mused. "But guilt about what exactly?"

I shook my head. "Wyatt? The guy practically has a panic attack ordering coffee. You really think he could plan a murder?"

"Sometimes the most anxious people snap the hardest," Jackson countered. "Back in college, my roommate used to stress-polish his desk during finals. One semester he just... broke. Took his laptop, marched to the communal kitchen, and put it in the freezer because he said it 'needed to chill.'"

Micah stared at him. "Seriously? He froze his laptop?"

Jackson huffed a quiet laugh. "Yeah. And of course it didn't fix anything. Campus wellness stepped in after that. He got support, but... it stuck with me. People don't always break where you expect."

"Speaking of snapping, Lucas and I overheard an argument between Lilith and Enzo," I said. "Turns out Lilith was Brad's drug dealer, and Enzo's been supplying her. She's behind on payments, and he's not happy about it."

"Hold up—what?" Micah leaned forward. "Our Lilith? Piano-playing, peace-offering Lilith?"

"The same," I confirmed. "From what we heard, Brad was causing problems. Maybe using too much or not paying. And Enzo..." I trailed off, still processing how different he'd sounded from his usual friendly demeanor. "Let's just say he's scarier than the guy who makes dad jokes during deliveries."

"If Brad was burning through product without paying..."

Micah started.

"Or threatening to expose her operation," Jackson added.

"It's definitely a motive," I admitted.

"And there's more," I continued. "Enzo has a grudge against Richard Bennington. Years ago, Richard outbid Enzo and his partner Bill for a warehouse. Enzo blames Richard for Bill's heart attack afterward. And now he's keeping an eye on Detective Martinez because of it."

Micah's eyes went wide, and she pressed a hand to her chest. "Wait, Martinez is involved?"

I nodded. "Yeah. Enzo met her the day his business partner died. She was a cop in Burlingame. Richard Bennington apparently saw her potential and helped nudge her career along. Enzo warned Lilith to be careful around her."

Jackson whistled softly. "So... we've got a detective who might not be impartial, and Richard Bennington pulling strings behind the scenes. Lovely." He drummed his thumb against the table's edge. "What about Irene?"

I actually laughed, the sound echoing oddly in the empty bar. But Jackson's expression stayed serious, the laptop's glow outlining the angles of his face. "Wait. You're not joking?"

"Think about it," he said. "She's usually on the sidelines quietly running routine tasks. But she was there the day Brad—"

"No." I cut him off firmly, my voice sharper than I intended. The thought of sweet, hardworking Irene being involved in murder felt absurd, almost offensive. "She's just trying to keep her family's business running."

I kept going. "If anyone's suspicious in that family, it's

Enzo." My hands moved animatedly, casting shifting shadows across the wall. "He's the one with shady connections. He's the one threatening Lilith about payments—not to mention his beef with Richard."

Jackson shrugged. "Ever notice how the most unassuming people are the ones who get away with the worst things?"

"Cass is right," Micah chimed in. "Come on, Irene? The same girl who we now know makes scented hand cream as a side hustle? Please."

The ice machine rattled to life in the far corner, the sound echoing through the quiet. Jackson glanced toward it, jaw tightening briefly before smoothing out again. I didn't know why it caught my attention, but I was grateful when Micah jumped in before I could start overthinking it.

"So who does that leave us with?" Micah asked, steering the conversation back to our other suspects. "Jordyn's got the rage, Wyatt's got the guilt, Lilith's got the drug connection, and Enzo's working behind the scenes."

"And I've got the detective breathing down my neck," I added dryly.

Jackson shut his laptop, his fingers resting briefly on the lid. "People overlook things when emotions are involved," he muttered, not quite meeting my eyes.

The words hit harder than they should have. "What's that supposed to mean?"

He shrugged. "Forget it. I'm not trying to start something."

"Hey," Micah interrupted, her voice deliberately light, "at least we can probably rule out the drag queens. Adda *lives* for the spotlight. Can you imagine her trying to be subtle about anything?"

The mental image of Adda attempting stealth in six-inch heels and a sequined gown broke the mood. We all laughed, though it felt forced. Even in laughter, the tension in the room didn't fully lift.

CHAPTER EIGHTEEN

The incessant buzzing of my phone dragged me from a fitful sleep. I fumbled in the dark, nearly knocking it off the nightstand before managing to grab it. Dolores's name flashed on the screen, my thumb hovering over the answer button. She never called this early unless there was a problem.

"Hello?" My voice was rough with sleep.

"Caspar." Dolores's usual warmth was gone, replaced with a tight urgency. "You need to come to the academy right away. Something's happened to Jordyn."

I sat up straight, fully awake. Lucas's warning about investigating alone echoed in my mind. "What happened?"

"Just… come quickly." The waver in her voice sent a chill through me. "And Caspar? Don't come alone."

I was already moving before she hung up, yanking on clothes. "Micah! Wake up!"

Through the wall, I heard her heartbeat shift from sleep-slow to fully alert. She muttered a curse as she stumbled out of bed.

"What's wrong?" Micah appeared in my doorway, hair disheveled but eyes bright with concern.

"Something happened to Jordyn at the academy." I pulled on my canvas sneakers. "Dolores just called."

Micah was tapping at her phone, ordering an Uber. "Five minutes away," she reported before disappearing to get dressed.

The pre-dawn air was crisp as we hurried outside. The distant rumble of early morning trains mingled with the flutter of crows on the power lines, and the gurgle of a coffee maker next door carried in the stillness. Beneath those ordinary sounds, though, the wail of sirens rose in the distance, drawing closer to the academy.

Tension knotted tighter in my body as our Uber wound uphill toward the school. Snatches of police radio chatter drifted from passing patrol cars, words like "unresponsive" and "possible overdose" crowding out every other thought. Micah squeezed my hand, her pulse racing.

Police vehicles blocked the academy's entrance, their lights washing the stone facade in alternating red and blue. Dolores stood near the steps, wringing her hands. When she spotted us, her face crumpled.

"Oh, Caspar." She reached for me, and I caught the salt-scent of tears she was struggling to hold back. "It's horrible."

Yellow crime scene tape sealed off the main hallway, forcing a cluster of early-morning students to detour around. Whispers drifted through the corridor:

"Just like Brad."

"Found this morning."

"Poor Jordyn."

The words clung to us as we neared the practice room. Through the open doorway, Jordyn's body slumped over the gleaming Steinway. Her cream blazer was wrinkled, one shoe half-off, ash-blonde hair spilling across the keys. She was always meticulous, so precise in her appearance.

The paramedics huddled near her, their low voices carrying, every word painfully distinct:

"No response to stimuli."

"Pupils fixed and dilated."

"No obvious trauma, but…"

The assessment stalled there.

Detective Martinez emerged from the crowd. Unlike the other officers radiating stress and unease, her pulse remained calm, unshaken. She gave me a small nod, a gesture weighted with meaning I couldn't quite decipher. Her glance briefly shifted to Micah, and I saw Micah push a strand of hair from her eyes. Without a word, Martinez pulled on a pair of gloves and stepped toward the body.

I drew a breath, sorting through the scents in the room. Beneath the pungent tang of fear-sweat from the gathered students and the metallic undertone that always seemed to accompany death, a familiar trace stood out—the same bitter scent I'd detected around Brad's body.

Before it could fully register, Martinez's voice cut through the murmurs.

"Anyone who saw Jordyn last night needs to come forward." She scanned the crowd, pausing briefly on each face. "No detail is too small."

A forensics tech in blue gloves approached Martinez, holding up a crumpled piece of paper sealed in an evidence bag. "Found this by the music stand, Detective."

Martinez studied it through the plastic. The handwriting

was instantly recognizable, the same elegant slope and curlicues I'd seen on setlists at the bar. Lilith's writing: *We need to talk. Now.*

Another tech hurried to Martinez's side, raising a smaller evidence bag with a scrap of foil dusted in white residue. "Detective, you need to see this."

I tuned into their hushed exchange.

"Traces of cocaine on her phone. It was in her tote—same as the Bennington case."

He reached back into the tote and lifted a small packet. "There's more. Suspected narcotics, in a makeup pouch."

The parallels were impossible to ignore. Beside me, Micah shifted.

Near the doorway, an officer had set up a laptop, playing back security footage from the previous night. The grainy video showed Jordyn and Lilith in what looked like a heated argument outside this very practice room. Jordyn's sharp, accusatory gestures cut through the static, while Lilith's stance stayed guarded, her fists clenched at her sides.

A viola student I recognized from Dolores's studio—Neve Riley, I thought—stepped forward hesitantly. Her voice trembled. "Lilith was here this morning. She... she was the one who found Jordyn."

Martinez's attention snapped to Neve, her posture shifting almost imperceptibly. I met Micah's wide eyes.

The officers parted the gathered students, and Lilith appeared, being guided forward. She stood in the hallway with her arms crossed tightly over her chest, her heart racing beneath her composed exterior.

"Tell me about last night," Martinez said.

"We argued, yes," Lilith admitted, glancing at the onlookers before her eyes lingered briefly on me. "But I left. She was fine when I walked away."

Martinez held up the evidence bag with the note. "Then why send her this, hours before she was found dead?"

Lilith pressed her lips together, and for a moment I thought she wouldn't answer. "Because I wanted to make amends," she said at last, her voice softer. "She reached out about forming a new trio. I thought... maybe I could help." She swallowed hard. "But when we met, she brought up the past. How I abandoned her when I left the academy. She didn't understand. She never understood what I was going through back then."

The forensic tech who had discovered the cocaine cleared their throat. "Detective, based on quantity, this doesn't read as casual use."

I thought of the bag I'd found tucked beneath a loose tile in the bar's bathroom. I'd turned it in, but no one had followed up.

Martinez studied Lilith for a long moment, weighing the evidence. When she spoke, her voice was cold, professional. "You were found at the scene. You fought with Jordyn hours before her death. And now she's dead, with drugs we know you source." She paused, letting each point land. "Lilith Fox, I'm taking you in for questioning."

The moment the handcuffs appeared, Lilith fractured. She stumbled back. "I didn't do this!" The words burst out with such force that several nearby students flinched.

The anguish in her voice rippled through the crowd, sparking a sudden uptick in heartbeats and a collective intake of breath. Beside me, Micah's pulse jumped.

Two officers stepped forward, taking Lilith's arms as they guided her toward the exit. Her voice cracked as she kept talking. "We were everything to each other once. Before I left, before everything changed. I came back to make things right, not to—" She broke off, choking on the words as tears spilled over.

I watched them lead her away, her distress palpable in the salt of her tears and the frantic rhythm of her pulse.

I closed my eyes, trying to cut through the scents and sounds crowding the practice room. Beneath the harsh chemical bite of forensic materials, that same bitter note threaded through the air. Fainter now, elusive, but unmistakably what I'd detected around Brad's body.

My eyes snapped open. The similarity couldn't be coincidence, but trying to explain it to Martinez would mean revealing abilities I couldn't. I glanced at the detective, now directing her team to process the scene. Her composure was unshakeable, yet a trace of doubt in her eyes hinted she wasn't fully convinced.

Micah touched my arm lightly. "We should go," she murmured. "There's nothing more we can do here."

She was right. As we stepped into the morning air, the sun crept over the academy's rooftop, gilding the stone walls in a soft gold that felt almost obscene against the darkness inside. A cool breeze carried the whiff of bay fog, but beneath it sat that bitter note in my memory, taunting me with its familiarity.

I couldn't shake the sense that we were missing a vital piece of the puzzle. The case against Lilith looked airtight, as it had once against me in Brad's death. But in the cold clarity of morning, with her anguished denial still echoing in my ears, I feared we were watching an innocent take the fall while the real killer moved free.

As Micah and I descended the academy steps, I cast one last glance through the practice room window. Martinez stood alone at the piano, her hand hovering above the keys where Jordyn had fallen, her face shadowed with the same uncertainty gnawing at me.

CHAPTER NINETEEN

The buzz of the fluorescent lights in the police station gnawed at my concentration. Every shuffle of paper, every keystroke, every hushed conversation struck like a pinprick. I tried to breathe the way Lucas had taught me. Slow, steady, and centered.

Micah's presence beside me helped too. Her familiar scent of coffee and vanilla grounded me, a reassuring counterpoint. Adda and Hella flanked us, both unusually subdued. Even Adda's larger-than-life energy sagged under the harsh institutional glow.

"I hate police stations," Hella muttered, her manicured nails drumming an anxious rhythm on the armrest. "The lighting is homophobic."

Despite everything, I nearly smiled. Trust Hella to critique the aesthetics of a crisis.

The humor slipped away, and I turned back to the hallway. Through the narrow window of the interrogation room, Lilith sat ramrod straight, hands folded on the table. The fluorescent lights burned harshly, highlighting the smudged eyeliner she hadn't fixed, the chipped edges of her once-immaculate nail polish, and the faint shadows under her eyes that whispered of sleepless nights.

I pictured her at the bar, commanding the piano bench like a throne, fingers dancing across the keys as she tossed sly smiles to the queens mid-number. The Lilith before me now was only a shadow of that performer.

Detective Martinez entered and I tuned out the station's background noise, narrowing my focus to their voices.

"Let's start with the basics," Martinez said, her tone professional but not unkind. "Tell me about your relationship with Jordyn."

"We were friends once. Close friends. Things... changed when I left the academy."

"And the drugs?" Martinez's question cut through the air. "Were you supplying her?"

I tensed, but Lilith didn't flinch. "Yes, I dealt. I won't deny it. But I never sold Jordyn anything. And I sure as hell didn't kill her."

Martinez slid an evidence bag onto the table, the crumpled note from the crime scene. "This was found near Jordyn's body," she said. "Explain it."

Lilith exhaled sharply. "I wanted to talk to her—to fix things. Jordyn reached out about forming a new trio, wanted my opinion on potential members. But when we met, things got heated. She was alive when I walked away."

I let my focus drift from the interrogation room. Beside me, Micah and Hella whispered to each other, their voices low, but nothing escaped my attention.

"She's been dealing for a couple years," Hella said with a light shrug. "What if someone wanted payback? God knows there are enough desperate people in this city willing to do anything for their next hit."

"Or maybe," Micah countered, absently tugging at a loose thread on her sleeve, "that's exactly what someone wants us to think. Frame the dealer. It's almost too perfect." Her eyes flicked toward the interrogation room. "Remember when Lilith first started performing again? She wouldn't even take aspirin without reading the whole label first. Everything she does is calculated."

Hella's expression softened. "She helped me get clean, you know, after that disaster with the touring company." She swallowed, and I remembered the night she'd stumbled into the bar, mascara streaked, shaking, desperate. Lilith had disappeared with her for some time. When they returned, Hella had carried herself differently. "She's not just our pianist," she said quietly. "She's family—no matter what."

Adda shifted closer, her perfume cutting through the station's institutional haze. "Honey, in all my years of devouring true crime novels—don't judge me—the truth is never that convenient." She folded her arms, her usual flair softened by a flicker of real worry in her eyes. "Someone's working awfully hard to make us look at Lilith instead of the real killer. Question is... why?"

Across the room, a knot of officers huddled around a laptop, their hushed comments tugging at my focus. I angled my hearing toward them while pretending to scroll my phone.

"Security footage from last night," one officer muttered. "Look, there's Wyatt."

From where I stood, I tuned in on the grainy feed. Wyatt's figure paced near the academy entrance, movements jittery and restless. He kept glancing over his shoulder, phone pressed tight to his ear, free hand slicing the air as if to punctuate his words.

The timestamp read 9:47 p.m., minutes before Jordyn was last seen alive. In the background, the scene unfolded like a casual play, the janitor trundling a cart as two students lugged instrument cases and a delivery driver balanced packages. Ordinary movements, yet there was a choreographed quality to them, too perfectly timed.

Then I saw it, a shadow at the edge of the frame. Someone stood just outside the light, their outline blurred, almost swallowed by darkness. They didn't move, didn't fidget, merely watched Wyatt with unnerving stillness. And then, as if aware of being observed, the figure stepped back and vanished from view.

I leaned in, studying Wyatt's body language. His shoulders hunched inward, defensive, like he was bracing for a blow. At one point he rubbed the back of his neck, but his jaw told the real story—clenched tight as his lips moved in rapid bursts. Whatever conversation he was having, it wasn't friendly.

The feed jumped. A flicker, a gap in the recording. When the image returned, Wyatt was gone. But in the spot where the shadowy figure had stood, a glint caught the light. I squinted, trying to pin it down. A reflection from jewelry? A weapon? Or merely a cruel trick of the grainy footage? Before I could decide, the officers switched the view to another camera.

Inside the interrogation room, Lilith's mask cracked. "I loved her!" The words burst out, ragged and unguarded. "Even if she didn't love me back..." Her voice splintered on the last word. "We were best friends once, before—" She cut herself short, swallowing hard.

The confession caught me off guard, reshaping memories I hadn't questioned before. I remembered overhearing Jordyn telling someone she'd "lost her best friend" when Lilith left the academy. Back then, I'd thought it was about choices, about Lilith's transition and her decision to walk away, a betrayal Jordyn couldn't forgive. But it hadn't only been about leaving. It had been about love, about fear, about all the words left unsaid until it was too late.

Martinez didn't flinch. Her attention stayed locked on Lilith. "Love has driven people to do worse things," she said evenly. "Are you sure there's nothing else you need to tell me?"

"I didn't do this." Lilith's fingers brushed the edge of the evidence bag containing her note, the gesture so tender it looked like she was trying to smooth away her own damning words. "I know how it looks, but I swear on everything... I didn't hurt Jordyn. I couldn't." Tears spilled over, leaving clean tracks through her smudged eyeliner.

I stepped away, finding a quieter corner of the station. I'd been seeing their interactions all wrong, noticing only the surface tension without grasping the depth beneath. With their history revealed, everything felt more complicated, layered onto a situation that had already seemed impossible to bear.

I felt Micah's presence before she spoke, her hand warm on my arm. "You look like you're about to combust. What's going on in that terrifyingly overactive brain of yours?"

I exhaled sharply, pressing my palms against my temples. "Something's not sitting right. If Lilith really did this, why does it feel like we're being pushed toward that conclusion? It feels... orchestrated."

Micah nodded slowly, thoughtful. "So what are we gonna do about it?"

I straightened, resolve hardening. "We find out who Wyatt was calling. And figure out what we're missing before someone else dies."

CHAPTER TWENTY

The pre-dawn hours at All Aboard Bar carried an eerie quiet. Chairs were stacked on tables like silent sentries, and through the partially open front door, the cool morning air drifted in, carrying the sweet scent of buttery pastries and cinnamon rolls from the bakery down the street.

Lucas stood before me, arms crossed, his expression the same familiar blend of patience and intensity. "You need to learn to control your senses before they control you," he said, his voice edged with authority. "Otherwise, you'll keep getting overwhelmed at the worst possible moments."

I nodded, recalling how during last night's shift I'd nearly dropped an entire stack of glasses when someone's perfume blindsided me. "I'm ready."

Lucas produced a black silk blindfold, holding it out. "Hearing and smell first," he instructed. "The others will follow once you master these."

I took the blindfold, the fabric cool and smooth against my fingers. As I tied it over my eyes, the world shifted. Not darker, exactly. Just different. Every sound tugged at my focus. The quiet whir of the refrigerator swelled into a continuous drone. Outside, a bird shifted on its perch, tiny claws scraping bark.

Lucas moved, or at least I thought he did. I turned my head, trying to track him, but too many sounds pressed in at once. Traffic rumbled three blocks away. An alarm clock buzzed in a nearby apartment. The rhythmic thud of a jogger's footsteps passed the bar.

"You're still fighting it," Lucas said, his voice carrying that same mix of patience and calm command. "Remember going back to work the day after you turned? How every glass clinked like a cymbal crash?"

I winced at the memory. That night had been a sensory onslaught, every sound amplified until my head felt like it might split open. I'd dropped three glasses before Lucas pulled me aside, teaching me how to build mental barriers against the assault.

"You've come far since then," he said, "but you're still trying to process everything at once."

Each lesson with Lucas revealed new layers of my abilities and new challenges. He'd shown me how to sift through scents like tuning a radio, how to lock onto a single voice in a crowded room. But it wasn't merely technical instruction. Lucas understood instinctively how crushing the flood of senses could be. What he never offered, and what we never spoke about, was the night I was attacked, and whether my new senses would ever allow me to remember.

"The thing about vampire senses," he continued, stepping closer, "is that they're not just sharper. They're more connected. Sound, smell, touch. They weave together into a complete picture. But first, you need to master them one at a time. Focus on just one thing. Find my heartbeat first, then work outward from there."

I took a deep breath, forcing myself to quiet the morning's symphony of sounds. Bit by bit, Lucas's measured heartbeat rose from the noise, followed by the whisper of fabric against his skin, the air shifting as he moved, and the trace of cedar and aged whiskey that always clung to him. He shifted again, and this time I turned with him, anticipating his movement before it finished.

"Better," he said. His tone stayed neutral, but I could hear the smile in it.

We fell into a rhythm after that, Lucas rearranging the bar, sliding glasses along the counter, dragging chairs across the floor, even tossing a bottle of water for me to catch.

"React, don't overthink," he said, tapping my shoulder lightly to jolt me back when my focus slipped. Each movement became a test of control. When Lucas slid a glass across the bar, I had to resist the urge to snatch it too fast; my strength could instantly shatter it. Instead, I practiced tempering my reactions, learning to let instinct and intention work together instead of against each other.

"Your body already knows what to do," Lucas said, circling behind me as I tracked another moving object. "It's your mind that's in the way."

He was right. The moment I stopped analyzing, my movements flowed more naturally. My muscles responded, no longer resisting my abilities but embracing them. The subtle displacement of air before an object shifted, the faint vibrations through the floor marking Lucas's steps, even the way ambient sound bent around motion. All of it sharpened into a clearer picture.

"The human in you wants to rely on sight," Lucas said, his voice drifting from different corners of the room as he moved. "But the vampire in you knows better. Trust it."

Gradually, I began to anticipate his movements more naturally, like learning to read music as a child. At first it was an overwhelming blur, too many notes and markings clamoring for attention, but with practice the patterns revealed themselves. Sound and scent became a map I could follow. I caught myself smiling when I pivoted as Lucas moved, earning a note of approval from him.

Then, in an instant, he was behind me. So close my pulse stuttered in my chest, the way it always did around him. His hands settled on my waist, firm yet careful. "You're letting your weight shift too far forward," he murmured, his breath cool against my neck as he adjusted my posture.

His hands anchored me in a world that had narrowed to only the two of us. The cool press of his fingers through my shirt sent a current racing up my spine, and I fought to hold my composure.

I felt the roughness of his palms through the fabric, the way he adjusted my stance. His chest didn't quite meet my back, but his body curved around mine as he demonstrated the posture.

The scent of him enveloped me, his breath stirring the fine hairs at my nape. A faint tremor ran through the fingers pressed against my sides, composure giving way as his pulse quickened.

The moment stretched taut, humming with possibility. I held perfectly still, afraid that even the smallest movement might break whatever was sparking between us. Every instinct urged me to lean back, to close that last sliver of distance, but fear, uncertainty, and the weight of everything unsaid kept me frozen in place.

The moment shattered like glass when the door opened, the bells overhead jingling softly. I tore off the blindfold as Jackson stepped inside, his eyes flicking between Lucas and me. Backlit by the morning haze, he carried an expression I couldn't look away from. Not anger, not jealousy, but a weightier truth: resignation laced with understanding. Somehow, that hurt worse.

The air shifted instantly, charged with a different kind of tension.

"Didn't expect to see you so early," I said, stepping away from Lucas so quickly I nearly tripped over my own feet in my haste to create space.

Lucas straightened to his full height, hands sliding into his pockets as though they hadn't been pressed against my waist. That easy composure reminded me of how effortlessly he could shift between intense mentor and casual bar manager, while I still fumbled to mask my reactions. The contrast only underscored how much better Lucas was at managing moments like this.

Jackson's smile flickered when it came, but his eyes stayed distant. He moved with the caution of someone approaching a wild animal. The worst part wasn't suspicion—it was the understanding in his eyes, as if he'd been bracing for this moment all along.

He parted his lips, then closed them again, swallowing back whatever he'd almost said. His attention didn't move, cataloging things I wished he wouldn't. Then he shifted his weight, drawing that easy expression back into place. "Micah texted me. We're heading to Daly City for breakfast at her parents' house."

As if her name summoned her, Micah stepped out of the back hallway. One glance at the tableau—me still awkward, Lucas carefully distant, Jackson overcompensating—and her brows shot up. A knowing smirk tugged at her lips, but mercifully, she held her tongue.

"Ready to go, Jacks?" Micah asked instead, snagging her jacket from behind the bar.

Jackson nodded, though his eyes paused on me a moment longer before he turned to follow Micah toward the door. I stayed rooted where I was, listening until their footsteps faded and the door clicked shut behind them.

"Focus, Reyes," Lucas said lightly, as if nothing had happened. But the rough edge in his voice belied the calm he tried to project.

♪ ♪ ♪

Later that afternoon, Micah reappeared at our apartment, arms full of containers of her mom's cooking. The scent of garlic rice and chicken adobo spread through the space, rich and comforting. She dropped onto our worn couch with her coffee in hand, fixing me with the look that meant escape was impossible.

"So," she drawled, her tone low and teasing. "That was some interesting tension back at the bar this morning."

I groaned, burying my face in my hands. "I like Jackson, okay? I do." The words came out muffled but honest. Jackson

STRING ME A MURDER

was everything I should want: kind, funny, normal. Safe.

Micah hummed, tapping her spoon against her coffee mug. "But?"

"It's not just attraction," I said, peeling at the label on my beer bottle. "With Jackson, everything feels... possible. Normal. He makes me laugh, he gets my music references, he's just... easy to be around."

Micah nodded, patient, waiting. She knew me too well to think that was the end.

"But Lucas..." The words caught in my throat. "Lucas understands parts of me Jackson can't. He's lived this. He knows what it's like when your whole world shifts sideways. And when he looks at me, sometimes it's like..."

"Like he sees everything you are and everything you could be?" Micah finished.

"Yeah." I exhaled, the admission leaving me almost lighter and heavier at the same time. "But he's also my mentor. My boss. He's supposed to be teaching me how to survive this new life, not... whatever this is turning into."

Micah set her coffee down and turned to face me fully. "Look, I've seen how Jackson looks at you, like you're this amazing puzzle he can't wait to solve. He's steady, he's kind, and he clearly adores you."

She paused, choosing her words with care. "But I've also seen you with Lucas. The way you orbit each other, even across a crowded room. How you both pretend not to watch when you think no one's paying attention."

"That doesn't help," I groaned.

"It's not supposed to help," she said with a sly smile. "It's supposed to make you think. Jackson is obvious. You two spark, it's cute, it's simple, it makes sense." She hesitated, then added, "But Lucas? Lucas is... complicated. And something tells me he doesn't mind being complicated."

I leaned back against the couch, closing my eyes. "Then I guess I need to figure out what I actually want before I ruin both things."

Micah grinned, equal parts sympathetic and amused. "Good plan. But maybe figure it out before things spiral into a tragic, broody love triangle." She took another sip of her coffee. "Although, I've gotta say... watching you stumble through vampire romance drama is way more entertaining than my Netflix queue."

I smiled, then lobbed a pillow at her. She was right, of course. I had to untangle my feelings before someone got hurt. Most likely me. The memory of Lucas's hands on my waist circled back, tangled up with the look in Jackson's eyes when he'd walked in. Both moments carried weight, but in such different ways I couldn't begin to reconcile them.

For now, I reached for the container of adobo, letting the familiar comfort of Tita Isa's cooking pull me back to the present.

CHAPTER TWENTY-ONE

Harmonic Brews Café near the academy buzzed with its usual early-afternoon energy, alive with the hiss of espresso machines and the low hum of students fueling themselves for practice schedules and theory assignments. The barista worked the machine, steam curling in the air, each hiss and tap falling into place, while the scrape of fingertips on laptop keys merged with the clink of cups and saucers.

I picked up my americano from the counter, the warmth of the cup a comfort against my perpetually cool skin. The rich aroma of freshly ground beans rose with an intensity I still hadn't learned to anticipate.

Jackson sat at a corner table by the window, nursing a flat white—two shots, oat milk, and the faintest trace of vanilla. His laptop screen glowed in front of him, multiple tabs open and reflecting in his glasses as he scrolled in absorbed silence. He took a quick sip from his cup and set it down again, aligning the handle so it sat perfectly parallel to the laptop's edge.

I slid into the seat across from him, the awkwardness from earlier this morning at the bar still hanging between us. Jackson's heartbeat quickened, enough to tell me he was thinking about it too.

"We don't have to talk about it if you don't want to," he said gently, his voice warm with that same unhurried patience he always carried. Even now, he was trying to make this easier for me.

"It's... complicated," I muttered, eyes tracing the black swirl of my coffee as if it might reveal the words I couldn't find. How could I explain what I barely understood myself? The pull I felt toward both him and Lucas. The way being a vampire had changed everything and nothing all at once.

Jackson leaned back in his chair, cradling his cup between his hands. "Complicated I can handle," he said, a slight smile playing at his lips. "I work in tech, remember? Debugging messy code is kind of my thing."

I huffed out a quiet laugh. "I don't think relationships work quite like programming."

"No," he agreed, his eyes meeting mine. "But they do require patience. And I've got plenty of that." He paused, taking a sip of his coffee before adding, "I'm not going anywhere, Cass. Whatever you need to figure out—with Lucas, with all of this—I'm here. No pressure, no deadlines."

There was a sincerity in his voice. He wasn't demanding answers or asking me to choose. He was merely... present.

"I don't deserve that kind of patience," I said quietly.

Jackson's smile softened. "That's not really your call to make." He reached across the table, and when his fingers met mine, the brief contact held my attention longer than it should. "Besides, you're worth waiting for."

He withdrew his hand and turned his laptop toward me. "Speaking of complicated," he said, "I think I found something about Wyatt you need to see."

Grateful for the reprieve, I leaned forward. "What did you find?"

"These," Jackson said, tapping the screen. "Emails between Wyatt and Diana Bloom."

Diana Bloom was practically royalty in the classical music world. Her patronage could launch careers overnight, opening doors that stayed firmly shut to anyone without the right pedigree. Worse, she'd had ties to Brad's family for years.

"Look at this one," Jackson said, highlighting a particular exchange. The words pulsed on the screen: *Brad is unpredictable. If the trio were restructured, our plans could move forward. Keep playing your part, and I'll ensure the right people notice.*

"What does she mean, 'Keep playing your part?'"

Jackson's expression turned grim. "From what I can piece together, if Brad was out of the picture, Diana was ready to sponsor Wyatt. He'd inherit Brad's connections. Maybe even secure a spot in the Philharmonic."

"The Philharmonic?" My voice faltered. "Wyatt's auditioning too?" My hands tightened around the cup. "Did Brad know? That would've put them in direct competition with each other and with me."

"Doesn't look like it," Jackson said, scrolling through more emails. "Diana mentioned she has connections and could secure him a position down the line, presumably."

I leaned back, letting the implications line up. Wyatt had more than enough reason to want him gone. With Brad out of the way, Wyatt would inherit his connections, secure a future with the Philharmonic, and finally step out of his shadow. The carefully worded emails painted someone who'd been waiting, planning, maybe even hoping, for an opportunity. The question was whether he'd acted on it.

Wyatt, with all his nervous energy and constant self-doubt, didn't seem capable of murder. But desperation could turn anyone dangerous. I'd seen how Brad's cruel remarks chipped at him, how years of being second-best had hollowed him out.

"So Wyatt wanted Brad out of the picture even before..." My voice caught before I could finish.

Jackson nodded, fingers tapping on his laptop. "And now Jordyn's dead too. Which either means—"

"—he orchestrated the whole thing," I finished, "or he thinks he's next."

A thought clicked into place, nudging me forward. "There's only one way to know," I remarked. "Dolores invited me to a recital at the academy tonight. Wyatt's performing."

Jackson arched a brow, a smile pulling at one corner of his mouth. "And you're hoping he slips up?"

"Something like that." I tried to mirror his smile, though my thoughts were already racing ahead, mapping out how I'd watch Wyatt without being obvious.

♪ ♪ ♪

Several hours later, I sat in the academy's intimate recital hall, the room glowing with soft ochre light that turned the polished wooden stage into a jewel. Dolores and Jules flanked me, close on either side.

"You think pre-performance jitters are bad now?" Jules said with a chuckle. "You should've seen the time Anna Korhonen downed an entire bottle of Bordeaux before her Tchaikovsky."

"Jules!" Dolores tried to sound scandalized, though I

caught the smile she was fighting to hide.

"What? It was fifteen years ago, and she's a respected professor now. Besides," he winked, "it made for a remarkable
interpretation of the piece. Very... experimental."

Their banter helped ease the room's tension, but my focus
snagged on a different thread entirely. Wyatt was hunched
near the back of the hall, gripping a silver flask as if it might
vanish if he let go. His pulse fluttered wildly, sweat beading
along his hairline, one foot tapping out an erratic rhythm
against the floorboards.

"That's not stage fright," Dolores murmured, her eyes following mine. "That's someone coming undone."

She was right. I'd seen plenty of pre-performance nerves,
but this was entirely different. Wyatt kept taking quick pulls
from his flask. Each swallow carried the smoky heat of expensive whiskey. Macallan, probably the 18-year. The kind of
drink you savor, not gulp in fear.

The recital began, and Wyatt stepped onto the stage with
his pianist. A slight tremor rippled through his bow hand as
he positioned his cello. Cassadó's Toccata in the Style of Frescobaldi. The name tugged a small smile from me, a memory
of wrestling through the same piece on viola. Its rich, flowing
lines could shimmer with elegance. Tonight, they carried a far
darker weight.

His playing was technically precise, years of training evi-
dent in every phrase, yet a subtle distortion lurked beneath
the polish. The tempo edged forward, rushed, as though his
body obeyed but his mind was elsewhere.

I closed my eyes, tuning out the rustle of programs and the
scattered coughs in the audience. Wyatt's heartbeat

hammered too fast, too frantic for nerves alone. This wasn't performance anxiety. This was terror.

Dolores must have noticed my intense focus because she touched my arm lightly. "You're not just here for the music, are you?" she whispered.

I shook my head, letting my focus slide back to the stage. Wyatt drove into the final passage, those ornate sequences of double stops and quick bow retakes. His left hand stalled where it should have glided, but the notes snagged under the tension in his bow arm, each stroke landing a shade too heavy. The phrases that should have blossomed rattled instead, pushed forward by a pulse that wasn't musical at all.

The pianist caught the shift instantly, her eyes flicking toward him as she recalibrated, adjusting her touch to stay with his accelerating tempo. But even she couldn't smooth the jagged urgency creeping through his sound. The fear radiating from him thinned the resonance, hollowing out the brilliance the ending demanded.

By the time he reached the last chord, it came not as a triumphant release but as a collapse—an exhale that barely held shape.

The audience swelled with applause, and Wyatt took a quick, almost mechanical bow before hurrying off stage.

"Excuse me," I murmured to Dolores and Jules. "I need some air."

I followed Wyatt at a distance, staying inside the hallway. I focused inward, sifting through the hum of voices and footsteps until I isolated his voice in the courtyard.

"I don't care what you think. I'm next, okay?" Wyatt's words shook with panic as he spoke on the phone. "First Brad, then Jordyn. We're being picked off one by one."

A pause. Whoever was on the other end responded, but the voice was too muffled to make out.

"No, I don't know who," Wyatt continued, desperation creeping into every syllable. "But it's not random. It can't be."

Whatever was happening, Wyatt truly believed he was being targeted. Which meant either he was putting on an incredibly convincing act, or someone really was systematically eliminating members of the Presidio Trio. And whoever it was, they were still out there.

I took a tentative step forward. Should I warn him? Let him know I might be able to help? Or would that only make things worse? Maybe even spook the real killer into acting faster?

CHAPTER TWENTY-TWO

The moment I stepped into All Aboard Bar, its transformation enveloped me. String lights crisscrossed overhead, casting a warm glow that softened the evening's usual stark shadows. Handwritten posters proclaiming "Justice for Lilith" plastered every wall, a unified response to the belief that she'd been arrested for a crime she didn't commit. The slight waver in some strokes revealed hands trembling with emotion as they wrote.

The typical pre-show chaos had given way to a focused urgency. Donation boxes and tip jars lined the bar, already brimming despite the early hour. Each soft rustle of folded bills and clink of coins was a small act of defiance against the injustice of Lilith's arrest.

Lucas stood behind the bar, quietly managing the influx of funds, while Irene sat beside him, her meticulous handwriting filling the ledger with exact calculations. Her quick mental math impressed me, calling out running totals faster than Lucas could tally them. Enzo hovered nearby, sorting donations into neat stacks, each motion shaped by years of managing Spirit Haven's books. Despite everything we'd learned about his side business with Lilith, Enzo was still part of our All Aboard family, his loyalty rooted in bonds deeper than any mistake or shady deal. I noticed Lucas's fingers linger briefly over certain notes, as if recognizing the scents of regular customers whose loyalty was woven into every dollar.

"Alright, my lovelies!" Adda's voice sliced through the hum of activity. She stood at the room's heart, commanding attention like a general rallying her troops. "This benefit needs to burn hotter than my heels at Pride, and trust me, those babies could melt concrete."

I couldn't help but smile as Adda outlined the evening's agenda. Even amid such weighty stakes, she balanced gravity with her signature flair. Her sequined sleeve caught the light with each dramatic gesture. "We've got performances to make you weep, speeches to make you think, and honey, wait till you see what we're auctioning off."

Nearby, Micah worked alongside Hella on last-minute costume adjustments. The faded Queen T-shirt Micah wore clashed strikingly with the elaborate gown she was refining. Her hand movements perfected details too subtle for most to notice, but impossible for me to overlook.

"Lilith was there for me," Hella said, a rare tremor of vulnerability in her voice. "My first real gig? I was terrified. She believed in me before I believed in myself." Her fingers traced the intricate beadwork on the dress she and Micah had donated for the auction. "Guess it's my turn to believe in her."

Adda reached over and adjusted a loose fold in Hella's gown. "Good. Because tonight, we give them a reason to believe right along with us."

The arrival of Micah's parents, Tita Isa and Tito Hector,

brought a wave of comfort and the mouthwatering aroma of fresh-baked Filipino treats. The air hummed with the buttery scent of empanadas, the sweet warmth of ensaymada, and the fluffy, tangy notes of mamon. They'd clearly been cooking all day.

"*Ay nako*, Cass," Tita Isa tsked, setting down a spread that could feed half of West Portal. "You're still too *payat*. Too thin! Here, try my new ube cheese mamon recipe."

I accepted the chiffon cake. Some gestures carried too much love to refuse. "Thank you, Tita."

Micah wrapped her arms around her parents, squeezing them tight. "*Salamat po*—thank you—Mom and Dad. This means so much to everyone."

Tito Hector's eyes crinkled as he patted his daughter's back. "*Walang anuman*—no worries—my *anak*. Of course we help. Lilith has always been kind to you, and we know she's important to this community."

"Your father and I raised you to stand by your friends," Tita Isa added, her hand finding Micah's shoulder. "Especially when they need it most." Her glance brushed mine, carrying an unspoken understanding before she smiled at the room. "We all face challenges we don't expect. What matters is who sticks by us."

"Besides," Tito Hector added with a playful wink, "your mother was running out of neighbors to feed. Yesterday I caught her trying to convince the mailman to take home a tray of pancit."

"Hector!" Tita Isa swatted his arm, laughing. The sound of their shared mirth made my chest warm with a bittersweet kind of happiness. This was what family should look like—

the gentle teasing, the unconditional support, and the way they all gravitated toward each other so effortlessly.

Micah rolled her eyes but couldn't hide her grin. "Dad, I swear you get worse every year. Next thing you'll be teaching our customers Filipino tongue twisters."

"Who says I haven't already?" Tito Hector shot back, making us all wince through our laughter.

Dolores and Jules had taken charge of the bake sale table, arranging everything to create a welcoming display.

"Caspar," Dolores called out, her teacher-voice in full effect, "if you don't help sell at least ten empanadas, it's scales and etudes for a week straight."

I groaned, not entirely serious. "You're not technically my teacher right now, you know."

"Tell that to the Bach suite waiting for you upstairs," she shot back, winking.

Standing there, I took it all in. Drag performers adjusted their wigs in the corners while customers excitedly examined the auction items. Neighbors from all walks of life gathering together were proof that even in darkness, light finds a way to shine through.

I made my way to the bar where Lucas stood quietly, keeping half an eye on the room. I could tell how much this place and these people mattered to him. He was proud of them, even if he'd never say it out loud.

Leaning against the counter, I watched him methodically polish a glass. Without looking up, he asked, "Taking it all in?"

"It's... a lot," I admitted, unable to keep the admiration from my voice. "You've built something here. A place where people actually take care of each other."

Lucas met my eyes, unwavering. "That's the point, Cass."

I lowered my voice, though the general bustle of the fund-raiser would cover our conversation. "If Lilith isn't guilty, then the real killer's still out there."

Lucas took his time responding, setting the glass back on the shelf. "You can't carry all of this yourself."

"If I don't do something, who will?" I challenged, but even as I said it, I knew he had a point. I let my attention drift across the crowd. "Wyatt's convinced someone's hunting him. And if he's right, we might not have much time."

Lucas shifted another glass into place. "You're putting yourself in the middle of a dangerous situation. You're thinking like a hunter, but you don't have control yet."

Before I could argue, the lights dimmed, and Adda took the stage. Her presence drew all eyes like a magnet, the room subtly shifting as heads turned toward her. "Alright, my darlings," she announced, her voice carrying that perfect mix of authority and warmth, "we might be standing in a bar, but tonight, this is a damn courtroom, and we're fighting for one of our own."

The crowd erupted in cheers. I felt the vibrations of their voices, a symphony of support and determination that made my skin tingle.

Hella stepped onto the stage in a stunning creation she and Micah had collaborated on, a layered gown of translucent mesh washed in iridescent pigment, its colors blooming and shifting with each step, almost as if it were made of liquid. She gave a brief, shaky nod to herself, fingers curling gently at her sides as she waited for the music.

The opening notes of *Rise Up* by Andra Day filled the bar, and Hella's performance transcended mere lip-syncing, each movement charged with meaning. I watched the audience respond, their collective heartbeats gradually syncing to the rhythm of the music. The air thickened with shared emotion, a potent mix of determination, hope, and fierce loyalty weaving silently through the crowd.

When Jules stepped up to the microphone after the second performance, his usual playful demeanor had softened into a tender sort of hush.

"When I first walked through those doors," he began, "I was a lost old man who didn't know where I belonged anymore." He went quiet for a moment, an unguarded softness settling in his eyes as they drifted to his hands. "After Rodney and I moved from New Orleans to San Francisco, he found a job as a lighting technician. He may have been behind the scenes, but Rodney lit up every room he walked into. We went to every opening night we could—the shows, the people, the late-night diner runs after curtain call... it felt like home."

There was a gentleness in his voice now. "But we lost so many friends during the epidemic in the eighties. And then when I lost Rodney a few years back..." He trailed off, fingers unconsciously brushing his ascot. "I wasn't looking for romance when I found All Aboard. I was looking for connection, for belonging again. And somehow, Adda and Lilith made me feel like family. They showed me it's never too late to find your people, even if you thought that part of your life was over."

"Jules, I swear, if you make me cry..." Micah fanned her face dramatically with a cocktail napkin from the side of the stage. "Wasn't ready for things to get this real tonight."

Laughter rippled through the crowd, tender rather than dismissive. In that moment, every person in the room was connected, bound by a force stronger than fear or suspicion.

I'd never had this growing up. In my parents' world of careful social calculations and rigid expectations, genuine community was as rare as the vintage wines they collected. But here, in this bar with its mismatched chairs and slightly sticky floors, people actually showed up for each other.

These people were fighting for Lilith because they believed she hadn't killed anyone and trusted her as one of their own. They weren't waiting for proof or permission. They were acting on faith and love.

Adda's voice carried both steel and velvet when she spoke of justice. Hella's movements told stories without words. And there was dignity in the way Jules revealed his vulnerability. I sensed layers of meaning in every gesture, every shared glance, and every spontaneous burst of applause.

Amid it all, I couldn't ignore what waited beyond these walls. Somewhere out there, a killer was circling. And while we rallied around Lilith, Wyatt might be running out of time.

As the night began winding down, I moved through the thinning crowd, collecting empty glasses and catching fragments of conversations about legal funds and next steps.

"You've been quiet," Micah said, appearing beside me and bumping her hip against mine. The familiar gesture carried the scent of fabric softener from her vintage T-shirt, mingling with the metallic tang of safety pins from last-minute costume adjustments.

I shrugged. "Just thinking."

"Dangerous hobby," she teased.

"Any word on Lilith?" I asked, keeping my voice low enough that only she could hear.

Micah's expression grew more serious. "Adda talked to her lawyer this afternoon. She's at County now. They honored her request to be housed with the women, which is something at least." She paused, watching me stack another glass. "The lawyer thinks we might be able to get her out on bail by next week, especially with all this." She gestured around the room at the evidence of community support.

"What if this isn't enough?" The words slipped out, heavy with doubt. "What if we can't help Lilith the way she needs?"

Micah's hand found my forearm. "We do what we can," she said, voice unexpectedly fierce. "And that's enough." Her pulse stayed sure, affirming her belief in the words even when I wasn't sure I could.

CHAPTER TWENTY-THREE

The day after the fundraiser brought an unusual quiet. Only a few regulars nursed their drinks in corners. Behind the bar, Lucas poured a pear martini for Jules, who sat on his usual stool, sharing more of his endless neighborhood stories.

"You'll never guess what Mango's done now," Jules, clearly amused, took another sip from the frosty glass.

"What trouble has he gotten himself into this time?" I asked, smiling despite everything weighing on my mind.

Lucas raised an eyebrow, bracing himself. "Don't tell me he's gone after the rooks now."

"Chess heists are last season," Jules said, giving a small, playful wave. "That feline felon has moved on to a far more ambitious enterprise. This week, it's laundry—Mrs. Nguyen's pride and joy, of all things. Linen napkins, cashmere socks... even a lone argyle from Mr. Petrenko's line, drying in the sun."

Lucas paused, his expression caught between disbelief and entertainment. "He's stealing laundry now?"

"She found them all piled like a multicolored nest under

her hydrangeas this morning," Jules continued, delighted by the escalation. "Says he's very particular about arranging them by pattern and warmth. The cashmere items get prime positioning, naturally."

I couldn't help but laugh. "Mr. Petrenko must be thrilled."

"Oh, he's resigned to it at this point," Jules said, finishing the last sip. "Apparently Mango has a very particular sense of style when it comes to his... acquisitions."

A light thump came from the direction of the windowsill. Jules leaned closer, whispering. "See? That's the pile growing. I swear he's adding to it as we speak."

Lucas shook his head. "Cats really do own neighborhoods, don't they?"

"Absolutely, *mon cher*." Jules rose, lifting his empty glass in a small toast. "I promised to help photograph the crime scene for their shop's Instagram—the one with all the pressed shirts and stain removal tips. They're documenting Mango's reign of terror for posterity." He paused at the door, glancing back. "Privacy is important for humans, but Mango? Let's just say he has his own agenda."

As Jules slipped away, the soft clatter of the bar returned, only to be interrupted by the bell above the door.

Detective Kerri Martinez stepped inside, removing her sunglasses and tucking them into her leather jacket pocket. Her eyes scanned the room, landing first on Lucas before finding me.

"Mr. Reyes," Martinez greeted, her tone that perfect blend of professional detachment and underlying warning she'd perfected. "We need to talk."

I exhaled, already feeling defensive. "I didn't do it," I

muttered, more out of habit than anything else. It wasn't fair to take it out on Martinez, but I did it anyway. I knew her composure had limits, even if she rarely let them show.

A faint smirk touched her lips, unimpressed. "And yet, here we are, having another conversation about a case you insist you're not involved in."

She leaned against the bar. "You're still under investigation," she stated bluntly. "And poking around isn't making it any easier. For you or for me."

I couldn't help the scoff that escaped me, frustration bubbling like carbonation in a shaken bottle. "Because it's easier to focus on me than the actual killer, right?"

Lucas angled his body toward us. "What exactly are we talking about?" he asked Martinez carefully. Neutral on the surface, but I could hear the protective edge beneath.

"Cass and his friends have overstepped their boundaries," Martinez replied, fixing me with a pointed look. "And made themselves noticeable to all the wrong people."

I bristled. "Noticeable to who? Richard Bennington?"

The name slipped out harsher than I intended, but I didn't stop. "Enzo seems pretty convinced you owe your career to him."

Lucas shot me a look, his eyebrows dipping—*what are you doing?*—but the words were already out.

Martinez's expression didn't crack.

"I see." She dragged her tongue across her upper teeth. "So that's the rumor Enzo's spreading now."

"I'm just saying," I countered, "it doesn't sound great from where I'm standing."

She looked me dead in the eye. "Let me make one thing

perfectly clear: no one owns me. Not Richard Bennington, not Enzo Dodson, and definitely not you, Mr. Reyes."

Lucas shifted closer to me, like he expected things to escalate.

Martinez took a composed breath, regaining control.

"Not that this is any of your business," Martinez said sharply, "but since you've already decided what kind of person I am, let me set the record straight." She straightened her jacket cuff. "Yes, Richard Bennington helped my career. I didn't ask him to. I didn't want him to. But when you're a young cop and someone with that much influence decides to 'support' you..."

She looked past me for a moment, as if sorting through memories she'd rather leave buried. "Donations to the department, recommendations, pressure in the right places—all framed as mentorship." She held still. "It wasn't mentorship. It was leverage. A way to claim he'd 'helped' me if he ever needed something in return."

Lucas's expression softened. "Sounds like you've spent your whole career proving you don't owe anyone anything."

She glanced over at him, a brief acknowledgment passing between them. "Exactly. Whatever rumors Enzo's spreading, whatever stories you've heard—I wasn't part of any game those men were playing. And I won't be used by them ever again."

Then she turned back to me. "So believe what you want. But don't mistake unwanted help for allegiance. I don't work for the Benningtons. And I sure as hell don't work for Enzo."

Lucas let out a breath beside me.

"Now..." Her posture straightened, the vulnerability gone.

"What I *do* see," she said coolly, "is you entangling yourself in an active homicide investigation when your own connection to the victim is still under review."

"I should investigate," I shot back. "Wyatt's scared out of his mind. I heard him say it himself: he thinks someone is coming after him next."

Martinez didn't react. She pulled out her notepad, flipping to a fresh page. "Go on."

I detailed the emails Jackson had uncovered, watching as she jotted notes. "Diana Bloom. You know her, right? Major patron in the classical world?" Her slight nod urged me on. "She was dangling Wyatt's future in front of him, practically suggesting Brad needed to be 'removed' from the equation."

Martinez raised an eyebrow, but her expression stayed neutral. The scratch of her pen against paper seemed unnaturally loud.

"And then there's the phone call I overheard," I pressed on, recalling every tremor in Wyatt's voice: *They're picking us off one by one. I'm next.* I didn't mention how I'd heard him from across the courtyard, or how the scent of his fear had been thick enough to taste. "If he's that scared, he knows something. Shouldn't that matter?"

Martinez didn't answer immediately. Instead, she tapped her pen twice—sharp little beats that made the hairs on my arms rise. I hated this tactic, her silence stretching until people felt compelled to fill it.

She snapped her notepad shut with a crisp sound that made me flinch. "You're not wrong that something's off," she admitted. "But that doesn't change the fact that you're too close to this."

I frowned. "I am this. This place, these people—it's my life."

"Listen to me carefully, Mr. Reyes. If the killer is still out there, and they know you're digging into this? You're making yourself a target."

My spine stiffened, but Lucas's reaction pulled my attention as his entire body went taut beside me, tense as a drawn bowstring.

Martinez glanced between us. "Consider that fair warning." She gestured to Lucas. "Soda, please. Still on duty."

Lucas reached for the soda gun; his motions stripped of his usual fluidity. Martinez took only two sips before setting the glass down.

"Stay out of trouble, Mr. Reyes." She paused. "And watch your back."

The bar door closed behind her with a soft jingle, leaving a tense silence in her wake. I ran a hand through my hair. "Are we just supposed to ignore everything now?" I asked. "Let Wyatt twist in the wind? Wait for another body to show up?"

Lucas cleared his throat and stepped around the bar. "Maybe it's time to let this go, Cass. Let the police handle the rest."

I turned sharply. "You're really saying that?" The words lashed out before I could stop them. Of all people, I hadn't expected Lucas to suggest backing down.

His voice lowered, tight. "You think I don't see what you're doing? Throwing yourself into this like you're invincible?"

"I know I'm not invincible—" I crossed my arms, bracing for whatever came next.

"Then start acting like it," Lucas cut me off. The edge in

his tone made me take half a step back.

I let out a thin laugh. "I can handle myself." The words rang hollow, more bravado than truth.

Lucas clenched his jaw, exhaling sharply through his nose. "You don't know that yet."

Instead of replying, I grabbed a rag from the counter and began wiping down tables, probably with more force than necessary.

Lucas shook his head and turned toward his office. He stalled for a beat, as if he had more to say but couldn't find the words.

I drew a jagged breath and let it go, gripping the rag until my knuckles went white. Martinez's warning echoed in my mind, but instead of scaring me off, it only strengthened my resolve. If someone was really hunting the Presidio Trio, time was running out. And despite Lucas's fears, despite Martinez's warnings, I couldn't—wouldn't—stand by and do nothing.

CHAPTER TWENTY-FOUR

The late-night hush of All Aboard Bar felt deceptive, like the stillness before a storm. Lucas sat behind the bar immersed in his spreadsheets. I was moving through the closing routine when my phone buzzed sharply in my pocket. A text from Wyatt: Please. Need to talk. Now. Harmonic Brews Café.

I stared at the screen. After Martinez's warning, I should've ignored it. But the urgency in Wyatt's message made that impossible.

Lucas glanced up from his laptop, his expression shifting into that unnervingly perceptive focus. "Trouble, Cass?"

I grabbed my jacket from the hook. "Gotta handle something."

Before I could reach the door, Lucas's cool fingers closed around my wrist. "Careful," he murmured, his voice a potent blend of authority and concern, making me feel both held and defiant.

I tugged my arm free, maybe a little more defensively than needed. "Yeah, I know."

The brisk walk to the café near the academy took under

twenty minutes. The sound of rustling leaves, distant traffic, even the soft patter of a stray cat blocks away was amplified with eerie clarity in the night. Harmonic Brews' neon sign hummed, its sickly yellow glow spilling over the near-empty sidewalk.

Through the window, I spotted Wyatt hunched in the corner at the same table where Jackson and I had held our impromptu investigation. His coffee sat untouched. His tan wool coat hung haphazardly over the back of the chair, as if he'd barely bothered to shrug it off.

The moment I stepped inside, my nose wrinkled at the intensity of his anxiety—a wall of bare, exposed fear. The tremor in his fingers wasn't mere caffeine jitters; his entire body thrummed with barely contained panic.

Wyatt's eyes locked onto mine, his jerky wave beckoning me over. "You came," he said, his voice tinged with shock more than relief.

I slid into the seat across from him, projecting calm despite the tension crackling between us. "You texted like someone was dying."

Wyatt didn't respond immediately, his fingers twitching at his shirt collar. "I think... I think I'm next," he said, his breath ragged and uneven. "Brad. Jordyn. It's not random."

Without warning, Wyatt shoved his phone toward me. Its screen glowed with texts from an unknown number, each one more ominous than the last:

You should've been more careful.

You're next.

You belong with them.

"Okay, slow down," I said. "How long has this been going

on?"

His knee bounced relentlessly under the table, sending vibrations through the floor. "A few days. At first, I thought it was just... stupid pranks. But they're getting worse. More specific."

I narrowed my eyes. "And you didn't think to tell the cops? Or Martinez?"

Wyatt reached across the table for his phone, his fingertips brushing mine as I passed it to him. The case was clear but worn, fine cracks spiderwebbing across its surface. Tucked inside was a photo of a young woman with the same deep brown eyes and tentative smile—almost certainly his sister. The edges were creased, as if it had been handled often, then carefully slid back into place.

"You don't get it," he said quietly. "Maybe I deserve this."

He caught me looking at the photo and flipped the phone over without a word. I looked away, but the image stayed with me.

"And why exactly would you deserve to be murdered?"

He exhaled. "Because, Cass... I should've walked away from that trio ages ago. Before things got this bad."

I leaned forward, catching the strain lacing his voice. "What do you mean 'this bad'? What aren't you telling me?"

Wyatt's fingers drummed an erratic rhythm on the table. Guilt etched deeper lines around his mouth, aging him since I'd last seen him.

"It wasn't just music with Brad," he said. "It was... connections. Favors. Things we kept quiet."

"Connections? With whom? Diana Bloom?"

Wyatt shook his head, already pulling back. "It doesn't

matter. None of it matters anymore."

"If it didn't matter, you wouldn't be saying you deserve this." I lowered my voice. The café's ambient hum—soft music, distant coffee grinding, murmured conversations—faded to static as I zeroed in on Wyatt. "Tell me what you mean."

His jaw clenched, tendons taut in his neck. "I should've walked away. Left Brad behind when I had the chance. It's complicated," he muttered, his hands twitching across the table.

I didn't let up, catching his evasion. "Try me."

His hands stilled, fingers pressed flat against the table. "My dad brags to the neighbors about my 'big competition,'" he said, staring into his cup. "He doesn't get that winning doesn't guarantee success. And my mom... she thinks chamber music means I'm set for life."

I watched his shoulders hunch inward, shielding something fragile.

"They believe if I just work hard enough..." He trailed off, eyes unfocused. "They sacrificed so much. They think talent plus effort equals success, and I—I know the world's messier than that."

He paused, a hint of vulnerability in his eyes.

"The worst part isn't that they're wrong. It's that I let them believe it."

"Wyatt—"

Without warning, he slammed his fist on the table. Coffee sloshed over his cup's rim, the heartbeats of nearby patrons spiking as they flinched. "You don't get it, do you?" he nearly shouted. "None of this was supposed to happen!"

My eyes locked on him with laser focus as the café fell

briefly silent. A few students glanced over, then quickly looked away, their pulses still racing from the outburst.

"Then why don't you explain what 'this' is, Wyatt?" I held myself in check, letting the challenge speak for itself.

Before he could respond, his phone buzzed against the table. Terror flashed across his face, stark and unguarded. I reached for the device, but Wyatt snatched it away.

"I need to go," he blurted, lurching to his feet so fast his chair screeched across the floor, jarring the air.

I stood too. "Wyatt, if you keep running, you'll end up like Jordyn and Brad."

For a moment, panic raged in his eyes before he shoved past me and bolted out the door. I didn't chase him, just stood rooted, watching him vanish into the night.

CHAPTER TWENTY-FIVE

The late morning fog hung heavy outside our apartment window as I sat with my viola braced against my shoulder. Shadows cloaked the living room, with only a glimmer of light struggling to pierce the gauzy curtains. From her room, Micah's sewing machine whirred, its familiar rhythm usually a comfort but today only amplifying my restlessness.

I drew a deep breath and tried to focus on the Sarabande, the emotional core of the suite. Slow, mournful, spare. It asked everything of you and offered almost nothing in return. No flashy runs, no technical fireworks to hide behind. Only long-held notes and the silence between them.

That silence was what terrified me most.

The slight scratch from the awkward catch of my bow stood out, and my left hand pressing too hard on the fingerboard made the pitch waver. I was playing too much, filling every space, afraid of what might surface if I let the music breathe.

The Sarabande was grief. Not the loud kind that screamed for attention. The kind that waited in your bones—patient, inevitable. It sat in empty practice rooms and late-night bar shifts. It lingered in the air where Brad's arrogance used to be, where Jordyn's careful ambition had once planned futures that never came.

I stopped mid-phrase, bow hovering above the strings.

Wyatt's panicked words from last night kept intruding: *I think I'm next.* The threatening messages. His confession about the pressure to keep up the illusion of success, no matter how far from the truth.

Play less. Mean more. That was what the Sarabande demanded.

I lifted the bow again, this time letting the silence settle first. Then I played—softer, slower—leaving space for the grief I'd been avoiding. For Brad's wasted potential. For Jordyn's stolen future. For Wyatt's guilt. For my own fear that I was in over my head, that every decision I made might get someone else hurt.

The truth lived in those silences, in the spaces between the notes, where there was nothing left to hide behind. Not technique. Not volume. Not speed.

My phone buzzed on the side table, and I reached for it, surrendering to the interruption.

"Cass, it's Dolores." Her voice was taut, controlled, but a subtle tremor undermined the fear she was fighting to suppress. Dolores didn't do fear. Ever.

Her next words came steadily but carried unmistakable weight. "I need you at the studio. Now."

I gripped the phone tighter. "What's wrong?"

"There's been a break-in." She paused, and I could almost hear her heartbeat quicken. "The police are on their way, but I need you here."

I was on my feet before she finished, my viola forgotten on the chair. "I'm coming."

I grabbed my jacket and keys, pausing briefly outside Micah's door, torn about asking for her help. Through the wall, her soft humming drifted as she worked. No, this could be nothing more than vandalism. Better to let her work in peace.

Hurrying down the bar's back staircase, my instincts sharpened. The musty scent of stale beer clung to the empty bar. A newspaper skittered on the sidewalk outside. Even the subtle shift in barometric pressure hinted at coming rain. My body felt coiled, poised to spring, as if sensing danger before my mind could catch up.

The streets of West Portal rested in a drowsy, liminal haze between the morning rush and lunch crowds. Yet the air carried an edge that raised the hairs on my neck.

When I reached Dolores's private studio inside the academy, the door hung ajar, its lock splintered and useless. Stepping inside, I crunched broken porcelain beneath my boot. Fragments of Dolores's favorite teacup, the one she always used during lessons, were shattered on the floor.

Sheet music lay strewn like fallen leaves, pages torn and crumpled. The music stand lay toppled, chairs upended, as if someone had torn through the room in a rage. Dolores stood by the window, hands tucked in her coat pockets, her face smooth and unreadable as I surveyed the disorder spread before us.

"What the hell happened?" I asked, forcing myself to stay composed.

She didn't answer immediately, staring out the window as if searching the foggy morning for answers that weren't there.

"I don't know. I got here this morning and found it like this." Her hands stayed buried in her coat pockets, fingers pressed flat against the fabric, as though she were restraining the urge to clench her fists.

I flashed back to the day a student collapsed during her master class. Dolores had calmly directed the emergency response while continuing to teach without missing a beat. When budget cuts threatened her program, she'd orchestrated a fundraising concert in three days, her voice steady as steel as she rallied support. Even when her mother passed, she'd channeled her grief into a memorial performance that left the audience in tears, her composure unshaken.

But now, as she kept that same careful posture, I noticed a slight tension around her eyes, like someone quietly working to stay grounded. Whatever this was, it seemed to reach her in a way I hadn't seen before.

I moved deeper into the room, surveying the destruction. This wasn't random. It felt intentional, calculated. Either someone had lost all control, or they were sending a pointed message.

The crunch of tires on gravel announced an approaching car, and Dolores turned her head. "That'll be Detective Martinez," she said, her voice steadier now.

Martinez swept in moments later, her leather coat unbuttoned, notepad tucked under her arm as she pulled on latex gloves.

"Nice to see you again, Mr. Reyes." Her voice was dry as sandpaper. "Starting to feel like we should schedule these run-ins."

I didn't reply, my attention fixed on the wreckage.

Scattered sheet music quivered, as if stirred by a disturbance hours old. Tiny scratches scored the chair's arm, shallow and uneven, where someone's fingers had dug in before throwing it.

One of Martinez's officers knelt near a pile of toppled sheets, lifting a folded paper that stood out from the mess. "Ma'am, Detective," he called, standing to offer the evidence with gloved hands.

Martinez unfolded it with care. Dolores and I edged closer. The blocky, jagged writing was pressed so hard into the page it nearly tore through: STOP LOOKING WHERE YOU DON'T BELONG.

Martinez turned the note over, inspecting both sides. "That's ominous." She pivoted, fixing me with a penetrating stare. "Looks personal. Any idea why someone would single you out?"

Before I could respond, Dolores crossed her arms tightly and stepped forward. "He's been digging into the murders. Someone didn't like it." Her words made me shift uneasily, torn between gratitude and discomfort at her defense.

"Detective," an officer called. He held up a scrap of tan wool, the same shade and weave as the coat Wyatt always wore.

Martinez crouched, her eyes narrowing as she scanned the wreckage, then rose to pin us with a stare. "Your friend Wyatt's deeper in this than we thought."

The officers moved like a chamber ensemble, seamless and unspoken, a current of silent theories flickering between them. When Martinez mentioned Wyatt, I caught a skeptical glance between two younger ones. They didn't buy it either.

Stepping deeper into the debris, I let my senses take over. The rustle of paper under the officers' boots roared like thunder. The subtle shifts in their breathing wove a symphony of anxiety and focus.

Then a faint, bitter scent—chemical, yet hauntingly familiar—appeared. My body stiffened the instant I recognized it.

That scent. I knew it. It had haunted the bar after we found Brad. It had seeped into Jordyn's practice room. And now, it threaded through the air of Dolores's studio.

I glanced at Martinez, then Dolores. Neither reacted. They couldn't smell it.

Only I could.

I gripped a nearby chair for balance. The scrap of wool felt like bait, the whole scene arranged to point in one direction. This wasn't mere vandalism or a warning.

It was the same killer.

Whoever did this wanted me afraid, wanted me to stop digging. The note wasn't mere words on paper... it was a display of power, of reach. They could strike anyone, anywhere.

And yet it reeked of desperation.

Which meant I was closing in.

Martinez's voice sliced through my thoughts. "Mr. Reyes? You look like you've seen a ghost."

I forced my face to neutral. "Just... taking it all in."

But as the officers worked around us, that bitter scent lingered in my nose, a silent warning.

CHAPTER TWENTY-SIX

"So, Mr. Reyes," Martinez said, her tone firm yet not unkind. "If this wasn't meant for Dolores, whoever did this was leaving a message for you to stop."

I caught the warning in her voice, but I couldn't back down. "What if I'm too deep to stop?"

She slid her notepad into her coat pocket, the paper's rustle cutting through the silence. "That's my worry. Keep pushing, and this could get uglier."

"So I should just step back and let you handle it? Like you handled Lilith's arrest?"

Martinez's expression remained neutral, but I caught the flicker in her eyes. "Lilith is still under investigation," she replied. "And now we have signs pointing to Wyatt's involvement."

I lifted an eyebrow. "Could be. But you don't sound convinced."

She tilted her head. "I don't like it when things line up too neatly." Her eyes drifted to the bagged piece of Wyatt's coat, then back to me. "And this? This feels...placed."

I rubbed my hands together, trying to chase off the jittery

edge. Somewhere behind us, a camera shutter clicked. At least she wasn't completely buying into the frame-up job.

Before turning to leave, Martinez leaned in toward me. Even though we were alone in this corner of the room, she lowered her voice. "You already know this isn't just about Wyatt. But tread carefully. You might be pushing buttons you don't even know exist."

The concern in her voice seemed genuine, which only made it worse. I nodded, trying to ignore the way my stomach curled at her words.

As the last officers filed out, Dolores stood by the console piano, her fingers tracing the edge of the keys without pressing them. Her usual commanding presence remained intact, but her stillness felt different. I stepped beside her, righting a toppled chair. "You doing okay?"

She hummed vaguely, as if weighing the question. "I've had worse mornings."

Tension tightened her lips and creased the crumpled sheet music she clutched. I didn't press her. Instead, I gathered the scattered pages—Bach, Brahms, Mozart—centuries of music strewn like worthless scraps. As we worked in silence, Dolores murmured, "You think this was meant for you."

I paused, a Mozart sonata half-folded in my hands. "Yeah."

Dolores continued organizing the music, but her voice carried the sternness she reserved for students teetering on folly. "I don't like this, Caspar."

"Neither do I."

She looked at me directly. "Then do me a favor. Don't be reckless."

I couldn't answer. We both knew I couldn't make that

promise.

Instead, I laid the stack of recovered sheet music on the piano. "If I find anything," I said, "you'll be the first to know."

Dolores nodded, a crisp movement that was pure her. A ghost of her usual smile flickered across her face. "Just don't make me have to bail you out of anything."

"I'll try," I said, the words ringing hollow.

As we restored order, a focused quiet settled between us. Despite the violation of her studio, Dolores moved with her characteristic purpose, her composure intact. But the way she paused a beat too long before touching certain items spoke of someone bracing against an unseen force. Her resilience remained unshakeable, but seeing these subtle cracks only fueled my determination.

♪ ♪ ♪

The bar's familiar hum of the refrigerator and the scent of stale beer guided me back toward a sense of normalcy. Lucas stood behind the counter, straightening the coasters in their holder even though the night had long since wound down, stalling until I arrived.

He didn't need to ask what happened. One glance at my face told him enough. Without a word, he grabbed the whiskey bottle and poured two glasses. The amber liquid splashed into them, catching the dim bar lights in tiny ripples. I slid onto the stool across from him, grateful to finally sit.

With a weary hand, I rubbed my scalp and laid it all out for him, starting with Martinez's skepticism about the evidence against Wyatt, then the threatening note that felt too blatant to trust, and finally the bitter scent only I could detect.

Lucas listened in silence, the small shift of his grip on the glass the only break in his calm.

He set his drink down. "Whoever this is, they're spiraling."

I swirled the whiskey, small whirlpools forming at the center, but didn't drink. "Desperate," I muttered. "Because I'm closing in."

Lucas's attention stayed on me. "Or because they want you to think you're close."

I knew what he meant, but it didn't change my decision. If I backed off now, someone else could get hurt. "I don't care. I'm not stopping."

He studied me, weighing his next move. "Figured you'd say that." His hand rested on the bar's polished wood. "You remind me of someone I lost long ago."

The barstool's cracked vinyl flexed under me when I shifted my weight. "Let me guess, they ignored warnings too?"

"George never listened to anyone—"

"Wait, George? As in George and Lucas?" I couldn't resist. "Insert Star Wars joke here."

He didn't crack a smile, and my humor died as his expression turned distant. "When Todd hired me at All Aboard, George worked here part-time. Photography was his passion—freelance work, commissions, anything he could build into a real career."

Lucas rarely mentioned Todd Rubio, All Aboard's owner. The tightness around his mouth drew my focus, the bar's hum fading around us.

"George landed a serious gig," He continued. "Documenting a private art collection. Great pay, professional client. Should've been routine."

"But it wasn't routine for him, was it?"

"George had a keen eye for detail, too keen sometimes," Lucas said, tracing the rim of his glass. "He noticed things in the pieces he shot—paintings that belonged in museums, sculptures stolen decades ago, documents that didn't add up."

A chill crept up my spine. How many times had I pulled at threads that unraveled too far? "What did he think it was?"

"An art forgery ring, maybe. Or an international theft operation. Something big, criminal—human." His hands braced on the bar. "We didn't know he'd stumbled into vampire business. Ancient vampires don't shop at Pottery Barn for their décor."

I pictured centuries-old vampires hoarding priceless art like others collect coffee mugs. Vampire Hoarders: Buried Alive for Eternity would make one hell of a show.

"So he dug deeper," Lucas said, shaking his head. "Researching online, contacting museums, asking about 'hypothetical' pieces. I warned him to be careful, but George thought he was dealing with ordinary criminals."

The parallels stung as I tallied the warnings I'd brushed off lately—Dolores, Martinez, now Lucas.

"The client called him for a meeting," Lucas continued, "to 'clear up inconsistencies.' Offered him money to stay quiet."

"Did he go alone?"

"He asked me to come along, worried about facing criminals by himself." His hands stilled on his glass. "I thought it was smart. I thought I could keep him safe."

I waited a moment. "Where did it happen?"

"An upscale gallery, after hours. Very professional, very

private. The vampires weren't there to negotiate. They were there to eliminate a problem." Lucas stared at the bar top, as if seeing that night laid out before him. "I set them off. Talked about involving the authorities, said George had backed up the files. Made it clear we wouldn't take their money and vanish."

I let the glass shift in my grip. "Was it... a hit?"

"We fought. Or tried to. You know what vampires can do when they drop the human act." His eyes locked on mine, burdened with guilt. "They dragged George away. Left me dying on the floor."

The bar's fluorescent lights buzzed, catching the tightness in his expression. I wanted to ask about George's fate, but the weight of Lucas's story told me he had no answers.

"Who found you?"

"Todd. He saved me by turning me."

All Aboard's owner was Lucas's maker? Todd Rubio being a vampire felt secondary to the fact that he'd turned him.

"When I woke, he was gone. Still is, ten years later," he said.

A decade. I tried to imagine carrying that weight for ten years, the unresolved loss, the questions, the guilt. I thought of that old photo hanging in his office, the man clinging to Lucas's back, laughter frozen in time, now with a name. George.

"You think I'm making the same mistakes he did," I said plainly.

"You're asking questions about things bigger than you realize. You think you're dealing with human problems. And when people warn you to be careful..." He shrugged. "How's your track record with listening?"

I wanted to argue, but my track record was dismal. "This is different, Lucas. What I'm chasing isn't supernatural. It's just—"

"Just what? Just criminals who might hurt you? Just people powerful enough to make you vanish?" Lucas leaned forward. "Cass, the supernatural didn't make George's situation deadly. It was powerful people who wanted to stay hidden. It was him poking into secrets they'd kill to protect. It was thinking he was smarter than those trying to silence him."

There was no arguing with the truth in his words. I had no defense against them.

"I'm not asking you to stop," he said softly. "I know you won't. But I'm asking you to think about what happened to someone like you."

I stared at my untouched whiskey. "Do you think he's still alive? George?"

"I don't know." Lucas's honesty cut deep. "But I think about him every day, wondering if I could've done something different, protected him better."

He's trying to protect me now.

"Be smart, Cass. There's a fine line between persistence and recklessness."

Lucas had watched over me since that night in the alley when he saved me from an attacker. This wasn't tactical advice from a mentor. It was personal.

He straightened, returning to his work behind the bar. "Just... don't make me save your ass again."

I smirked but held my tongue. "No promises."

CHAPTER TWENTY-SEVEN

S prawled on the worn leather couch in the back office, I flipped through invoices for Lucas, nursing lukewarm coffee. Busy work, handed over without comment, as if the routine of it might keep my thoughts from running ahead. The fading warmth of the mug offered small comfort amid the dull rhythm of paperwork and bar operations, a rare normal morning.

My phone buzzed against the counter, Professor Yates's name lighting the screen. Everything in me went quiet. Any academy contact felt heavy with complications, and I dreaded re-entering that world.

Lucas glanced up from his desk, his dark eyes probing. I sighed and answered the call.

"Professor Yates," I said.

"Caspar," he replied, his usual authority tinged with tension. "I hope I'm not catching you at a bad time."

I neatened the invoice stack. "Not at all. What's this about?"

"The academy, with the Bennington family, is organizing a memorial concert for Brad and Jordyn." Yates paused, letting the words settle. "Given your history with Brad and your standing at the academy, you'd be an ideal performer."

A memorial concert. Of course the classical music world would lean into its ceremonies to mourn. But performing to honor two murder victims—one I'd slept with, the other a part of my musical circle—felt surreal.

"I..." I faltered, catching Lucas's raised eyebrow. "When is it?"

"We're meeting this afternoon at five to plan. It's short notice, but we'd value your presence."

The smart move would be to decline, but refusing might draw scrutiny, especially with Richard Bennington involved. But accepting meant stepping into the spotlight, exactly where I shouldn't be.

"I'll be there," I said, reluctance heavy in my voice.

After hanging up, I turned to Lucas, who watched me with an unreadable look.

"A memorial concert," he said, voice flat.

"Yeah." I shrugged, feigning nonchalance. "Hard to say no to something like that."

"Be careful with Richard Bennington, Cass. From what you've told me, nothing he does is random."

I tried to brush off his warning, but his tone lodged in my mind. Lucas didn't spook easily, and his instincts about people were rarely wrong.

"I'll watch my step," I promised, though we both knew I might not.

♪ ♪ ♪

The Bay Area Music Academy's concert hall hovered above,

its polished marble facade gleaming in the late-afternoon sun. I paused at the entrance, memories of performances, late-night rehearsals, and triumphs and failures flooding back. Now, a dark veil tainted those golden moments.

Inside, the grand chandeliers cast a warm glow over the auditorium, but their light seemed muted, as if the space itself mourned. Musicians and faculty sat in small clusters, their whispers contained but constant.

This was how the music world gathered—quiet, polished, grief and concern folded neatly into rows and rules. It was nothing like the fundraiser at the bar, where fear had turned into solidarity, messy and held together by hands instead of protocol, all in service of protecting one of their own.

Professor Yates stood by the gleaming Steinway, one hand resting on its surface. His commanding presence was more subdued. Behind him, Richard Bennington sat like a statue, his tailored suit impeccable, his expression coldly neutral.

I slipped into a middle-row seat, trying to blend in, but Bennington's gaze tracked me. My skin prickled. Every instinct urged me to move, to escape his line of sight, but I forced myself to stay put.

"Thank you for coming," Yates began, his voice carrying both authority and compassion. "As we plan this memorial concert, we're here to acknowledge the loss of two musicians who were part of this academy—students, colleagues, and members of a community that extends well beyond these walls."

He paused, clearing his throat. "Grief doesn't stay neatly contained in one place. It reaches teachers, ensemble partners, and families. This concert is our way of recognizing shared loss and giving it proper form. The Bennington family has worked with the academy to ensure this is done thoughtfully, with respect for the music and the people we're honoring."

Around me, tension rippled in subtle gestures. A cellist's fingers tightened on her bow, a pianist squared his stack of pages, and Wyatt, at the front row's edge, twisted his sweater's hem until the knit frayed.

"The program will open with a solo performance by Caspar Reyes," Yates announced.

My head snapped up. Opening the program? That honor typically went to a prestigious performer. Stares weighed on me, and I fought the urge to shrink in my seat.

"Caspar and his instructor, Ms. Larsen, will select an appropriate piece," Yates continued, leaving no room for discussion.

I nodded mechanically, grateful for Dolores's presence a few rows back. Her fierce confidence, unwavering even when I doubted myself, gave me something solid to hold onto.

Yates outlined the rest of the program, concluding with, "...and Wyatt Cross will close the concert with Cassadó's Toccata in the Style of Frescobaldi."

I glanced at Wyatt. His pianist squeezed his arm, but he barely registered the gesture; his eyes remained distant.

The meeting blurred through rehearsal logistics and scheduling details. Polite nods met each announcement, but I caught hitches in breath and quickening pulses. These weren't merely performance slots. They were obligations shaped by Richard Bennington's influence.

Throughout it all, I could feel Bennington's attention, like the weight of a spotlight I couldn't escape. When he stood to

leave, adjusting his platinum cufflinks, his eyes locked onto
mine. He offered a slight nod that felt more like a warning
than a greeting.

As the crowd began to disperse, I stood, stretching my
arms, when movement at the back of the hall caught my eye.
My vision honed in instinctively, cutting through the dimness
to focus on a figure slipping through the side door. They wore
a muted brown coat, and their petite frame and distinctive
gait felt familiar. Irene? But before I could be certain, they
vanished.

I stood there, frowning. If it was Irene, why was she here?
She had no connection to the academy, at least none I knew
of. I pushed the thought aside, focusing instead on gathering
my things. No need to add another layer of complexity to an
already tangled situation.

As I made my way out of the hall toward the building's
entrance, the temperature dropped. My senses snapped into
overdrive, picking up… something. A presence? A lingering
energy? The air felt charged, like the moment before a lightning strike.

I stretched my senses further, straining to pinpoint what
had triggered my instincts. Overhead, wiring hummed with
at an irritating frequency. Somewhere, water dripped in an
even rhythm. But there was something else, lying beyond my
grasp, eluding identification.

Then it was gone, leaving me wondering if I'd imagined it
all. Was I cracking under the pressure?

As whatever had set my instincts off slipped away, nothing
distinct remained. That was the problem. No familiar scent,
no hitch in a heartbeat, no disruption in the air. Whoever had

passed through hadn't vanished so much as blended in, leaving nothing for my senses to catch hold of.

I pushed through the front doors into the late afternoon sun. The memorial concert was meant to honor Brad and Jordyn, to bring closure to a grieving community. Yet somewhere in that tangle of emotions and motives, a killer remained hidden, perhaps already choosing their next target.

I pulled out my phone to text Lucas: Meeting's over. You were right about Bennington. Something's off, but I can't pin it down.

His response came quickly: Trust your instincts. They're usually right.

I stared at his message for a long moment before pocketing my phone. I couldn't shake the suspicion that the meeting had altered the landscape, that pieces were moving on a board I couldn't fully see. My instincts told me the memorial concert was more than a tribute. It was bait.

CHAPTER TWENTY-EIGHT

The familiar rhythm of pre-opening preparations filled All Aboard Bar. As I arranged chairs, each scrape of wood against wood echoed through the quiet, creating a low, almost musical cadence. Behind the counter, Lucas stocked shelves, the gentle clink of glass bottles forming a soft symphony.

Footsteps approached from the back hallway, accompanied by the familiar screech of cart wheels. Enzo and Irene emerged, pushing a battered delivery cart that looked long past replacement but still serviceable by his standards, stacked with cases and loose bottles.

"Morning, boys!" Enzo's booming voice filled the space with his usual charm as he set down a case of wine with an exaggerated grunt. "Beautiful day for heavy lifting, eh?"

I caught Lucas's subtle head tilt, a signal to act normal despite what we knew about Enzo's dealings with Lilith. I managed what I hoped was a casual nod, continuing to arrange chairs.

"Hi, Cass," Irene said, barely meeting my eyes as she opened a box labeled 'Premium Liquor' in bold black letters.

Lucas stepped around the bar, extending his hand to Enzo.

"Let's check that manifest," he said smoothly, guiding Enzo toward the office.

I grabbed a bar towel, wiping my hands as I approached Irene. "Need help with those bottles?"

"Thanks." She smiled, unpacking with care.

I cleared my throat. "Hey, I was at the academy yesterday. Thought I saw you slipping out the back of the concert hall."

Irene's fingers stilled on the cardboard flap of a case. "Yeah," she said. "Richard Bennington asked Spirit Haven to handle the liquor for the memorial concert reception. I had a meeting with him and Professor Yates about the orders." She adjusted another bottle. "Thought I'd scope out the academy since I've only been there for a few concerts. Checking where we'd set up, storage for bottles, that kind of thing."

Irene's explanation was perfectly reasonable, delivered without hesitation.

As she set bottles on the back bar shelf, I reached for one she handed me. The moment the glass touched my fingers, a scent—bitter, sharp, and hauntingly familiar—slammed into me. It was the same scent I'd detected at the crime scenes. Up close, I could tell it wasn't a single note, but tangled with floral sweetness.

I forced myself to keep moving, to act natural as Irene continued explaining liquor logistics. I nodded at appropriate intervals, but my focus was locked on that scent clinging to the bottles she touched, likely transferred from her hands. Was it perfume? A cleaning product?

I opened my mouth to question her, but the back entrance burst open. Micah stormed into the bar, her pulse thrumming with excitement.

"Guess what?!" Micah slammed her bag onto the counter. "My mom just got hired to cater the memorial concert reception! By Richard Bennington himself!"

Her face glowed with pride as she planted her hands on her hips, clearly expecting an enthusiastic response. "Mr. Bennington called her this morning. I just got off FaceTime with her. And she's already planning the menu—" she began ticking off fingers as she listed them, "prawn lumpia, mini takeout boxes of pancit noodles, savory pastries... she's going all out!"

I blinked hard, trying to process this news while still reeling from the scent discovery. As far as I knew, Richard Bennington had never crossed paths with Micah's family. It felt... suspicious. Tita Isa was an incredible cook, but she'd never catered anything this high-profile before. Why now?

I tried to mirror Micah's excitement, but my mind was racing with connections. Spirit Haven handling the liquor. Tita Isa catering. Me opening the concert. Each piece was innocent enough on its own, but together...

"That's... a lot of coincidences," I muttered, not realizing I'd spoken aloud until Micah's smile wavered.

"You're kidding, right?" The hurt in her voice stung.

I hesitated, knowing I should stop but unable to resist. "No, I just mean... Richard Bennington's pulling in so many people we know for this event. Doesn't that seem odd to you?"

Micah's expression twisted, hurt flashing across her face. "Oh my God, Cass. Can you, just once, be happy about something instead of spinning conspiracies?"

"Micah, that's not—"

She cut me off. "You're seriously standing here, acting like my mom's first big catering gig is some... calculated chess move to spy on you?"

I rubbed the back of my neck, my paranoia having hijacked the moment. "That's not what I meant—"

"Fine. Whatever." Micah grabbed a bottled soda from behind the bar, twisting the cap with more force than necessary.

I knew I'd blown it. "I'm an idiot. I'm sorry."

She took a long sip, then rolled her eyes. "You are an idiot. My mom gets one good thing, and you turn it into a problem. Not everything is about you, Cass."

She moved to where Irene was restocking bottles, slipping into a conversation about signature cocktails for the reception. I hung back, watching them chat. When Irene stepped away from the shelf, I leaned in, inhaling deeply. The bitter scent lingering where she'd stood was unmistakable now.

After finalizing the order, Enzo and Irene grabbed their clipboard and left. Micah headed upstairs to work on Hella's dress, leaving the bar quiet except for the soft clinks of Lucas and me prepping to open. I wiped down the counter, pretending to focus, though I could feel Lucas's eyes on me as I moved.

"Alright," he said. "How long you gonna stand there pretending you're not freaking out?"

I sighed, tossing my rag onto the counter. "You noticed?"

"I always notice. Is it that thing with Micah?"

I planted my palms on the bar, lowering my voice. "Yeah, I hate how I handled it, but I'll talk to her later. Something else is nagging me, though..." My fingers drummed on the counter. "I smelled it again, Lucas. That scent. It was on the bottle Irene handed me. Faint, but unmistakable."

The slightest shift in his expression told me he'd caught it too. "Same scent as before?" he asked, his voice careful, as though he were assessing the strength of my perception.

I nodded, the bitter aroma from the crime scenes still vivid in my memory. Even now, traces lingered in the bar, a ghostly reminder of Irene's presence.

Lucas folded his arms. "Trust your gut, then. But don't spiral into accusations without proof."

"I know it's important. I just don't know how it connects yet."

Lucas held my gaze for a long moment, his eyes searching mine. "Be careful, Cass. Drawing conclusions based on a scent alone could wreck a business relationship, and friendships."

I didn't argue. As he spoke, a new pattern took shape. I should have been able to place the bitter scent, and the fact that I couldn't, despite how often it had surfaced, kept needling at me. But it was no longer mere coincidence; it was a clue.

CHAPTER TWENTY-NINE

I tried to focus on propping chairs onto tables, but my attention kept drifting to Micah's movements behind the bar. The sharp snap of receipts being sorted, the crisp clicks of the register drawer, and her frustrated sighs were the only sounds she'd directed my way all night. I'd really messed up this time. Our usual easy rhythm was gone, replaced by stiff efficiency and pointed silence. Even the regulars noticed, with Jules's casual jab about "lovers' quarrels" earning twin death glares from us both.

In the post-closing hush, I watched Micah reorganize the already neat receipt stack for the third time, a classic Micah avoidance tactic. When upset, she rearranges everything in sight. Last time we fought, she color-coded my entire sock drawer.

I took a deep breath and approached the bar, clearing my throat. "Hey." My voice came out low, rough with guilt. "I was a jerk earlier."

Micah's hands stilled on the receipts, her eyes fixed downward. "What specifically?" When she looked up, one eyebrow arched—an effortless expression she'd mastered.

I scratched my scalp, grimacing. "The catering thing. What I said about Richard Bennington pulling strings to get your mom that gig. It wasn't about her. I just... noticed co-incidences and spiraled. You know how I get."

She sighed, setting the receipts down. "Yeah, I know." The edge in her voice softened, though a trace of hurt still colored her tone. "You're an ass." Her lips twitched into a smile. "But at least you're a self-aware ass."

My shoulders eased. In Micah-speak, this was as close to forgiveness as I'd get tonight. I reached for the coffee I'd brought, a quiet peace offering, hoping it'd seal the truce.

"I invited Jackson over," I said, aiming for casual. "Thought we could go over the suspects again." When Micah's eyebrow arched higher, I rushed on. "I could really use your help on this. The case, I mean," I clarified quickly. "But also, you know... in general."

Micah studied me for a moment, then nudged my elbow. "Fine, but only because you clearly need help in every aspect of your life."

I exhaled, the knot of tension between us loosening.

The bar's door swung open, carrying in a gust of cool night air along with Jackson, his laptop bag slung over one shoulder. He strode in, every inch the focused programmer, neatly rolling up his sleeves. The dim light caught his restless hands—likely too much caffeine—and his glasses slid exactly three millimeters down his nose. Faint shadows under his eyes hinted at late-night coding sessions.

We settled into our usual corner booth, the vinyl seats creaking under our weight. Micah slipped behind the bar, returning with a pitcher of IPA and three glasses, then slid into the seat beside me. The hoppy scent wafted over, laced with citrus and pine.

Jackson cracked his knuckles before flipping open his laptop. I knew that every question we asked pushed us a little further outside the rules. But until the real killer was found, suspicion wasn't just hanging over my friends. It was over me.

"Alright," he said. "Who're we hyper-fixating on tonight?"

I took a deep breath, bracing myself. "We need to look at Irene again."

Micah snorted, beer foam nearly escaping her nose. "Oh my God, Irene? Again?" She swiped her lips with the back of her hand.

Jackson tilted his head. "Didn't you rule her out last time?"

"Yeah, well," I admitted, a little too engrossed by my glass. "Maybe I was too quick to judge."

Jackson let out a slow exhale and pulled the laptop closer. "Alright. Gimme a minute." He tapped a few keys, then frowned. "Huh. That... shouldn't be there."

He typed faster, mumbling half-formed tech terms under his breath. "Port filters... redundant firewall... rate-limiting herself... Irene, what are you doing?"

Micah shot me a questioning look, and I shrugged. Neither of us had a clue.

"She sandboxed her apps. Wouldn't have pegged her as someone who'd bother with something that technical."

He tried again. A soft curse.

"...okay, nope, wrong folder. Ignore the coupon database." He backed out, cheeks warming. "Let's try this from the top."

I bit back a smile as he reworked the approach, moving with more caution than bravado now. Micah muttered "Tech foreplay" out of the side of her mouth, earning a quick elbow from me.

A moment later, his eyebrows lifted. "There we go. Got her personal files—finally."

I leaned over, squinting at the screen despite the awkward angle. Jackson scrolled through meticulously organized digital folders: Irene's Apothecary – Ingredients / Testing, Alternative Oil-Free Recipes.

"She's got serious chemistry research here," he said, clicking through documents. "Spreadsheets tracking batch ratios, supplier invoices, notes from failed test runs... yeah, this beauty product side hustle is no joke."

He opened a file labeled Current Formulations. Highlighted in yellow was an ingredient that immediately stood out: hydrolyzed almond protein.

"That's... curious," Jackson said, his tone deliberately neutral.

"She's been using almond protein across her formulations," I said. "And Brad—"

"Was fatally allergic to nuts," he finished. The booth fell silent, the only sound the quiet hum of his laptop fan.

Jackson's fingers danced across the keyboard as he pulled up scientific articles. "Okay, hydrolyzed almond protein is almond proteins broken down into smaller bits via hydrolysis," he said, nudging his glasses up. "It's common in beauty products. Great for moisturizing skin and hair."

He paused, scrolling further. "Here's the kicker: because it's broken down, it's absorbed faster than regular almond protein. Think protein shake versus whole chicken breast. Ready for your skin to soak up."

"And potentially deadlier for someone with a nut allergy," I said, my voice grim.

"Yeah, that's what makes it nasty," Jackson said, his expression darkening. "Especially if it's ingested. The hydrolysis process makes it more bioavailable, so Brad's body would've processed it faster than regular almond protein."

Micah leaned back, raking a hand through her hair. "Well, that's horrifyingly impressive. Remind me never to mess with anyone slinging DIY beauty products."

I managed a tight smile at Micah's quip. She saw the world in sharper lines than I did. Bad people did bad things for clear reasons, justice was straightforward, motives simple. But we'd barely patched things up after our last fight, and I wasn't about to spark another over her way of coping with the horror. Instead, I took a long pull from my beer, letting Jackson's typing fill the quiet.

Jackson navigated to Irene's Instagram, the screen blooming with perfectly staged photos of handmade beauty products, each caption detailing ingredients and benefits.

"Look at this," Jackson said, pointing to a post dated exactly one week before Brad's death. "Her latest hand cream formulation."

I read the list aloud, catching every pixel of the carefully filtered photo: "Lanolin, beeswax, hydrolyzed almond protein, sweet orange, jasmine…"

"It's right there," Jackson murmured, angling the screen for us all to see. "She wasn't hiding it."

My mind raced, but before I could process, Jackson dove deeper. "Hold on, there's more," he said, pulling up a YouTube video from the Hillsborough High archives.

The grainy footage showed a younger Irene on stage during our junior year, her violin tucked perfectly under her chin. We watched in silence as Irene played, her talent shining through the fuzzy video. Each note was precise, passionate, delivered with an intensity that stirred my fingers in quiet awe.

"She sounds incredible," Micah breathed. "Hard to believe anyone could've beaten her."

"Irene was the best," I admitted, memories flooding back. "But the judges picked Brad, handing Irene second place. No one was shocked. We'd seen it before. Plus… Brad had that flashy Guarneri violin."

I stood, drifting to the small stage in the bar's back corner where we held drag shows. My fingers brushed Lilith's keyboard.

Then I caught it—the same bitter note that had haunted me since Brad's death. Instinct did the work for me, teasing apart the layers. Sweet notes of jasmine and orange rose first, meant to distract from what lay beneath.

But the bitterness didn't disappear. It ran through the sweetness, more intricate than I'd first realized. An almond-like trace followed, restrained but unmistakable, altered enough to escape immediate recognition.

I brushed my fingers along the keys again, the slight tackiness of Lilith's hand cream still clinging to the surface. The scent rose with the contact, clearer now that I knew what I was looking for.

My head snapped up. "Lilith uses Irene's hand cream."

Micah's brow furrowed. "Okay… and?"

"I've smelled it before," I replied. "At the crime scenes."

Jackson's typing halted. "But Lilith was in custody when Dolores's studio was broken into."

"Okay, hold up," Micah said. "Are you saying someone else is using that hand cream? Or..." She trailed off, her words hanging in the air.

Jackson's fingers resumed their dance across the keyboard. "If Lilith and Irene aren't working together," he said, his tone driven like he was debugging intricate code, "we need to check who else uses the hand cream. Who knew about Brad's allergy? Who'd want to frame Lilith?"

I turned to him, determination flaring in my chest. "Can you pull a list of Irene's clients? Who's buying this stuff?"

Jackson was already typing. "On it."

CHAPTER THIRTY

The grand concert hall's massive chandeliers cast a golden glow, softening the somber mood. I pushed through the heavy wooden doors and the familiar sounds of dress rehearsal for the memorial concert filled the space. Dress shoes padded softly on carpet and musicians tuned their instruments in a continuous drone. Near the stage door, someone munched a granola bar, their heartbeat running far ahead of their chewing.

The hall felt off tonight. Maybe it was the deep red drapes, swallowing more than mere sound, or the music stands gleaming too brightly under the chandeliers. This wasn't simply about honoring Brad and Jordyn anymore; it was a parade of wealth and status cloaked in mourning.

Faculty members sat off to the side, their whispers drifting across the hall. Professor Yates stood near the front, clipboard in hand as he checked his watch for the third time in two minutes. Richard Bennington sat among the patrons, posture immaculate but expression set, as if grief had been folded away rather than processed. Even from here, I caught his expensive cologne—leather and tobacco layered heavily, as if applied to compensate for the unsteadiness beneath.

"Places, everyone," Yates called, his voice ringing through the hall. "Mr. Reyes, you're opening with the Bach."

I took my place on stage, adjusting my stance as I lifted my viola. The hall's acoustics sharpened, every sound crystalline. As I drew my bow across the strings, the notes rippled through the cavernous space in precise mathematical patterns, sound waves bouncing off walls to weave complex harmonics I wouldn't have noticed before... before turning.

Dozens of gazes pressed against my skin, their collective attention almost palpable, and I caught small shifts in heartbeats as the music stirred them. One stood out—too controlled. Irene, seated in the back row, watched without reacting.

I finished to polite applause, catching Dolores's approving nod before she turned to Neve Riley. The younger student buzzed with nervous energy. I didn't mind Dolores's shift in focus. Neve needed her encouragement more. Once, I'd craved that reassuring smile, that gentle guidance, but now I carried my own weight.

"Mr. Reyes?" Professor Yates's voice sliced through my thoughts. "You can take your seat."

Right. Brooding at the audience from center stage wasn't exactly selling my 'normal musician' act.

I settled into an empty seat, trying to focus on the next performer. But my mind kept snagging on the sense we were all pawns in someone's meticulously staged show.

Restlessness pulled me out of the hall into a side corridor. The air shifted—cooler, laced with the faint creak of warped floorboards under decades of footsteps, the hum of music vibrating through the walls, and... voices.

Hushed whispers drifted down the hallway. I followed, my steps silent on the worn carpet, until I reached a corner near the break area. A small knot of alumni, faces familiar from scholarship programs, had gathered there. I pressed against the wall, ears straining.

"Do you know how many times I outplayed Brad in master classes and auditions?" A violinist with intricate braids spoke, her fists clenched. "Didn't matter. His name carried more weight than my work ever could. Scholarships meant nothing. Always overshadowed by the rich kids."

A pianist, recognizable from past recitals, shook her head. "And Jordyn? Acting like she wasn't part of the problem? Scooping up opportunities I bled for?"

"Why do you think we're even here?" another student cut in, voice dripping with cynicism. "Not because they care. They need us to make this concert look like they do."

A sudden clarity cut through my thoughts. I'd always known privilege shaped music, skewed perceptions of talent. But hearing it in their voices made it all too real.

My thoughts spiraled back through years of competitions, auditions, opportunities. How much of my success was talent? How much was the right teachers, the right background, the cushioned upbringing? I'd been blind to it, coasting on privilege, never questioning why some doors swung wide for me while others found them locked.

In an instant, the murders took on a new weight. Was this someone's warped sense of justice? A strike against a system that had sidelined them for years?

"Shh... someone might hear," a voice hissed.

I melted deeper into the shadows as the group scattered, their footsteps used to slipping through these halls. When they were gone, I remained there, sifting through what I'd heard.

If there was a connection, a motive shaped by years of being shut out, this case was bigger than I'd imagined. Could resentment have pushed someone to kill? Had being overlooked for so long pushed them over the edge?

Returning to the rehearsal hall, I spotted Wyatt perched on the stage's edge, fingers gripping his cello case. Nervous energy crackled around him, a visible aura of fear and anticipation that set my own nerves buzzing. Every few seconds, his eyes darted between exits, audience members, and side doors, while his fingers unconsciously picked at his sweater's cuff, fraying the wool into tiny pills.

I shifted my attention to the back rows, where Irene sat, half-shrouded in shadow. Unlike the other observers who watched the performers with varying degrees of interest or boredom, she was detached from the music entirely. Her eyes roamed the room, as if she were taking inventory rather than listening.

I tried to rationalize her presence. Spirit Haven was handling the reception. That part tracked. What didn't was where she'd chosen to sit. Instead of clustering with the other event staff, Irene had tucked herself into the darkest corner of the hall. I caught the trace of her hand cream again and reached for my phone.

Before I could second-guess myself, I sent Jackson a quick text: Any luck with Irene's client list?

His reply came faster than expected: Still digging, but

I've uncovered some intriguing connections.

I typed back instantly: Cross-reference with academy alumni, especially violinists.

The thought had been gnawing at me since I learned about Irene's hand cream business. Musicians needed oil-free products; greasy lotions could ruin their grip on their instruments. How many current and former academy students might be using her products? The pool of suspects could be far larger than we'd realized.

Wyatt stepped onto the stage, his pianist giving his shoulder a reassuring pat that did nothing to ease the haunted look in his eyes. As he lifted his cello, his hands trembled so violently he nearly dropped his bow. Wyatt's playing carried a trace of unease. Though his bow strokes were technically precise, a small quiver lurked beneath the surface.

Professor Yates stood at his podium, projecting a facade of calm as he directed the rehearsal. "Again, from measure 57, please," he called, his voice steady despite the undercurrent of tension. "Mind the ritardando this time."

Wyatt's playing grew increasingly erratic, his interpretation drifting as if mirroring his scattered thoughts. Tempos shifted without musical logic, and dynamics swung wildly. At one point, he halted mid-phrase, fingers trembling against the fingerboard. Closing his eyes, he took a shaky breath, then forced himself to continue.

When Wyatt finished, he packed up his cello, his face showing no relief—only the haunted look of someone who knew what was coming and could do nothing to stop it.

Then it happened.

A phone chimed. Then another. And another. The sound

rippled through the hall like falling dominoes, each notification igniting a fresh wave of tension. My phone buzzed in my hand.

The message was stark: You're next.

I scanned the room. Other musicians stared at their phones, their faces draining of color.

Whispers swelled into frightened murmurs.

"Who sent this?"

"Is this some sick joke?"

"Is this real?"

I closed my eyes, tuning my hearing beyond the panicked clamor. I tried to isolate each heartbeat, searching for one that might betray guilt rather than fear. But every pulse thrummed with terror pulsing through their veins.

Wyatt's breakdown was the most alarming. His breathing had quickened to near hyperventilation. He stood abruptly, shoving his phone deep into his coat pocket. For a moment, I thought he might bolt. Instead, he collapsed back into his chair, gripping the seat as if it were the only thing tethering him to reality.

I moved instinctively, crossing to him and crouching until we were eye to eye. "Wyatt," I said, "talk to me. Is this a bluff?"

He barely managed to shake his head, still focused on the nearest exit. "I don't know... I don't know."

Professor Yates strode down the center aisle, bow tie askew. "Everyone," he called, projecting authority. "I understand this is unsettling, but I strongly urge you to stay."

Yates's words did little to quell the panic. Several musicians edged toward the exits, clutching their instruments like shields.

Dolores stepped forward to join Yates. "Leaving only empowers whoever sent this," she declared, her voice firm yet nurturing.

As if pulled by an unspoken instinct, my focus settled on Richard Bennington. He sat perfectly still, his face an unreadable mask, observing with the calculated detachment of someone watching a chess match rather than a crisis.

As Yates opened his mouth to resume damage control, Wyatt lurched to his feet. The movement was so sudden and violent that he toppled a nearby music stand, sending sheets of paper fluttering to the floor like startled birds.

Every eye in the room snapped to Wyatt. The silence that followed was absolute.

"I… I need air," Wyatt stammered. Without waiting for a response, he bolted for the doors, abandoning his cello case.

His exit shattered the fragile restraint holding others in place. Like a dam bursting, musicians surged through the aisles, grabbing cases and coats as they fled. Professor Yates watched them go, exhaling sharply through his nose but making no move to stop them. Even he recognized that pretense and professionalism could only stretch so far when people feared for their lives.

Whispers and murmurs swirled as those who remained debated what to do, but I couldn't stay still any longer. My legs carried me toward the exit before I'd consciously decided to move.

I stepped into the academy's shadowed courtyard. My grip on the wrought iron railing made the metal creak under my fingers. This was no bluff or prank. The killer was still out there, playing their game, and they weren't done.

My phone felt heavy in my pocket. I pulled it out and sent another text to Jackson: Have you cross-checked the lists?

His reply came instantly: Just got it. Two-factor authentication and a locked backend slowed me down. Cross-checking now.

Dread crawled up my spine. I typed: Please hurry.

CHAPTER THIRTY-ONE

The day of the memorial concert dawned with an ominous weight, the sky a gray shroud mocking the weather forecast's promise of clear skies. I approached the Bay Area Music Academy; its imposing structure loomed larger than usual, the classical architecture turning gothic under heavy clouds.

Yates made the call before sunrise, sending out an email informing us that the memorial concert would proceed as scheduled, with security arranged and police presence approved. He didn't say *mandatory*, but he didn't have to. The decision had already been made, carrying the expectation that we would fall in line without debate. By the time I reached the venue, campus security and SFPD officers dotted the perimeter, their rigid postures and vigilant eyes deepening the charged atmosphere. Their presence, meant to reassure after last night's threats, only underscored the lurking danger.

"Well, this is cozy," Micah muttered beside me, adjusting her blazer. "Nothing says 'memorial concert' like a SWAT team reunion."

I managed a weak smile at her attempt to lighten the mood, but my attention splintered in a dozen directions.

Fragments of radio chatter—coordinates, security proto-cols—mingled with the nervous shuffle of arriving musicians.

I entered through the main doors with Micah and Jackson flanking me like stylish bodyguards, Lucas trailing behind, hands casually tucked into his pockets. But I knew better. His relaxed stance was pure theater. Beneath that facade, he was scanning every movement, braced for trouble.

"You good?" he murmured.

I adjusted my viola case strap. "As long as nobody gets hurt during the Bach suite, I'll be all right."

Micah snorted. "Way to set the bar low, bestie."

Apparently, this was my pep talk.

The reception area, usually stark, buzzed with an almost festive air. Long tables were laden with meticulously arranged finger foods. Prawn lumpia nestled beside delicate hopiang baboy—rich pork filling wrapped in flaky pastry—a fusion that screamed Tita Isa's touch.

"*Anak*," Tita Isa called when she spotted me, her face light-ing up. "Come, tell me if the arrangement looks okay." She gestured to a towering display of petit fours, elegant yet tee-tering on precarious.

"It's beautiful, Tita," I assured her, catching the subtle jit-ter in her hands as she nudged a plate. Even she wasn't immune to the evening's unease. "Everything's perfect."

Tito Hector stepped in beside her, easing a loaded tray into place before his warm hand landed on my shoulder. "Good luck tonight, Cass. Show 'em what you've got, ha?"

Micah and Jackson pitched in with the setup, Micah seiz-ing control of the aesthetics while Jackson deftly averted disaster, steadying a tray of champagne flutes as a harried event coordinator nearly crashed into it. The coordinator mumbled apologies, his pulse hammering like a bass drum.

Across the room, Jules cut a striking figure in his deep blue suit, the matching silk ascot neatly tied. He was deep in conversation with Professor Yates, each of them maintaining a fragile facade of normalcy that failed to mask their unease.

"*Mais non*," Jules said, hands gesturing expressively, "we cannot let fear dictate the evening. Music must triumph over tragedy, *n'est-ce pas?*"

Before Yates could reply, Adda and Hella swept into the room, their entrance nothing short of spectacular. Hella's take on evening menswear outshone every tuxedo in the room, the jacket cut lean and angular, its silhouette unmistakably her own. Several musicians paused their nervous warm-ups to stare.

"Darling, you're making everyone else look positively pedestrian," Adda declared.

"That's the goal," Hella replied with a wink. "But it'd be nice to get through the night without another incident."

Adda and Hella approached me, their cologne mingling with an undercurrent of concern.

"Sweetheart," Adda said, sweeping me into a quick hug, "Lilith sends her love. She knows you'll be magnificent tonight."

"How is she doing?" I asked, concern for our friend tightening my voice.

"She's holding up," Hella replied, adjusting her impeccable tie. "Said she's sure you'll deliver. No pressure."

Adda gave Hella's lapel a quick, appraising pinch. "Honestly, darling, you look flawless, but you could've steamed that pocket square."

"It *is* steamed. It's called structure, Adda. Not everything has to drape."

"Draping is timeless, darling. Structure is a trend," Adda murmured as they walked off.

"Please. Trends wait for me to make them timeless," Hella shot back.

Inside, the concert hall buzzed with musicians milling about in formal black, a sea of anxiety cloaked in wool and silk. Beneath it all, the scent of Irene's hand cream surfaced, its trace of bitterness imperceptible to anyone who wore it. Once a distinct clue at each crime scene, it was now maddeningly ubiquitous.

I recalled what Jackson had uncovered about Irene's hand cream, now a trending must-have among classical musicians. After the dress rehearsal, Micah had been eager to share the news.

"Jackson found something juicy," she'd said, eyes gleaming with excitement. "Irene's hand cream? Over half the academy's students use it. It's blowing up on classical musician TikTok, of all places."

I froze mid-step. "What?"

"Yeah, who knew, right?" Jackson had replied. "I hadn't seen it before, but students are posting 'get ready for a performance' videos featuring Irene's hand cream. The oil-free formula's apparently a big deal."

The bitter scent I'd been tracking was everywhere now, clinging to the hands of countless performers who'd touted their "holy grail oil-free hand cream" on TikTok. Just what I needed. As if solving a murder wasn't complicated enough without social media beauty trends muddying the waters.

Dolores glided through the room like a vibrant ship parting dark waves, her flowing kaftan a burst of jewel tones amid the sea of black concert attire. She touched shoulders, adjusted bow grips, and murmured encouragement. When she spotted me, her smile held that familiar blend of pride and warning—her "don't you dare mess this up" look, softened by genuine affection. I'd seen it countless times before recitals and competitions, but tonight it carried an extra weight.

"Remember to breathe," she said softly, her hand briefly squeezing my shoulder. "The music knows what to do. Trust it."

I nodded, comforted by Dolores's reassuring support.

After setting my viola case down backstage, I went back to the reception area to clear my head and spotted Irene calmly directing her staff. Her attention stayed fixed on the "tribute cocktail" she'd created for tonight. Unlike the other servers, who moved easily through their tasks, she wore latex gloves as she handled the drink setup, the only one taking such precautions. The detail gnawed at me, like a wrong note in an otherwise flawless phrase.

"The tribute cocktail must be perfect," Irene murmured to a staff member, her gentle voice taut with intent. "Mr. Bennington requested it specifically for his son Brad's memorial."

Brad's name sent a chill down my spine. I scanned the room, noting the drinks laid out in strict rows, the tribute cocktail's crimson liquid glinting ominously.

A few steps from the bar, Detective Martinez stood against a wall, stone-still but coiled beneath the surface, attentive to every nuance. Beside her, speaking in low, controlled tones, was Richard Bennington.

They both looked my way at the same moment.

Were they talking about me? Was he about to corner me? Accuse me?

He offered Martinez a parting word and started toward me with the authority of someone who made every room move to his rhythm, the space seeming to bend around his presence. His slate-gray cashmere overcoat hung loose, draped rather than buttoned, as if even grief couldn't wrinkle him.

"Mr. Reyes." His voice was deep and sonorous—courteous, not at all cold. "Thank you for being here today."

My throat tightened. "Of course," I managed.

"I wanted to speak with you before the program begins," he continued. "I personally requested Mr. Yates offer you the opening position. You and Brad performed together for many years. It felt right that someone who understood his musicianship—and his history—would begin the evening."

I had no words. Only disbelief.

Richard glanced toward the far end of the room, where guests made their way into the concert hall, before returning to me with the steadiness of a seasoned negotiator.

"I'm aware," he said evenly, "that our families have… decades of disagreements behind them." He straightened his overcoat, smoothing the lapels. "I know your father never held me in high regard."

It was perhaps the most diplomatic way to describe a feud that had shaped much of the Bay Area's commercial real estate.

"But today isn't about old rivalries," Richard continued. "It isn't about property battles or anything that came before your generation." He paused for a breath, letting the veneer of the CEO slip. "It's about honoring my son. And I appreciate that you agreed to be part of it, despite everything."

His words carried the weight of battles I'd only ever heard in muffled fragments from the hallway outside my parents' kitchen.

I swallowed, the fog in my mind beginning to lift. Only then did I realize I'd been holding my breath.

"Yes. Whatever history our family has—what you and my father carry—doesn't matter today. Today is about Brad."

Richard inclined his head with impeccable restraint. "Thank you, Caspar."

Then he turned, returning to Martinez with that same authority he'd entered with, a thinning ribbon of warm tobacco trailing after him. Grief, disbelief, and inherited resentment had tangled around our exchange in ways I wasn't quite ready to process.

A hand brushed my elbow.

"Hey, you okay?" Jackson's voice jolted me from my focus. He'd appeared at my elbow, concern etched on his face. "You're pale as a sheet."

I forced a weak smile. "Just pre-performance jitters," I lied. "You know how it is."

"Right," he drawled, clearly unconvinced.

Before I could respond, a harried graduate student with a clipboard rushed up. "Reyes! Two minutes! You're up first!"

The stage manager's announcement snapped me back to reality. My attention flicked to Irene across the room, where she was checking the display of cocktails, making a small adjustment before stepping aside to direct a staff member. I wanted to act. Pull Martinez aside, confront Irene, prevent her from carrying out whatever she was planning. But I couldn't. Not yet. Not without proof. If I made a scene now and was wrong, I'd ruin any chance of catching the real killer.

"Did you hear me?" The stage manager's voice climbed an octave. "Two minutes!"

"Yeah, I heard you," I said, my voice steadier than I felt. "Just... getting in the zone."

She shot me a look that said my "zone" had better include being on stage in exactly 120 seconds, or else.

"Break a leg," someone called as I passed.

Given recent events, the phrase felt too on the nose.

I nodded, forcing myself toward the stage. The lights cast a warm wash on my skin as I stepped out to generous applause. The crowd stretched before me like a dark ocean, familiar and unfamiliar faces blending in the dim house lights. Donors in tailored suits, musicians in performance black, and faculty struggling to maintain composure watched expectantly, their smiles tight and eyes sharper than usual, all too aware of the danger threading through the air.

CHAPTER THIRTY-TWO

I lifted my viola, my fingers finding their positions by muscle memory alone. Thank goodness for the countless hours of practice spent mastering control over my strength. The Bach Suite had become my sanctuary, a space where I could channel my newfound abilities rather than resist them. Each practice session was an exercise in restraint, teaching me to temper my strength so it enriched the music rather than overwhelmed it.

Tonight, though, felt different. This wasn't simply another performance. It was a tribute to two fallen colleagues, with the shadow of their killer looming, perhaps ready to strike again.

Dolores's words echoed in my mind: *Let the music breathe. Don't overthink. Let it tell its own story.*

I tightened my grip on the bow, drawing in a slow breath. Time seemed to pause as my body settled into the ritual of performance.

The first note reverberated through the hall, deep and haunting. Each phrase flowed seamlessly from my bow as I modulated the subtle variations in pressure and speed. The

Prelude poured out of me, every note imbued with restrained emotion, every phrase weaving a story of loss and resolve.

I felt the audience holding their collective breath, ensnared by the music's spell. For a fleeting moment, we were united in this shared tapestry of sound and emotion.

"*Mon dieu*," I heard Jules murmur to Dolores between movements, "I've never heard him play like this."

I hadn't either. Something had shifted, not only in my technique, but in my connection to the music itself. Every note pulsed with life under my fingers, each phrase a distinct narrative. Perhaps this was part of my transformation, a deepening attunement to the pure mathematics of sound and a growing ability to perceive music in its most elemental form.

With each note of the Allemande, my hearing sharpened, catching the nervous rustling of programs, a student frantically mouthing their memorized piece in the wings, and the distant click of heels on marble in the hallway alongside the music itself. Every sound wove into a complex tapestry of tension and anticipation, threading through my performance like an unseen counterpoint.

My bow danced furiously across the strings in the Courante, my mind detaching enough to process the world around me. In this state of hyper-awareness, it became clear. Irene had always been there, lurking in the shadows—at the bar when Brad died, meeting with Jordyn on her final day, touching every bottle that passed through All Aboard. I'd seen her in each of those moments without really seeing her. Her presence was unremarkable, yet she had been perfectly positioned every time it mattered.

As I drew out a mournful phrase in the Sarabande, my

senses latched onto that bitter scent. It had lingered at the bar, in Jordyn's practice room, even in Dolores's vandalized studio. The hydrolyzed almond protein wasn't only evidence of the killer's presence, it was Irene's signature, altered enough that I hadn't known what to make of it at first. Her hand cream became wildly popular in the classical music community later, turning it into the perfect cover.

Brilliant, I thought. I forced the revelation aside as my bow found the strings again, channeling the turmoil into the music ahead.

The first Minuet flowed from my viola, light and composed. My fingers danced across the fingerboard, shaped by years of careful study and discipline, learning how to deliver a performance that was polished and controlled. This was the courtly minuet, refined and elegant by design.

But as I moved into the second Minuet, the darker, more rustic phrases demanded a different kind of truth—the version hidden beneath the polished surface. My bow pulled heavier across the strings, drawing out the earthier tones Bach had buried in the contrast.

Two dances. Two faces. One light, one dark. The pairing was essential. You couldn't understand one without the other.

Like Irene.

Sweet, timid Irene—that was her first Minuet, the face she showed the world. But was she bitter enough to turn resentment into a weapon? Clever enough to hide it in a product people trusted without a second thought?

My fingers nearly faltered on a shift, yet I stayed with the music, refusing to lose the thread. How many musicians in this very room had her products on their hands? How many had shared her DIY beauty hacks, unwittingly masking a murder weapon in plain sight by making it trendy?

Hydrolyzed almond protein wasn't simply a moisturizing ingredient. For someone with Brad's severe nut allergy, it was lethal. And Irene, with her background in chemistry and cosmetics, would have known exactly how to use it. She'd taken an ingredient meant to heal and beautify and turned it into a weapon... murder wrapped in self-care.

My fingers trembled slightly on the fingerboard as I brought the second Minuet to its close, but I willed them back under control.

The implications struck as my bow danced through the Gigue's rollicking finale, alive with wild leaps and double stops. Irene had known about Brad's nut allergy since high school and had access to the Brazilian banana liqueur bottle at Spirit Haven. She'd met with Jordyn on her final day, though Jordyn lacked Brad's allergy. Her work in beauty products meant she understood chemistry well enough to manipulate ingredients in ways no one would think to question, not just the hydrolyzed almond protein.

And now, she was handling the drinks for the reception, poised to strike again. Tonight. Here. The tribute cocktail she'd been meticulously preparing wasn't a mere memorial gesture. It was another weapon.

A small tremor in my arm nearly disrupted the bow's arc. The note wavered slightly, but enough for Dolores to straighten in her seat. I gritted my teeth, wrestling control back. I couldn't lose it now. Instead, I channeled the surge of fear into the final, spirited passage of the piece.

My attention snapped from inward reflection to the

periphery of the hall. Shadows pooled deep in the wings beyond the stage lights, sheet music stirred on the stands from the ventilation's breeze, and bodies shifted in their seats as the music surged toward its climax.

As I drew the final note to its lingering close, my attention drifted to the back of the hall. Irene was there, but unlike the audience, transfixed by the closing measures, she was already moving.

If she slipped away now, if she finished what she'd started with the tribute cocktail...

I couldn't let that happen. Not again.

The audience erupted into applause, but it was mere white noise, distant and hollow against the urgency surging through my veins. I offered a curt bow, barely acknowledging the standing ovation. My mind was fixed on one thought: *Irene cannot leave this building.*

As I strode offstage, I caught Micah and Jackson at the front row's edge. Their faces shifted the instant they saw mine. Micah half-rose, but I gave a subtle shake of my head. I couldn't wait for them, couldn't risk losing Irene's trail.

Without hesitation, I pushed past the heavy curtain into the dim backstage shadows.

CHAPTER THIRTY-THREE

The applause still echoed through the concert hall as I set my viola down backstage, but it barely reached me. My body had shifted into predator mode, every supernatural sense honed to a single purpose. I moved toward the reception area, muscles coiled with the certainty of my revelation.

The transition felt jarring, almost surreal, like shifting between two disparate realities, from the ordered elegance of classical music to a darker, more perilous world. But I couldn't hesitate. Irene was slipping away toward the side exit, and if I delayed even a moment longer, she'd vanish. As she had after Brad's death. As she had when Jordyn died.

I locked onto her the moment I entered the reception area. Irene's slight frame cut away from the hall, her stride even, a silver serving tray balanced in her latex-gloved hand. The tray held several identical glasses of deep-red liquid, her "tribute cocktail," specially prepared for tonight. Her fingers gripped the tray's edge, keeping the glasses perfectly steady despite her swift pace. As she descended a narrow concrete stairwell, her footsteps echoed softly against the worn steps.

I followed at a careful distance, listening for anything that might give me away as fabric whispered with my movements, my shoes tapped faintly on the concrete, and my breathing stayed measured. The stairwell spiraled deeper beneath the concert hall, leading to an unfamiliar corner of the academy I'd never explored in all my years here.

I stared down into the dark. It yawned below me, cool and still, like the open mouth of a long-forgotten cello case. Irene's heels echoed somewhere in the depths, dissolving into the shadows.

I pulled out my phone. No signal.

I could run upstairs. Grab Lucas. Call the cops. Do the smart thing.

But by the time I explained, by the time they believed me... she'd be gone. Or worse, someone else would be dead.

Lucas's voice echoed in my head: *Don't go alone.*

Then another lesson surfaced. One Lucas hadn't meant to teach me, but had anyway: Sometimes, the music doesn't wait for you to be ready. You simply have to play the next note.

I took a breath and stepped into the dark. The air grew colder, thick with the musty scent of neglect and abandonment. The basement level opened before us like a forgotten catacomb, a maze of narrow corridors branching in every direction. Bare concrete walls replaced the elegant wood paneling above, and the uneven floor bore spider-webbing cracks. The space felt oppressive, almost suffocating after the soaring ceilings of the concert hall.

The walls' soundproofing muffled the performance above to a faint whisper. An eerie stillness dominated, amplifying every small sound. The distant drip of water from rusted pipes and the soft rustle of Irene's movement carried through the silence.

Abandoned relics of the academy's past cluttered the corners. Dust-caked music stands leaned against the walls, piano benches warped and water-damaged, and piles of yellowed sheet music scattered like forgotten memories. Together, they bore witness to the academy's slow decay.

How did Irene know this place so well? She moved through the darkness with unwavering confidence, never hesitating at intersections, never pausing to orient herself, as if she'd walked this route before. Even I, who had spent countless hours exploring every corner of the academy above, felt disoriented in this underground maze.

How many times had she come down here? What had she been plotting in these forgotten corridors?

Irene wasn't only at ease here, she was in her element. Every step, every turn, every shadow felt choreographed, as if she'd rehearsed this moment countless times. Nothing was improvised.

I wasn't pursuing Irene. She was leading me exactly where she wanted.

She stopped abruptly two doors down a narrow side hallway, setting the silver tray beside a storage room door. It stood ajar, revealing a thin wedge of deeper darkness through the gap.

Before my senses could process what was happening, she reached inside. A soft metallic click signaled a mechanism locking into place. Then she slipped into the room, vanishing into the shadows beyond.

The silver tray remained where she'd placed it, the crimson liquid in its glasses catching the dim light filtering from above. Tiny ripples danced across each drink's surface, stirred by the vibrations of the performance upstairs, a Chopin nocturne unfolding under a pianist's steady hands.

I edged forward, past the abandoned tray, toward the partially open door. Every instinct screamed to stop, to retreat, but I couldn't let her vanish again, not when I was so close to unraveling her crimes.

The door slammed shut behind me with a crisp metallic snap. The sound reverberated through the concrete walls, echoing from all directions until it faded into utter silence. No footsteps. No breathing. No trace of Irene.

My jaw clenched as I lunged for the handle, fingers wrapping around the cold metal. It didn't budge. I pressed harder, but the mechanism held fast. Images of that fateful night in the alley when I was attacked flashed through my mind, but I shoved them aside.

I tensed my muscles, channeling power into my core, readying for the precise strike Lucas had drilled into me during training. One controlled blow and—

A crunch of glass underfoot shattered my focus. My heart sank as I glimpsed the remains of a small glass ampoule. Its liquid was already evaporating, releasing a thick cloud of concentrated fragrance into the confined space.

"No," I whispered, but it was too late. The toxic vapor saturated the air, its heavy, overpowering musk scorching my throat with each breath.

I stumbled back. My vision blurred as the room tilted and spun, my reflexes betraying me as every sensation surged beyond control.

My hands trembled as I pressed them against the cool

concrete wall, desperate to anchor myself. My knees buckled, and I slid partway down, the scrape of my clothes against concrete piercing with excruciating clarity. Even as my mind clouded, one truth burned clear: this attack was meticulously orchestrated. Someone knew exactly what I was and had crafted a trap to neutralize me.

Through the haze, a heavy shadow took form in the darkness. Enzo Dodson stepped into view, his friendly demeanor gone, replaced by a stare as sharp as a blade's edge.

Before I could fully process the betrayal, I caught the abrupt intake of his breath and the whisper of air as he lunged. He slammed into me, his strength propelling me backward. The impact sent me staggering deeper into the toxic cloud, forcing the last air from my lungs.

Enzo didn't hesitate or gloat. In one fluid motion, he grabbed my shoulder and throat, driving me into the darkened space beyond as my legs gave out beneath me.

"Should've minded your own business, kid," he muttered, his voice stripped of its usual warmth.

I tried to fight back, to summon the supernatural strength that had become second nature, but my body felt distant, unresponsive.

The rattle of chains pierced the room, drilling into my skull. Before I could gather my scattered thoughts, cold metal cuffs snapped around my wrists. The chair beneath me was bolted to the floor. They had prepared for this.

Through dimming vision, I caught lighter footsteps—measured, assured—approaching. I forced my head up, lightning-bright pain tearing through my fractured mind. Irene stepped into view. The timid, sweet persona she'd worn fell away, her eyes now hard and assessing. The true face of a killer who had orchestrated everything from the start.

"Comfortable?" she asked, her voice stripped of its usual uncertainty. "Don't worry, Cass. Soon you'll have a front-row seat to the finale."

CHAPTER THIRTY-FOUR

I shifted my weight, testing the restraints binding me to the chair. The metal cuffs bit into my wrists. Under normal circumstances, I could've snapped them with ease, but my co-ordination was shattered, dulled by the perfume's assault. Even breathing had become a risk, each inhale drawing fresh waves of that devastating scent.

Enzo loomed near the door, his stance deceptively casual—arms crossed, shoulders relaxed—radiating the detached neutrality of someone carrying out an unpleasant but necessary task. He wasn't the mastermind. He was following orders, ones that had escalated far beyond his usual shady dealings.

Irene stepped into the flickering light cast by the single bulb overhead. The shy, demure woman who once faded into the background gave way to someone entirely different—incisive, unyielding, and fully in command.

"I knew you were sensitive to smells," she mused. "But I didn't realize just how much until now."

"You've been watching me," I managed.

Her lips curved into a small, satisfied smile. "Of course. I had to be certain it was hyperosmia," she said, articulating each syllable clearly.

"Hyperosmia?" I echoed, barely forcing the word past the burning in my throat.

"A heightened sense of smell so intense it can interfere with daily life. Fascinating how quickly it developed in you." She tilted her head as she studied me. "I watched you at the bar, you know. Following scents, mastering your bartending skills practically overnight. It was like watching someone suddenly develop a superpower."

She had been analyzing my changes, but didn't understand their true nature. To her, this was a medical condition, not a supernatural transformation.

"It got me thinking," she said, her voice slipping into an almost academic tone. "If smell is your strength... what happens when it's used against you?"

She lifted a small glass capsule into the dim light, the viscous liquid inside catching the glow. "Jasmine absolute to disorient, ylang ylang to sicken, and black amber essence to overwhelm. Each one concentrated to full potency." Her latex-covered fingers twirled the vial. "I take it from your response that the combination is effective?"

"Why Brad?" I rasped. "Was it really just about the competition?"

Irene crouched before me, her once downcast eyes now locked onto mine.

"Do you ever wonder what it's like to watch someone like Brad win over and over, when you know... you *know*... they don't deserve it?"

The measured calm in her tone carried the weight of years of resentment. Darkness simmered beneath her composed exterior, festering behind polite smiles and quiet compliance.

"You were there," she went on, her eyes gleaming in the dim light. "At Hillsborough High. You saw how it worked. Brad's family makes one phone call, and suddenly he's first chair. One donation, and he gets the solo. One word from his father, and doors just... open. While the rest of us, the ones who actually worked, who actually deserved it... we had to watch. Stand in the background. Smile and applaud."

I wanted to respond, to push back against her twisted logic, but another wave of the chemical cocktail left me fighting to stay conscious.

She began pacing, her fingers trailing along the edge of a dusty music stand. "I overheard my father talking to Lilith on the phone. She was complaining about some high-strung client needing more product. Said he was stressed about competitions and auditions. It wasn't hard to figure out who she meant. Brad's cocaine habit wasn't exactly a secret, was it? And the Fischer competition, the Philharmonic audition. Everyone in my old circle wouldn't shut up about it on social media."

The sterile detachment in her voice made my skin crawl.

"I had just sourced hydrolyzed almond protein for my skincare line," Irene explained. She slipped a small bottle from her pocket, tilting it so the clear liquid inside caught the dim light, its movement thick and almost oily. "The molecular structure is fascinating, really. Nearly odorless, water-soluble, perfect for blending into any liquid medium."

Pride edged her tone as she described her work, like a twisted artisan admiring her own craft.

"I tested it first, of course," she continued. "A few drops in tea, in cocktails. Nothing too dramatic, just enough to understand how it would behave." Her eyes stayed fixed on me, filled with probing interest. "But you noticed it somehow, didn't you? Not by taste, but by smell. That's when I knew you were different."

I swallowed hard, my head spinning. "I... I couldn't ignore it," I admitted, voice hoarse.

"When my father mentioned the Brazilian banana liqueur he was so excited to share..." A small, satisfied smile curved her lips. "Well, it was perfect, wasn't it? The strong, cloying sweetness masked any trace of bitterness. And Brad was always a sucker for being the first to try something new and trendy."

She detailed how she injected the protein into the bottle, ensured it dispersed evenly, and left no trace behind.

"I thought it would just make him sick," she went on. "Just enough to ruin his chances at the competition."

"But he didn't just get sick."

"The concentration was higher than I anticipated," she said with a casual shrug that struck me as rehearsed, a well-worked act of innocence. "Twenty-three percent protein content, broken down into amino acid chains through hydrolysis." She pronounced the scientific terms with almost reverent care, like a musician speaking of a beloved piece. "I didn't realize how quickly it would absorb."

I understood with horrifying clarity that she was proud of her work, even if the outcome had gone far beyond her intention.

"At first, I thought I'd gotten away with it," she said. "Then I noticed you."

Her expression shifted—a glint of calculation in her eyes.

"You started asking questions, talking to people differently. Following leads like some amateur detective." She paused, and for a moment her pulse quickened. "But it wasn't just that. You changed. Your appearance, your movements, your sudden sensitivity to scents..."

She had attributed the changes in me to something mundane, one that fit neatly within her scientific worldview.

"But why Jordyn?" I asked, trying to shift in the chair, only to have another wave of dizziness crash through me.

"Jordyn was," her voice softened, "an unfortunate necessity. She thought she was helping me—pulling me back to music, making plans, acting like she was doing me a favor."

Irene shook her head. "But she posed a unique challenge. No convenient allergies to exploit, no connection to Lilith's clientele. I needed something different."

She drew out a small vial marked with an official medical label.

"Botulinum toxin, or Botox, as it's commonly known. Research showed it could be lethal if ingested," she explained, lecturing as though to a classroom. "And I already had an appointment at the beauty clinic that day with a friend, eager to discuss collaborating on my new balm line. When she stepped out to gather samples, well... accessing their refrigerated storage was almost embarrassingly easy. No one noticed the exchange."

Every detail accounted for, I thought.

"Then everything aligned perfectly. Jordyn reached out about the trio proposition just as Lilith asked me to prepare a gift basket. Two opportunities, handed to me at once." She paused, and a slight crease appeared between her brows before smoothing away. "I knew if I timed it right and planted just enough evidence, the police would follow the path I set for them."

The smirk that flickered on her lips was fleeting but unmistakable, a flash of genuine pleasure at her own cunning. "And they did. Like sheet music, every note played exactly as written."

I fought to hold on to consciousness as the weight of her manipulation crystallized, forcing myself to stay alert.

"At the meeting, the setup was almost too perfect. Jordyn was so eager to discuss the trio, she didn't even notice when I volunteered to pour the drinks. The beauty of botulinum toxin is its delayed effect," she explained. "By the time Jordyn felt the symptoms, I was long gone."

Her voice hardened. "People like Brad, like Jordyn... they take up space they don't deserve. Talent, hard work. None of it matters when some wealthy patron's child gets pushed ahead. Merit means nothing when money speaks louder."

The suffocating fog thickened as her fingers clenched, the scent of rubber threading through the air.

"I was supposed to be where you are. I was supposed to have a real career in music."

She paused. "You know, Cass, you were always kind to me in high school. But you did the same thing Brad did. Did you really think you earned first chair viola on talent alone? Your family's wealth, their connections... they opened doors while the rest of us stood in the shadows."

How blind had I been to my own privilege? Guilt flared, but even as it rose, I knew it couldn't justify murder. Nothing could.

"But why kill Jordyn, when she was trying to help you?" My voice was raw, the concentrated perfume searing my airways.

"Just another wealthy musician playing savior. Lifting up the poor, talented girl who couldn't afford college." Irene scoffed. "Like I should be grateful for her pity. But that's what people like her do, isn't it? They take control, make everything about their generosity, their kindness. Never once stopping to ask if we even want their charity."

"You killed them because you didn't get the recognition you thought you deserved?" The words tore from my throat like shards of glass.

Irene's reply was chilling in its simplicity. "I killed them because they stood between me and what was mine."

She gestured toward the small silver tray glinting through the gap in the door. "Tonight's tribute cocktail is a special one," she said, her voice lifting into an unsettling lilt, like a familiar melody played in a minor key.

"A final toast," she added. "To honor the fallen. Isn't that what memorial services are for?"

CHAPTER THIRTY-FIVE

"Irene, a word," Enzo barked, his voice firm with authority. "Now."

Her voice faded as she turned to argue with her father, granting me a fleeting moment to gather myself.

My breathing had gone shallow, too fast to pull in anything but the perfume, locked into a useless rhythm. Lucas's training sessions surged into my mind. I could almost hear his gentle, reassuring voice: *When your senses overwhelm you, don't fight them. Acknowledge each one, then let it slip into the background.*

I forced slow, deliberate breaths, shifting my focus to other sensations. The icy bite of metal cuffs cinching around my wrists became my anchor. Beneath the overpowering floral notes, the metallic tang of rust emerged, mingling with the damp stone underfoot.

Breathe. Let the perfume fade. Find your center.

My mind cleared, and I subtly tested the chains tethering me to the chair. As my senses steadied, my strength began to return. I rolled my wrists, probing for weaknesses in the corroded steel. The cuffs were old, worn by years of moisture, but reinforced, likely by Enzo, anticipating my resistance.

Lucas's voice echoed in my memory: *Leverage matters more than brute power.* I experimented with different angles, testing the metal's response to pressure. A faint creak rewarded my efforts, a weak point. If I could only find the right angle...

Beyond my restraints, Irene and Enzo argued in hushed, urgent tones.

"You've done your job!" Irene hissed, her usually composed tone fraying. "Just keep him here!"

Enzo's reply came slower, weighted with hesitation. "This is going too far. He's not the one who ruined your life, Irene."

I tucked that exchange away. Enzo's wavering loyalty could be an advantage.

Irene was right about one thing: I'd stood on stages others weren't allowed to touch. Doors had opened for me without my even asking, and I'd let them. I'd told myself that being kind was enough, that I wasn't part of the problem if I didn't actively play the game.

I couldn't change what had opened for me, or what hadn't for her. But I could choose what came next. And I chose to stop her from hurting anyone else.

While they bickered, I adjusted my grip on the chains. The cool metal bit into my palms as I twisted my wrists. Sensing the brittleness in the aged cuffs, I pinpointed where years of moisture had eroded their structure.

With measured pressure, I worked on the weak spot. The chain strained, metal fibers parting. Only a bit more...

SNAP!

The crack of breaking steel rang through the room. Irene gasped and spun toward me, too late. I was already moving, the chains clattering behind me as I lunged forward.

For a split second, time almost froze. Irene's eyes widened in shock, Enzo's stance shifted, muscles coiling, and the air swirled from my sudden motion.

I launched forward, instincts seizing control as the perfume cleared from my system. My face shifted, fangs extending fully, tearing past the restraint I kept for blood bags as adrenaline surged. Irene's heartbeat thundered, fast and uneven.

I drove my shoulder into Enzo, channeling my strength into a brutal impact. He crashed into a pile of discarded chairs with a deafening clatter.

Irene's gasp sliced through the air. "What are you?" she demanded, staring at my transformed face.

I pivoted toward her, the turn and the step merged into one smooth, unbroken motion. Her eyes widened as she stumbled back, colliding with the silver tray of drinks she'd meticulously prepared. Cocktails splashed across the dusty floor, liquid fracturing into rivulets. A thin, oily sheen of poison rose to the surface, glinting in the dim light with sickly iridescence, eating into the grime-caked concrete.

The scent of alcohol, laced with a synthetic note, wafted from the spreading puddle. By instinct, I picked out gin and Campari, grapefruit and pineapple juice, maraschino liqueur, simple syrup, and orange bitters. Underneath it all was the bitter signature of botulinum toxin, the same slow-acting poison that had killed Jordyn.

Enzo recovered faster than I'd anticipated, his burly frame deceptively agile as he lunged. His fingers clamped onto my arm, trying to force me down, but my strength had fully returned. I felt every point of his grip, each finger digging into my skin.

With a sharp twist, I turned his momentum against him. Enzo's bulk became his downfall as I redirected his charge, sending him crashing into a stack of music stands. The metal frames collapsed in a deafening clatter, shaking the room and kicking up clouds of dust.

I took a deep breath, my features settling, fangs retracting. The transformation had been involuntary, driven by survival, but I needed clarity now. I couldn't let the vampire side consume me.

Irene stood before me, her heartbeat skittering loud and erratic. "You don't understand!" she spat, her voice shrill. "They never let us win! They never give us a chance!" Her words erupted like venom.

Before I could respond, she pounced, uncoiling like a striking snake, her manicured nails slashing toward my face. I dodged back, reflexes kicking in right in time. Her nails sliced the air, missing my face by millimeters. The whoosh of displaced air grazed my skin. She was faster than I'd expected, her movements fueled by sheer desperation and adrenaline.

Irene stalked forward, her delicate features contorting into pure ferocity, lips curled in a snarl and eyes blazing.

A metallic screech of chair legs against concrete snapped my attention. My head whipped around as Enzo, recovered from his fall, gripped a heavy metal music stand, knuckles white around the steel frame.

"I'm done playing," he growled, eyes gleaming as he adjusted his grip, measuring the distance between us.

The music stand whistled through the air as Enzo swung

it toward my head. Time slowed, my reflexes surging. I tracked the weapon's arc, the rush of air slicing toward me, the hum of vibrating metal. As I ducked, the stand missed my head by inches, crashing against concrete with a deafening clang, sending fragments scattering across the floor.

Seizing the brief respite, I assessed the situation with preternatural clarity. Enzo was strong but predictable, his attacks blunt, relying on brute strength over finesse. His breathing grew labored, a sign of fatigue—pulse stuttering faintly, a tremor running through his overworked muscles.

Irene, by contrast, moved with erratic speed, her actions fueled by emotion rather than strategy, like a cornered beast. Yet beneath her desperation, a calculating mind steered her every move. Her racing heartbeat and rising scent carried a darker edge.

A flicker of motion caught my peripheral vision as Irene darted for the overturned tray, snatching a small glass vial.

"Stay back!" she barked, voice cracking with panic, and hurled it before I could react.

The vial spun through the air, shattering against the wall inches from my head. Glass shards grazed my cheek, and a chemical sting hit my nose, unleashing a wave of concentrated fumes far more potent than before. My vision blurred, and my stomach churned as droplets trickled down the wall, each one releasing fresh bursts of the overpowering perfume cocktail.

I staggered, battling to hold my balance as the room spun. Lucas's voice echoed in my mind: *Control your senses, don't let them control you.* I forced focus, my system fighting to purge the toxin.

Gritting my teeth, I shoved past the suffocating perfume and tuned into the world around me as footsteps thrummed through the floorboards and Irene's breath rasped nearby. The perfume pressed in, potent, but I refused to let it over-whelm me. Surrender now, and I was dead.

CHAPTER THIRTY-SIX

Muffled applause filtered through the thick walls from above. I picked out multiple sets of footsteps, their rhythms quick and purposeful. The concert had broken for intermission. Help approaching. But I wasn't sure it would arrive in time.

A shift in Irene's breathing signaled her awareness of the sounds. Her heartbeat surged as panic gripped her.

Enzo's massive frame stirred at the edge of my vision. Though dazed from our earlier clash, deadly intent gleamed in his eyes, his jaw set hard as he shifted forward.

"You're not going anywhere," he snarled, his voice rougher with strain. Despite his fatigue, his strength remained formidable as he reached for me.

My body tensed, instincts flaring at the desperation in his movements. He wasn't merely restraining me now; he was fighting to shield his daughter, to bury their deadly secrets.

The footsteps above grew sharper, closer. Time was running out for all of us.

A primal surge coursed through me, slicing through the jasmine and ylang-ylang fog. The perfume still seared my airways, but beneath it, my strength coalesced. An ancient force, deeper than physical power, rooted in my very core.

In the dim basement, every bead of sweat on Enzo's face gleamed, each muscle twitch telegraphing his next move. Without thought, I launched at him, muscles driving me forward with devastating force. The impact sent us staggering, but I held control, steering our momentum.

Enzo's back slammed into the metal storage cabinet with a deafening crash. A moment later, a dull crack echoed as his head struck the corner. His body jolted, then stilled. His eyes unfocused, tension draining from his frame as he slid down the cabinet, no longer commanding his weight. The coppery whiff of blood from a small scalp cut stung my nostrils. His breathing, shallow but even, and his pulse, weak yet persistent, confirmed he was alive, though unconscious.

Irene's gasp split the air like a gunshot. Her pulse stuttered, adrenaline flooding her system. She stumbled back, fingers twitching uselessly at her sides.

"This isn't fair," she breathed, her voice cracking, its ripples cutting through the air. Her eyes darted between me and Enzo's unconscious form, grief and disbelief warring across her face. "I was supposed to prove them wrong. Strip away what they took for granted."

"You proved you'd rather destroy than create," I said, my voice low but unyielding.

Irene flinched as if struck, the motion so abrupt my reflexes tensed. But instead of the desperate counterattack I braced for, her shoulders slumped, the fight draining from her in faint tremors.

Her hands trembled violently, the latex gloves crinkling as

she folded her arms across her chest, as if shielding herself from the crushing weight of defeat. As she accepted the end, her heartbeat slowed, her breathing steadied, and the strain in her presence dissolved into resignation.

A sudden crash shattered the silence as the door was kicked open, the shockwave reverberating through the basement. I winced as metal slammed against concrete, vibrations pulsing through the soles of my feet.

Detective Martinez's silhouette filled the doorway, gun drawn and fixed. Her trigger finger held expert control, her pupils dilating in the dim light, her breathing measured—a testament to years of training behind her calm authority.

It had only been a matter of time before they found me. I'd trusted Lucas to make sure of that.

"Irene Dodson, step away, now," Martinez commanded, her steely voice slicing through the room.

Lucas slipped in like a shadow, his face a mask of neutrality. He surveyed me first, checking for injuries, then flicked to Enzo's unconscious form before settling on Irene. His fists clenched briefly, but he stayed silent, yielding to Martinez.

Irene stood, head bowed, strands of hair falling across her face. Despite her carefully laid plans and the lives she'd taken, she appeared almost small in defeat.

Martinez advanced. "Irene Dodson, you're under arrest for the murders of Bradley Bennington and Jordyn Hurst," she declared, her voice heavy with authority.

A uniformed officer stepped past Martinez, handcuffs ready. Irene didn't resist or protest; she simply stood there, motionless.

A low groan escaped Enzo as he twitched on the floor. His

heart pulsed sluggishly, movements uncoordinated.

With the danger past, my body registered the fight's toll. Adrenaline faded, leaving bone-deep exhaustion. Through the haze, a familiar presence neared. Lucas's hands gripped my shoulders, his familiar scent cutting through the lingering perfume.

"You alright?" he asked, his voice low, concern layered in his tone too complex for my weary mind to unravel.

I managed a rough nod, swallowing against the dryness in my throat. "Yeah," I rasped. A vital instinct gnawed at me, a warning I couldn't ignore.

"The cocktail," I said, my voice strained but gaining urgency. "She poisoned it. The memorial drink. They're still serving it upstairs."

Lucas's eyes met mine. He squeezed my arm, looking past me toward the stairs.

And then he was gone.

Not walking, not running. Just... gone. A blur of movement so fast it could have been a trick of the light, leaving only the faintest displacement of air where he'd stood.

I blinked, expecting confusion, expecting Martinez to shout questions. But when I looked up, she was already watching the empty space where Lucas had vanished.

She didn't flinch. Didn't gasp. Her heartbeat remained steady as stone.

Our eyes met across the basement, and in that shared glance, everything shifted. She knew. Had always known, maybe.

Neither of us spoke. We didn't need to.

The officer finishing with Irene's cuffs glanced around.

"Hey, where'd the other guy go?"

Martinez didn't respond, simply cast a brief glance toward the shadows where Lucas had disappeared. Then she keyed her radio.

Static crackled. A voice came through: "Detective, cocktail service halted. Some guy came out of nowhere. Said not to drink anything. Then he was gone."

Martinez nodded to herself, calm as if she'd expected exactly that response.

Of course he did, I thought, relief washing over me as I leaned against the wall. *Definitely not Batman.*

"Copy," Martinez said into her radio. "Secure the perimeter. Shut down all beverage service. Nothing leaves the bar."

She turned to the officer. "Finish with her. I'll help him."

As the officer began escorting Irene toward the stairs, I slid down the wall, knees weak. Martinez crouched beside me. "Not bad, Mr. Reyes," she said.

"Just connecting the dots," I managed.

A second officer entered, moving to check on Enzo, who was beginning to stir with confused groans. The officer knelt beside him, trying to make sense of the situation.

Lucas reappeared as silently as he'd left, stepping from the shadows near a support beam as if he'd been there all along. He didn't speak, simply positioning himself within reach.

Martinez rose, her coat swaying as she prepared to follow the others upstairs. As she passed Lucas, she glanced at him. No words, only a look of understanding that said everything and nothing.

I watched as Irene was led up the stairs. Martinez followed, already issuing instructions to the officers, her voice fading as they climbed toward the light. I kept my eyes on them until they disappeared.

When I turned my head, Lucas stood beside me, hand extended.

I took it, letting him pull me to my feet.

The basement air remained heavy with the remnants of Irene's perfume trap, jasmine, ylang-ylang, and black amber weaving a suffocating veil that clung to every surface. Beneath those overpowering notes, fainter scents emerged in the rust-tinged tang of old pipes overhead, the damp must of the concrete walls, and the clean, reliable presence of Lucas still beside me.

I drew a deep breath, releasing it slowly. For the first time since this nightmare began, I could truly exhale.

CHAPTER THIRTY-SEVEN

The television above the bar hummed with the news, the anchor's voice blending into the familiar afternoon buzz of All Aboard. I tried not to dwell too closely on the details I'd only just lived through.

"…in a stunning development, local business owners Irene and Enzo Dodson have been arrested in connection with the murders of Bradley Bennington and Jordyn Hurst…" The anchor's measured tone couldn't conceal the story's sensational weight. "Sources indicate the murders stemmed from a deep-seated rivalry within the classical music community…"

I leaned against the bar. The comforting scents of wood polish and stale beer steadied me as the reporter laid out Irene's scheme. Stripped down to clinical facts, the hydrolyzed almond protein used to kill Brad, the botulinum toxin stolen with Jordyn in mind, and the final attempted poisoning at the memorial concert all sounded surreal. The anchor's voice faltered at the mention of the "DIY beauty product connection," as if she struggled to believe it herself.

The front door swung open, ushering in a gust of cool air and the familiar blend of coffee and leather that clung to

Detective Martinez. Beneath those notes lay a trace of gunpowder residue, hinting at a recent visit to the shooting range.

Lucas glanced over from the chalkboard mounted on the wall, where he'd been updating the specials. "Detective," he greeted, wiping his hands on a bar towel before reaching for a glass. "The usual?"

Martinez settled onto a barstool, her leather jacket creaking softly. I straightened instinctively, but her dark eyes glinted. "Relax, Reyes. You're officially off my suspect list."

Lucas placed a club soda with lime before her.

"Though I'll admit," she continued, nodding her thanks for the drink, "you had me wondering for a while. Not many would keep digging after being named prime suspect."

I shrugged, aiming for nonchalance. "Guess I'm just stubborn like that."

"That's one way to put it," Lucas muttered under his breath.

Martinez curled her fingers around her glass, the ice cubes clinking softly as she tilted it. "The evidence was airtight," she said. "Jackson pointed us in the right direction. We built the case the proper way. Once we traced Irene's beauty supply orders to that Latvian manufacturer, the puzzle snapped together."

"Just following the trail," I said, glancing toward Lucas. "Couldn't have done it alone."

"I kept an eye on you, you know. Waiting for a misstep. But you? You just don't quit." She tipped her glass towards us. "I get the feeling this won't be the last time we cross paths."

She turned to leave, then asked over her shoulder, "By the

way... is Micah seeing anyone?"

I choked on my coffee, the hot liquid searing my throat. Lucas's smirk radiated beside me.

Before I could muster a response, Martinez winked. "See you around." The door swung shut behind her, leaving only the fading traces of leather and resolve.

I turned to Lucas, his insufferable smirk still firmly in place. "Did that just happen?"

"Oh, that absolutely happened," he replied. "Our detective's got a crush."

I groaned, dropping my forehead to the bar. "Micah's never going to let me live this down."

Lucas's soft laughter filled the bar, warm and genuine. For a fleeting second, the air felt lighter, as if the room had tilted back toward normal.

The back hallway door swung open, and Micah, Adda, and Hella spilled through, their excitement crackling in the air.

"Cass!" Micah called, seizing my arm. "Come on! Lilith's train is pulling in!"

I barely had time to set down the glass I was wiping before she dragged me toward the door. Lucas gave me a wry nod, silently urging me to go.

The West Portal Train Station stood across from All Aboard, its familiar blue archway gleaming gently in the early afternoon light. I caught the distant rumble of the approaching train before the others, a growing thrum building in the tunnel. As the Muni car's doors slid open with a dull thunk, I spotted Lilith instantly. She stepped out cautiously, shoulders braced as if expecting a blow. Her signature sharp eyeliner was as precise as ever, but her eyes held a new vulnerability, a fragility I'd never seen before.

Micah didn't wait for Lilith to fully step onto the platform before surging forward, wrapping her in a fierce embrace. "About time," she murmured, her voice thick with emotion. "The neighborhood's drama isn't the same without you."

The scent of Lilith's relief mingled with the barest trace of industrial soap still clinging to her clothes. But as Adda and Hella stepped forward, that institutional undertone softened, overtaken by their perfumes and the comfort of chosen family.

"The queen has returned!" Adda proclaimed, arms flung wide. "Prepare a feast! Release the doves! Someone alert the media... oh, wait, they're probably still camped outside the academy." She winked, coaxing a faint smile from Lilith.

I held back at the edge of the group, watching the reunion unfold. Lilith's gaze met mine over Hella's shoulder, and she offered a subtle nod. In that small gesture, I read volumes. Gratitude, acknowledgment, and perhaps the first stirrings of forgiveness for my earlier doubts.

"I feel like I should be pissed," she said, her voice rough with emotion. "I just got out of a jail cell, after all."

"You're allowed to be mad," I offered, stepping closer.

"Mad doesn't begin to cover it," Lilith said, though her tone carried less venom than I'd braced for. Her fingers brushed the skin of her wrist where the handcuffs had left their mark. "I spent days in jail while the real killer walked free. But..." She looked up at me, her old directness resurfacing. "At least I had people fighting for me out here. Even if some took their time believing in me."

I winced at the pointed jab, though I caught the uptick at the corner of her mouth. Fair enough, I deserved that.

"So," Adda declared, clapping her hands with theatrical gusto, the sudden crack making me flinch. "We're throwing you a 'Congrats on Not Being a Murderer' party."

I dragged a hand over my face, unable to stifle a groan. "That's a terrible name." Through my fingers, I glimpsed Micah struggling to suppress a laugh.

"You don't get to judge," Adda retorted, her sparkling lamé coat glinting under the station lights as she swept a dramatic gesture. "You've been mincing around like some viola-playing Poirot, if he shopped at Hot Topic. At least my party names have flair."

The comparison startled a laugh from me. I sensed the group's postures ease as the tension began to melt away.

Lilith shook her head, smiling. "You're all ridiculous," she said, warmth breaking through her feigned exasperation.

"We prefer family," Hella countered, striking a pose in her cropped faux-fur jacket, its neon-lime fluff impossible to ignore as she treated the platform like a stage. "It hits better."

Lilith's laugh was soft but genuine. Piece by piece, she was reclaiming herself.

As we crossed back to All Aboard, I glimpsed Wyatt through the front window. He sat at the bar with Lucas, his posture steadier than the jittery energy I'd come to expect. His hands, now calm, cradled a glass of water, his eyes clear with sobriety.

He looked up as we entered. "Not here for whiskey," he said. "I just... need to talk."

Lucas gave me a subtle nod, and I guided Wyatt to the back office. Behind us, Adda was already orchestrating party plans, her exuberant voice weaving through Micah and Hella's suggestions. "We need glitter," she proclaimed. "Metric tons of glitter."

"You do realize who's cleaning that up, right?" Lucas replied dryly, drawing a faint smile from me.

The noise of the bar dimmed as the door clicked shut behind us.

"I'm done," Wyatt said, hooking his thumbs into his pockets. "With the competition, the politics. All of it."

I waited, sensing more beneath his words. The even cadence of his pulse revealed a decision rooted not in fear or haste, but in conviction.

"But," he continued, a spark of hope lighting his voice, "I think I can do something better." He straightened, an understated resolve settling into his posture. "I've been talking to Dolores about starting a scholarship fund through the academy for underprivileged musicians. She's agreed to mentor me through it. And not just tuition," he added, his voice firm, "but instruments, travel, and master classes—the things that can make a difference between innate talent and mastery."

I couldn't help but note the irony. This was exactly what Irene had needed years ago.

"Finally, the difference someone needs," I said.

"The academy's board is actually listening. The publicity from the arrests, plus some... strategic pressure from certain donors, is forcing them to confront the wealth disparity issues. I can't fix everything," he admitted, "but maybe I can ensure no one else loses their dream like Irene did."

The heaviness around him didn't disappear, but it loosened enough to let a softer light settle in. "How about joining us out there?" I suggested warmly, nodding toward the bar where the others were still plotting the celebration. "I'm betting Adda's about to mandate group hugs or something equally theatrical."

Wyatt smiled but shook his head. "Thanks, but... I need to stay clear-headed for a while. There's a lot of work ahead. I just wanted to thank you, Cass. For everything."

As he moved toward the door, I caught a final glimpse of the resolute set of his shoulders. Change was underway, not only in Wyatt, but in the entire system that had led us here. It wasn't perfect, but it was a beginning.

Later that night, after the crowd had dispersed and the buzz of Lilith's celebration had faded, I found myself absently wiping down tables. The familiar rhythm turned meditative, my fingers tracing the fading warmth where hands had rested, sensing the faint salt crystals from spilled tears of joy that wove a story of celebration and relief.

Lucas leaned on the bar, his calm presence a cool anchor in the hushed space. "You actually did it," he said, his voice blending pride with a deeper note I couldn't quite place. "Solved your first murder."

I paused, the damp cloth twisting in my hands. "Not my first mystery, though." The words carried more weight than I'd intended, heavy with the memory of that night in the alley. The attack that had upended everything. This was the first time I'd let myself acknowledge it.

Lucas's shoulders stiffened, his usual calm fraying, replaced by a heavier shadow. "Your attacker. He's still out there."

"Still out there," I repeated, the words echoing in my head.

"Whoever it was..." Lucas began, his words measured. "They weren't like us. Not the vampires who've adapted to blend into this world. There was something wilder. Something... wrong."

I held still, waiting for him to go on.

"When I found you that night," he continued, his voice thinning, shaded with restraint, "there was a scent I didn't recognize. Ancient. Feral." He stepped closer, his cool aura brushing against mine. "The way he fled when I arrived... it wasn't normal. Not even for our kind."

My mind raced, grappling with the implications. If vampires unlike Lucas and me existed—wilder, unadapted to coexist with humans—what did that mean for us all?

"And you're going to find him." I said, determination pulsing in my voice.

"We both will. But first, you need to complete your training. Whatever's out there..." He paused. "It's older than anything I've faced. And far more dangerous."

I cracked a small smile. "So, you're saying I need a training montage? Should I queue up 'Ride of the Valkyries' while honing my vampire skills?"

Lucas's lips twitched, though he fought to hold his serious expression. "I was thinking more 'Gonna Fly Now' from the original *Rocky*, but whatever gets you moving." His deadpan delivery drew a choked laugh from me.

"Did you just make a pop culture reference? Who are you, and what've you done with Lucas?"

He rolled his eyes, but a slight quickening in his pulse hinted at his amusement. "I'm not that old, Cass. Besides," he added with a pointed glance, "someone in this bar has to keep up with your awful puns."

The banter lightened the moment, but his revelation

stayed with me. Whatever had attacked me that night wasn't done, and now I knew even Lucas feared it.

I moved to the front door to lock up for the night when movement outside caught my eye. Through the glass, Jackson stood with his hands in the pockets of his dark jeans.

As I opened the door, a gust of cool night air carried Jackson's heartbeat to me. "You did it," he said simply.

I let out a soft laugh, struck by how much had changed since our first meeting at yoga. "We did it," I corrected. Without his tech skills and steadfast support, I might never have pieced it together.

The silence that followed crackled with possibility as Jackson stepped closer. His pulse quickened, a subtle shift in his scent hinting at anticipation. He tilted his head, studying my face, and time appeared to slow.

When Jackson closed the distance between us, I didn't pull away. His fingertips bushed my jaw, the warmth of his touch radiating through me. His breath brushed my cheek, his pupils darkening in the dim light. Every shift of his body stirred a deep longing within me.

Jackson's lips pressed softly against mine, sincere and certain. His pulse thrummed close, a calm rhythm syncing with my own. His scent enfolded me like a warm embrace, anchoring me as the world beyond faded.

I leaned into it, tempering my supernatural strength to draw him closer. For this fleeting moment, I could savor this simple, profound human connection, even if I was no longer entirely human.

Lucas's presence across the room crept into the edge of my awareness. A subtle chill radiated from him, mingling with the even cadence of his breathing—acceptance, not jealousy. He offered a small nod before turning away, granting us privacy while keeping vigil over the bar.

I rested my forehead against Jackson's. The warmth of his skin against mine underscored how much had changed. Yet that difference felt right, a step toward weaving my old life with this new reality.

"I've been waiting to do that," Jackson admitted, his grin lighting up his whole face.

"Me too," I whispered, a genuine smile breaking through for the first time in what felt like forever. Those truths hadn't loosened their hold—the murders, the transformation, the mystery of my attacker still shadowed the edges of my thoughts. But this moment, imperfect and complicated as it was, felt like its own kind of victory. Not an ending, but maybe the right kind of beginning.

For now, it was manageable. For now, it was enough.

CHAPTER THIRTY-EIGHT

I sank into our thrifted couch, my viola case propped against the coffee table like a loyal companion, scrolling mindlessly through my phone when a notification chimed.

One new email from the San Francisco Philharmonic.

My breath snagged in my throat. For what felt like an eternity, I hovered there, anxiety surging. The slow dance of tiny dust motes drifted through the sunbeam, and sunlight warmed the couch at my side.

I tapped the email.

"Congratulations! We are pleased to offer you a position as a violist in the San Francisco Philharmonic."

I read the line once. Twice. Three times. My brain stumbled over the words, as if they were in a language I couldn't grasp. The phone quivered in my grip as I forced myself to read on.

A sound tore from my throat—half gasp, half laugh, and faintly hysterical. This was it. Everything I'd fought for, dreamed of, feared I'd lost after being turned.

I read the email again, every pixel and font gradient searing into my mind. It was real. Undeniably real.

The apartment door flew open, and Micah burst in—a whirlwind of energy, rainbow fabric swatches spilling from her arms.

"Hey, I found the perfect sequins for Hella—" She froze mid-sentence, her pulse spiking. "Wait, why do you look like you won a million bucks or found a body?"

I opened my mouth, but words failed me. Micah's excitement shifted to concern, her pupils dilating, mouth agape, fingers tightening on the fabric.

"Oh my God." Her voice fell to a whisper. "Who died?"

I found my voice, though it wavered, embarrassingly thin. "I got in."

Micah blinked. "Into what? Witness protection? Because after everything, Cass, I swear—"

"The Philharmonic!" I shouted, thrusting my phone toward her.

Her scream tore through the air, so shrill it made me wince. Fabric swatches flew as she flung her arms up, a kaleidoscope of colors fracturing into threads and textures in the air.

She punched my arm, hard enough to sting despite my durability. "You couldn't lead with that?! I nearly called 911!"

"I'm still processing!" I protested, rubbing my arm more from habit than pain. "I just opened the email!"

"You're impossible," she declared, her grin so wide I could hear her cheek muscles straining. "Absolutely impossible. I can't believe you made me think someone died again."

For a split second, I thought of my parents.

The idea stalled there. Too much had changed. Where would I even start? And even if I tried, would they pick up?

Micah was already dialing her phone. "Mom!" she

bellowed into it. "Cass got into the Philharmonic. Get the food ready!"

She hurled my phone back at me without missing a beat. My reflexes snapped it from the air. "Call Dolores before she hears through the grapevine and curses your viola with impossible tuning."

I fumbled with the phone. The screen glowed with Dolores's contact, and I held my breath as it rang, each electronic pulse jolting in my ears.

She answered on the third ring. "Caspar? Everything okay?"

"I got in," I managed.

A piercing yell exploded through the phone, so loud I flinched, pulling it from my ear. Even Micah, still buzzing about food plans with her mom, spun at the sound.

"Caspar, darling!" Dolores's voice brimmed with pride. "This calls for champagne! I knew you'd do it, but you still gave me heart palpitations!"

I heard her bustling about. "I'm calling Jules now. We're meeting at All Aboard."

The warmth of Micah's enthusiasm flooded over me. After everything, her unwavering support meant more than I could ever say.

She practically hauled me down the stairs, her excitement pulsing off her in waves. Lucas looked up from behind the bar as we entered, a smile tugging at his lips.

"Proud of you, Reyes," he said simply, warmth threading his calm tone.

"Oh em gee, you were totally eavesdropping with your vampire super-hearing!" Micah accused, jabbing a finger at him. "So unfair. I nearly had a heart attack finding out!"

I frowned at Lucas's understated reaction. "That's it? No grand toast? No heartfelt speech?"

His mouth twitched, a glint in his eye as he reached for a bottle on the top shelf, his private reserve of Japanese whiskey. "You think I'd waste a speech before pouring the good stuff?"

"Wait!" Micah gasped. "What am I going to wear? More importantly," she turned to me with narrowed eyes, "what are you going to wear? You can't celebrate getting into the Philharmonic looking like a bartender who spilled last night's secrets all over their outfit."

"Hey!" I protested, even as I cataloged every wrinkle in my shirt and the coffee stain on my sleeve I'd prayed no one would notice.

"No arguments," Micah declared, tapping on her phone. "I'm texting everyone. You just focus on not passing out from shock."

I opened my mouth to insist we didn't need balloons or decorations. The presence of my closest friends was enough. But looking at her excited face, at Lucas's pride, at the way the bar already seemed to hum with anticipation... I couldn't bring myself to dampen their joy.

"Fine," I conceded. "But no glitter cannons."

"No promises!" Micah sang, her phone's chime punctuating her grin.

CHAPTER THIRTY-NINE

A few hours later, the bar pulsed with life, brimming with the bright fizz of champagne and a riot of color from the outfits Micah had miraculously coordinated on short notice. The air thrummed with joy, and it felt like a new chapter was unfolding. For once, I let myself bask in its glow.

Across the room, Hella and Micah huddled, already scheming future designs for Philharmonic concerts, their excited whispers mingling with the scratch of pencil on paper as they sketched ideas. Dolores clinked glasses with Jules before sweeping over to plant a dramatic kiss on my cheek.

"I knew you'd triumph, dear," she said, her voice a perfect blend of pride and vindication. "With your fierce dedication, how could you not?"

Jules, sipping champagne with his usual elegance, shot me a playful wink. "And we didn't even have to murder anyone to get you here."

The table fell silent for a moment, a collective breath catching.

Micah sighed heavily. "Jules, you can't say that."

Jules tilted his head, feigning innocence as he switched to

French. "*Pourquoi pas?* Why not? It's the truth, *non?*"

I couldn't help but laugh, sending ripples of relief through the group. Some things would never change, and honestly, I wouldn't have it any other way.

The front door swung open, flooding the bar with the mouthwatering aromas of Filipino cuisine. Tita Isa and Tito Hector swept in, bearing three enormous trays that released the sweet-savory scent of pancit noodles studded with carrots and celery, the crackle of perfectly fried lumpia, and the rich, spiced aroma of lechon belly that burst through the air like a full-blown flavor explosion.

"*Anak!*" Tita Isa called, her voice brimming with pride. "You think I'd let my adopted son celebrate without proper food?"

They set the trays on a table where the drag queens were prepping for their performance. Tita Isa, with her seemingly endless supply of containers, swiftly produced plates and utensils, while Lilith cleared space by pushing aside an unrolled mat of makeup and brushes.

I watched as Tito Hector cornered Lucas by the bar, brandishing a plate piled high with food like a weapon. "You're too skinny," he declared, brushing off Lucas's attempts to protest. "All those hours working, not eating properly. Here, the lechon will build muscle."

Lucas shot me a desperate look that screamed *help me*, but I simply grinned, relishing the rare sight of someone mother-henning him. He sighed, accepting the plate, knowing resistance was futile against the Velasco family's mission to feed everyone in their orbit.

"You too, Cass!" Tita Isa called, already assembling

another plate. "Musicians need fuel!"

Before I could reply, Adda's commanding presence swept through the room. She grabbed my arm, her perfectly manicured nails glinting under the bar's lights. "Alright, baby legend, I know you're the star tonight, but some of us still need to prep."

Behind her, Lilith adjusted her wig pins, a playful glint in her eyes. "Don't think we've forgotten you," she smirked. "We're dedicating a song to you tonight."

I let out an exaggerated groan. "If it's *I Will Survive*, I'm out the door."

Hella, scrolling through her phone, smiled without looking up. "Relax, boo-boo. We don't do basic."

Adda gave me a slow once-over, her brow lifting at the sight of the slightly pilled beige cardigan I'd insisted was 'dressy enough.' She didn't say a word, just lifted her chin and moved on.

"Tonight," Adda proclaimed, "we celebrate Cass and the triumph of justice." She paused for dramatic effect. "And I'm debuting a new wig. Try not to weep at its beauty."

Every strand of that wig caught the light in mesmerizing detail. The intricate color variations and styling—clearly the work of hours—were exactly the kind of spectacle Adda lived for.

From my spot near the stage, I caught Lucas behind the bar, his posture relaxed yet vigilant. A slight softening around his eyes suggested genuine contentment, a rare departure from his usual measured control as he watched the celebration unfold.

I slid onto a barstool. "You're doing that thing where you

pretend not to be emotional," I teased.

Lucas scoffed. "And you're making everything dramatic, as usual." He reached for two champagne flutes, their crystal rims chiming softly as they met.

We clinked glasses, his fingers lingering a touch longer than needed. "Thanks for everything," I murmured, my words carrying far more than tonight's celebration.

Lucas's eyes met mine, and for a moment, I glimpsed beyond his carefully guarded facade. "Anytime," he replied, his voice heavy with sincerity.

Adda clapped sharply. "Alright, my beautiful disasters, we have a show to ignite! Drag excellence waits for no one!"

I watched as Lilith rolled her eyes but followed dutifully, her heels clicking against the floor. The familiar clamor of the drag queens prepping for their performance filled me with an unexpected wave of gratitude. This was home, this was family, this was everything I never knew I needed until it found me.

As the whirlwind of pre-show preparation swirled around me, I wove my way back to our corner table, where Jackson waited, his eyes crinkled at the corners as I settled beside him. His fingers brushed my arm, a touch so light yet vivid, each point of contact sparking warmth from his skin. It was softer than the electric tension I felt around Lucas—warmer, more tender, an assurance without urgency or expectation.

"You know," Jackson murmured, "I think this is the first time I've seen you truly relax since we met."

"You know what?" I replied with a soft laugh. "I think you're right."

"And," Jackson added, "I always knew you'd make it."

I turned to him, catching the pride in his eyes, and the way the bar's dim lighting traced the angular planes of his face. "Even when we were too busy playing detective for me to practice?"

"Especially then. Your stubborn streak shines when you want something. It's kind of your thing."

For the first time in what felt like ages, I let myself truly relax. The cacophony of sounds and scents that usually over-whelmed me melted into a gentle background hum. Here, surrounded by those I loved, everything felt right.

I closed my eyes, letting the distant click of the perform-ers' heels, the melodic laughter spilling from the bar's corners, and the familiar scents of home mingled with cele-bration wash over me. All of it threaded together into a perfect snapshot of contentment, one I longed to hold on to forever.

"You're doing that thing again," Jackson teased, amuse-ment lacing his tone.

"What thing?" I asked, opening my eyes.

"That thing where you get all intense, like you're trying to etch every moment into memory."

I looked back at him, his soft, knowing expression stirring my dead heart. "Maybe I am," I admitted. "Is that weird?"

Jackson shook his head, his smile broadening. "Nah. It's kind of beautiful, actually. In a very you way."

More patrons streamed into the bar, their collective energy surging with anticipation for the show. I registered each arri-val as a new heartbeat joining the symphony I'd tracked all evening, their rhythms weaving into a familiar chorus. Waves of perfume and cologne layered over the rich, lingering warmth of Tita Isa's cooking. Through it all, I caught Lilith's distinct footsteps heading toward the piano, as unique to me as a fingerprint.

As soon as the crowd began to settle, a ripple of energy moved through the bar's front, sharpening my focus as breaths caught and bodies subtly shifted toward the entrance.

Murmurs rose above the ambient hum, drifting to me like leaves on a stream:

"She's... wow."

"Look at those pearls."

"That Birkin though."

"Is that real Chanel, or just very convincing?"

The voices carried awe and curiosity, but I knew that reverent whisper too well. More snippets drifted through the air:

"Who is she?"

"Must be someone important..."

"Did you see those shoes?"

"Has to be old money. Period."

I turned slowly, catching her reflection in the bar's mirrored wall. Angela Hawthorn Reyes, my mother, was immaculate in her Chanel suit, the gold-threaded tweed catching the bar's soft glow, not a hair out of place.

The warmth I'd basked in all evening vanished and the celebration dimmed—colors muted, sounds dulled—as if her presence alone could sap the life from the room.

Every eye in the bar turned to her. Even Adda, mid-stride onto the stage, froze, her drag queen instincts recognizing a rival who could command attention as fiercely as she did. I heard her murmur under her breath: "Oh, honey, this is going to be good."

My mother's eyes swept the room in clinical arcs, scanning the mismatched furniture and the disco ball glinting above the stage. A twitch at the corner of her mouth and the tightening of her grip on her handbag betrayed her unease.

But this was my world now. Drag queens and chosen family, barbacks and musicians, vampires and humans woven together. Everything she'd tried to shield me from. Everything I'd claimed as my own.

And now she was here, her world colliding with mine.

Angela moved through the crowd, her grace honed by habit, Ferragamo heels clicking against the floor. Each step carried the weight of years of etiquette training and social polish. Her perfect posture, measured pace, and the slight tilt of her chin radiated authority and refinement.

The crowd parted instinctively before her, yielding a clear path through the bar. The contrast between her Birkin-bag elegance and the bar's warm informality drew every eye.

Micah stepped toward me, protective instinct quickening her pulse, but I raised my hand. The subtle gesture carried the weight of my tangled emotions—hold on, stay, let me handle this. Jackson's fingers tightened around mine, his familiar pulse a warm anchor against my cooler skin.

My mother halted precisely three feet away, adhering to the upper-class protocol for serious conversations. Her perfectly lined lips pressed into a thin line, her French-manicured nails digging into her palms.

"Caspar," she said, her voice measured, loud enough to cut through the bar's ambient buzz without seeming raised.

She inhaled softly, a careful, restrained breath. The silence hung between us, balanced on the edge of resolution, like a cadence left unfinished.

Then she spoke. "Your father. He's dead."

The world stilled, broken only by the drum of my own heartbeat.

ACKNOWLEDGEMENTS

THANK YOU to my editors: Haily C. and Lisa H., for sifting through the rubble and unearthing something worth polishing. Your thoughtful edits and guidance brought clarity to the chaos and helped the story take its final shape.

To my cover artist: Julia H., for sharing your artistry and for your endless patience through all my nitpicking. You took my ideas and turned them into something far better than I imagined.

To my beta readers: Elge P., Kelly P., Mark J., Nikki D. and Shae P., for your honesty, sharp eyes, and generous feedback. You helped strengthen the story, and in doing so, helped me grow as a writer.

To my steadfast cheerleaders: Emmy C., Jae G., and Miguel S., who rooted for me through every draft, rewrite, and crisis of confidence. I truly wouldn't have finished this without your voices in my corner.

To the friends and family who gave me a space to create when I needed an escape: Leah S. & Rachel A., Viola D., and Lori D. & Max C. at Binu Bonu—thank you for the sanctuary, the laughter, and the many glasses of wine that powered me through edits.

To my mom and mom-in-law: Carmen R. and Cindy R., your faith in me and in every odd little venture I dive into means more than I can say.

To my husband: Christian R., for reading that first messy scene and saying, "You should write this." Your insight and creative eye have shaped this book in ways only you could.

To San Francisco: your foggy streets, hidden corners, and wild, beating heart made the perfect stage for a queer vampire mystery.

And finally, to all my readers, for letting me tell you a story. I hope it makes you feel seen, thrilled, comforted, or maybe just entertained for a little while.

On The Horizon

Return to the fog-drenched streets of San Francisco in the next installment of the **All Aboard Bar Mysteries**:

Book Two
Pluck Me a Scheme
Money gone missing. A newcomer with fangs. Notes that fall out of harmony. In a family full of shadows, not everything is as it seems.

★ Plus… a new mystery unfolds in the heart of Salinas: ★

Boxed Up and Empty (working title)
Book One of the **Sari-Sari Sunset Market Mysteries**
A clutter consultant. A family market. Folklore that won't stay buried. Because some secrets can't be boxed up or swept away.

From Behind The Bar

LUCAS'S PEAR MARTINI

JUST LIKE SINKING YOUR TEETH INTO ONE OF
THOSE LUXURY WINTER PEARS WRAPPED IN GOLD.

**2 fl. oz. Grey Goose La
Poire**

¾ oz. St-Germain

¾ oz. fresh lemon juice

splash of soda

Add all ingredients to a
shaker filled with ice. Shake
well until thoroughly chilled
and strain into a frosted
martini glass. Garnish with a
lemon twist.

www.ingramcontent.com/pod-product-compliance
Lightning Source LLC
Chambersburg PA
CBHW050028120726
47903CB00006B/1951